Angus Smyth studies psychology at th
His main research interest focuses on
people with cancer. This has led to his ass
Lynch Centre at Belvoir Park Hospital, B
Editor with *The Psychologist,* and a past Editor of *Psych-talk.*
Angus lives in Comber, Co Down and has one daughter, Jade. This
is his first novel.

In memory of my father, George

Friends of Montgomery House

Belvoir Park Hospital, Hospital Rd, Belfast BT8 8JR.
Registered Charity No: XN87255

The author has dedicated his payment – 10% of net profits from the sale of *It wasn't me!* to the cancer charity *Friends of Montgomery House* at Belvoir Park Hospital, Belfast.

Montgomery House was the original name given to the hospital in 1953. *Friends,* was launched in 1984 and is made up of a dedicated team of hospital staff and the general public. Since its formation, almost £3 million has been spent by *Friends* to improve patient care and treatment.

If you would like to make a direct donation you can do so by sending a cheque made payable to:
Friends of Montgomery House

to:

Friends of Montgomery House
Belvoir Park Hospital
Hospital Road
Belfast BT8 8JR.

Angus Smyth

It wasn't me!

Ownlee Publishing

Ownlee Publishing,
10 Longlands Drive, Comber, Newtownards, Co. Down, N. Ireland, BT23 5AL.

Published by Ownlee Publishing 2000.

Copyright © Angus Smyth 2000

A catalogue record of this book is available from the British Library.

ISBN 0 9539090 0 X

The author asserts the moral right to be identified as the author of this work.

This book is entirely a work of fiction. The names, characters and happenings in this book are the works of the author's imagination. Any resemblance to actual persons, living or dead, happenings or communities is entirely coincidental.

Printed and bound by
W & G Baird Ltd, Caulside Drive, Antrim,
Northern Ireland, BT41 2RS.

All rights reserved. No part of this book may be reproduced, stored in a retrieval system or transmitted, in any form or by any means, electronic, mechanical, photocopying, recording or otherwise without the prior written permission of the author and publisher.

Chapter 1

Tullydeen, Co Down, Northern Ireland
Summer of 1968

'And-and John Wayne punched him hard. BANG!'
'Be careful, Simon. You'll fall and hurt yourself. Did the baddie die?' Susan Patterson asked.
'Yes. John Wayne always wins. Did you not watch it? Everybody watches John Wayne.'
'I don't like him,' Susan said. 'I like Romper Room and The Magic Roundabout. I love Dougal. Daddy says he will get me a dog like him.'
Simon walked faster.
'Wait for me, Simon. Wait for me.'
'You're only a girl. Only girls watch Romper Room.'
'No, they don't.' Susan kicked him.
'They do. And ...you're only a girl and a big cry baby.' Simon ran towards the tiny school in Tullydeen. Susan stood, her head bowed towards the ground. He stopped at the entrance. 'See, you're only a cry baby and ...that didn't hurt ...so there.'
  Mrs Jordan sent him out to find Susan Patterson. She was sitting in the tall, seeded grass on the verge, sniffling and cuddling Peggy-Sue, her stupid doll. Simon was fed up telling her that the doll wasn't a real person.
'Mrs Jordan says you're to come to school.'
'Go away.'
Susan would not get up. It took him a long time to convince her to

move. He had to promise not to call her a cry baby and to say that he liked Romper Room and The Magic Roundabout. Anything to get her moving. Susan's big hazel eyes leaked rivers down her cheeks. She continued to sniff as he helped her up, however she trailed her feet along the road because she knew that annoyed him.

After school they skimmed stones on the shore behind Simon's house. She could only make them bounce once. He was tired showing her how to do it. Eventually, he gave up and put it down to her being a girl. They watched the new colour television together. The first colour television in all of Tullydeen. His dad had bought it as a surprise. Susan just loved Dougal, in colour. Simon pretended not to watch.

All summer long they fished for mackerel. Susan squealed when they jumped. They watched the apollo rockets take off, in colour, from Cape Canaveral. They even built their own rocket from a cardboard box. At night they looked at the moon. Simon was determined to become an astronaut and Susan hoped that he would wave to her. He knew she would probably want him to wave to that stupid doll, as well. But he agreed. Susan's flight of fancy made her spot the apollo one night. However, Simon told her it wasn't the apollo. It was only Captain Kirk and Spock. They had been up there for a long time and if she had been a boy she would have known that.

The townland of Tullydeen fired their imagination. The little strip of shore behind the Rogers' home welcomed the salt lough, an inlet from the Irish Sea. It could be what they wanted it to be: sometimes a desert; sometimes the moon; sometimes Cape Canaveral; and sometimes it was just Tullydeen. The scrawl of rocks where they sat fishing could easily change into monsters or giants. At other times they stormed over the top to kill Germans or Indians, and sometimes they just sat and complained about adults and their stupid ideas.

That was where they were sitting when she told him about moving to Drumfiddy. They borrowed the atlas from his parents' bedroom and sat on the rocks looking for it. They argued about how to spell Drumfiddy. He told her he thought Colombo lived there. Susan said he didn't because Colombo lived in America. Her dad had said.

She told him Drumfiddy was sixty miles away. Then they reckoned it must be in America. Simon told her about riding his bike to Matt Young's house; how tired he was; how long it took him; away past the boat yard and up the big hill. And, that was only two miles. They underlined every town in America with their fingers: no Drumfiddy.

They looked at Africa. Sixty miles away could be Africa, he reckoned. That was where Tarzan lived with all the snakes. She squealed as usual and said she didn't want to go if it was in Africa. However, he reassured her that Tarzan killed all the snakes and took care of everyone, even girls and stupid dolls.

They could not find a Drumfiddy in Africa, either. It sounded mysterious and they reckoned it would not be as nice as Tullydeen, wherever it was. Susan asked him not to be Sarah Galway's friend when she left Tullydeen. Simon promised as they walked to Matt Young's house. Simon wanted her to see how far two miles was. She was frightened because her legs ached. He was sure Drumfiddy was in America. Simon told her if they walked another two miles they would probably be in America. He gave her a piggyback part of the way home. As far as the old boat yard. Then they rested a bit.

The next day Susan ran into the house and told him Drumfiddy was in Co Antrim. They checked the atlas, but it *still* didn't say Drumfiddy. They caught mackerel that day and he made her touch one of them. He figured there would be no mackerel in Drumfiddy. That made her sad and how she wished she was not frightened of them jumping about. Susan made him nurse Peggy-Sue. He did so because it was Susan's last day in Tullydeen. He made sure no one was looking and he placed the stupid rag-doll on his knee. She said he could feed her if he liked. It was a lucky break because Peggy-Sue said she wasn't hungry. They reckoned she'd miss Tullydeen as well.

Her dad was dressed in his best suit. The one he wore on Sundays. Her mother wore a red dress. The black Morris Minor sat in the yard. Everyone was kissing and hugging. Susan wore her blue dress. The one she wore when something important was happening. She told him to watch out because her mother would kiss him, too. It was one of those days for kissing.

The four adults crowded around him. Susan's mother kissed him on the cheek and marvelled at how tall he had become. Simon knew that he would miss Pearl, and her raisin buns. His dad told him to say good-bye. It came out as a mumble. Simon darted past his father's legs and ran into the field. He heard them laughing and the car coming to life.

The field was all rutted where the tractor had been. He stayed close to the hedge. He could get to the gate before them. When he looked over his left shoulder he almost stumbled. Her mum and dad smiled and waved, as they reached him at the crest of the lane. Simon stood on the patchy tarmac. Susan stared back, resting her chin on her tiny hands. She did not wave. Susan just stared from the little half-moon window. The big bundle of suitcases on the roof flapped and rattled, as the car grunted towards the end of the lane. His body seemed to free again. Simon ran like he never ran before. Mr Patterson tooted the horn, as they turned right towards Tullydeen village.

Simon skidded to a halt and gazed up the narrow road. He could still hear the car chugging into the village on its way to Drumfiddy. Soon, it was silent. She was gone. Only his breath was with him. Sarah Galway wouldn't listen to him about John Wayne. How he wished he had not said terrible things to Susan and pulled her hair when they fought. Simon decided, there and then, that he would watch The Magic Roundabout every day. His shoulders were hunched, his hands deep in the pockets of his beige shorts. There was nothing beautiful about Tullydeen that day and he doubted if there ever would be again. He ambled about the road, kicking a stone. That's when he noticed Peggy-Sue.

Chapter 2

Summer, 2000

I stare at the page, wondering about the impact it will have.
'No leads on who these two are?' Rory asks.
'Not a thing. I don't think they're important. Sort of front men. Probably paid a few quid to look the part,' I reply.

He looks at me briefly and then back to the photograph of the two men, relaxing by the swimming pool of a villa in Malaga. 'The hotline's set up for the policyholders. I'm happy with the proof.' He pauses, pats his thinning fair hair, and smiles. 'Well done, Simon. Great pictures, Mandy. Where will this end?'
'Nugents, you're buying.'

We take the well-worn path from *The Irish Scribe* via the underground car park, past the presses and into the cutting sunlight of Belfast. A Belfast blistering in a heat wave.

Nugents is packed. It must be to quench thirsts, earned in the blistering heat. Usually, it's to shelter from the rain. Rory makes his way to the bar. Mandy and I negotiate our way towards the table in the corner, grappling with the smell of pub grub and inquisitive stares. Most men stare at Mandy and imagine what they could do with her flowing blonde hair. At least I did when we first met. Then, she informed me we were both after the same thing.

Rory arrives with three pints, with the usual glint in his eye, in anticipation of the first mouthful. 'To the downfall of the Andrews Corporation and the power of investigative journalism,' he proposes.

'I'll drink to that and my three weeks away from this place,' I smile.
'Where shall you go, Rogers?' Mandy asks.
'Ach ...I'll just hang about home. ...Do a bit of fishing. Just relax.'
'You need a woman in your life again, Rogers.'
'Aye ...Mandy's right. Ye can't tar them all with the same brush, Simon. Ye can't just work-work-work. After all, ye are a doctor, now. Women always go for doctors,' he smirks.
'Ach ...Rory,' I plead.
'Dr Simon Rogers. Imagine that, our Simon is a doctor. I'm surprised he still speaks to us, Mandy.'
'He's not a medical doctor, Rory. Rogers is a crap-talking doctor instead.'
'A doctor's a doctor,' he jibes back. 'Aye ...the wee women always fall for doctors. Oh Doctor Rogers why am I so unhappy?' he recites, as if he's nursing a baby. 'Can ye make me happy again?'
'All the willie-nillies that cannot face up to life will be calling on Rogers, Rory. Most of it is a load of old gibberish. What sort of people would want to kill themselves? Why don't they get off their arses and get on with life. How pathetic ...cutting your wrists.' Mandy pauses to sip her beer. 'Why do you want to associate with people who cut their wrists, Rogers, and all the losers in life? They cannot hack it. I would bloody well tell them. If you want to die, go ahead and die.'
'Ach ...Mandy.'
'Ach ...Mandy nothing, Rogers. They should bloody well let them die. I have no time for their sort. Hummh ...running around crying and wallowing in self-pity. Such a load of nonsense.'
'Are you telling *us* Mandy, or are you trying to convince yourself?' I slip in. Mandy's blue eyes sour like milk in August.
'How dare you, Rogers! How dare you say that!'
'Say what?'
'You ...you miserable little shit.'
'Hey, less of the miserable, Mandy.'
'Damn you, Rogers. Good bye, Rory.'
    Mandy makes it to the door and stops. She's on her way back. My shirt takes her fist-grip. 'You better be in the gym tomorrow morning, Rogers. Remember we have a challenge.'
'Ach ...Mandy, I won't be able to make it. I pulled a calf muscle.'
'Ha. Calf muscle. Be there, Rogers. Or else.'
'Ach ...Mandy.'
'Ach ...Mandy nothing. Be there.'

'I've a pulled calf …'

'Be there, Rogers. You conniving little weasel.'

Rory and I drink up and stroll along Royal Avenue. We talk about the Andrews Corporation and their crooked dealing. Hordes of shoppers pass, laden with bags, puffing in the heat.

'I wonder how many of these ones are in for a shock in the morning, Rory.'

'Aye …it's no joke. Ye think you have put your money past for a rainy day and all the time it's been spent by a load a crooks.'

'Aye …Rory …a rainy day in the middle of a heat wave.'

'It's always the honest folk who get caught. Take a look around you. Just ordinary folk out trying to earn a living. They stick their wee bit of savings into the Andrews Corporation, thinking it will do for maybe wee Jane's wedding. Ahhh. I even hate breaking news like this. Ah well …they have to find out. Some of these investment companies get away with murder. They send out a slip of paper each year …sure they could put anything on it, nobody would be any the wiser,' Rory says, shrugging.

'That was their plan. Most people had paid in for ten years or so. It was only when they went to collect that this came to light.'

'That's some money, Simon. …Take a tenner a week. That's £520 a year, £5200 never mind the interest on ten years,' Rory calculates quickly.

'Well the tip-off was due to lift £680,000 or thereabouts. Naturally he didn't want to be traced. I tried. And he knew I'd try. All I know is that he was from the Antrim area. One of his phone calls was from Portrush … a call box,' I explain.

We stop at the corner of Manford Street and the sun reflects off *The Irish Scribe* building. Rory's white shirt and blue tie square up to me. I figure he wears this colour scheme to remind him of his native Glasgow. As usual, his shirts are immaculately clean, ironed to perfection. Maureen wouldn't let him out of the house if he looked scruffy …or, knowing her, let him iron his own shirts. She would do all that; have his dinner ready and his clothes ready and waiting for the golf course, too. Just the way my own folks did. Sort of a generational thing.

'Keep in touch, Simon. If you've nothing to do, take a run over, Maureen is always asking for you. Bring wee Grace with ye. Enjoy your holidays …don't worry about the story. All the others have to come through me if they want to latch onto it.'

'Cheers, Rory.' We almost hug, but end up gripping each other's arms instead.

'I know you're the psychologist, but you need to put the Pauline thing behind ye, Simon. Then your folks dying ...well, it hasn't been easy for you, son. Ye deserve a bit of luck. If you had a wee woman like my Maureen, you'd be fine,' he nods.

'Does your wee Maureen know you're slipping a *wee* drop of sugar into your tea again, Rory?'

'Och, how many terrorists in Belfast do you know who killed folk by slipping a wee drop of sugar into their tea?'

I watch a plane skim the sky and smile as he mumbles on about Maureen fussing. I don't mind Rory Hamilton giving me his opinion. He's like a father to me, instead of a boss. You really feel it when someone has your best interests at heart. Mandy's the same although she huffs and puffs ...but she's genuine. So's Big Paul. I look at Rory, the man who gave me a job all those years ago when no one wanted a psychology graduate. I took it as a stopgap; little did I know how things would develop. I love what I do and that's thanks to his guidance and wisdom. I had held the stereotypical image of an Editor as a hard drinking, tough talking, sleazy type of person from the American TV shows of the seventies. Any one who knows Rory Hamilton could never put him down as that. In a way he uses his gentleness as part of his subtle technique. On my first day he told me not to ask too many questions. Investigative journalists observe. That way people don't become suspicious, stop doing what you suspect them of doing in the first place. His philosophy was simple and effective. He knew I wasn't the sort of person who liked asking questions, either. I hate people asking me questions. I get all jumpy and flustered.

I engulf him in my arms and pat his back. 'Thanks, Rory.' Quickly, I release from our embrace and walk towards the underground car park of *The Irish Scribe*. I turn around, where the shadows meet the day. Busy brown bodies and a street singer somewhere don't distract Rory's stare.

Chapter 3

I could imagine, Mandy pacing about in the gym and calling me a weasel. I didn't show. Instead, I called Grace and arranged to pick her up. Like many other dads I had stopped at the door while Pauline, my ex-wife, aimed the offspring at the waiting vehicle, and Grace came running with Cornpop, her doll, bobbing about under her arm. I had always found that bit hard. It opened up the wound of Pauline's unfaithfulness. Waving from the door was enough. We shouted when we talked.

Grace hit me with the latest cartoons and the trouble she was having getting Cornpop to sleep at nights. I asked how she was sleeping: 'Sometimes I need a glass of water, Dad.' After checking that Cornpop was able to see out properly, she began humming a song that I didn't know. Next, the radio received its usual poking and prodding until an appropriate music channel blasted out. Her fair hair, with ponytail, framed her mischievous smile. We stopped at the park, where I waved when she reached the top of the slide and waited by the roundabout as she circled. We were there for nearly two hours, the energy of a five-year-old, despite the heat.

It had always been my dream to have a daughter and live happily ever after. Gradually I was beginning to realise that *happily ever after* meant divorce and living single. The pain of being cheated upon was still raw, yet watching Grace enjoy herself made up for that somewhat. Maybe I'm different, but I just wanted my kid to like me. I'm probably a bigger kid than her, becoming a parent seemed to revive my own childhood. We ended our few hours together in Menary's Cafe in Newtownards. We both ate fish and chips. Grace was asleep before I dropped her off. I carried her to the door where a waiting Pauline cradled her gently. Good old Tom's car was there so I set Cornpop on the doorstep and walked back to my Toyota. I didn't acknowledge Pauline's thank you, and I didn't want her asking how I was coping. Stuff her, anyway.

I cruised back to Tullydeen, taking my time and soaking up the gentle breeze drifting in. I had Eric Clapton blaring and I planned what I might do on my holidays. The barns needed painting and a spot of fishing was a possibility. Grace was quite interested in camping out on the islands, as long as there were no alligators. I assured her Ireland had run out of alligators, but I offered to order her one on the Net, if she wanted.

I'm almost asleep as I drive up the lane. A white Ford Fiesta is parked close to the door, which brings some alertness to my mind. A woman with black hair is walking about, looking lost or out of luck.
'Simon Rogers? Simon, it's you,' she smiles, rushing to hug me. I manage to tell her shoulder that I'm him. She is wearing a blue dress that maybe just looks expensive.
'You don't know who I am, do you?' her perfect white teeth flash. They're real, but almost too real to be real.
'No …no …'.
'I'm Susan …Susan Patterson. Remember? Remember I used to live over there before I moved to Drumfiddy,' she says, flinging an arm in the direction of her old cottage.
'Susan …that Susan. Ach …it's years. It must be thirty years anyway,' I reply. She's all smiles and clasping her hands together in front of her belly, bending her knees with excitement — either that or she needs to pee.
'It's thirty-two years …I think, Simon, or thereabouts. We're both nearly the same age. I'm thirty-eight past.'
'Yeah, me too,' I cut in, raising my brows and blowing.

She drinks water. I have a Harp and we walk to the picnic bench in the garden. Susan Patterson saunters over to the wall and watches the gulls. The tide is teasing off the seaweed and it's preparing for sleep in the ebbing hours. I finish my beer and walk over to her. We talk about our families and how time had brought sad things and moments of joy. She tells me about becoming a nurse. She looks like a nurse …whatever that means. I'm trying to recapture the little girl that played with me all those years ago. I find it hard to connect her to her present age. Susan used to twitch her shoulder when she talked. Maybe people lose that with age. 'How's Peggy-Sue?' I ask, catching her off guard. 'Peggy-Sue,' I prompt again. Her face is getting flustered. 'Your doll,' I add, when her eyes are dancing around.

'Oh ...Peggy-Sue's fine,' she says, pushing out a huge sigh and smile. 'What brings you out to Tullydeen ...old times sake?' I ask as my stomach takes the impact of her lie. She goes silent and looks down at her toes. I pick up my Marlboro and light up.

'I'm in trouble, Simon,' she says, leaning on the bench.

'What sort of trouble?' I ask, trying to play along with whatever is going on.

'Man trouble. I thought you could help. I often read your stories,' she says, softly. 'Well, I'm being followed by a stalker. I went to a nightclub some time back and it started from there. First the phone calls asking for dates, then bumping into me in the supermarket, that sort of thing.' She pauses and looks at a wagtail on the wall. I let the silence run. She takes sly glances at me and twists at her fingers as if they are loose or something. 'It's Trevor Mulholland,' she continues. 'Trevor Mulholland, the accountant from Belfast. He won't take no for an answer. He's making my life a misery.'

I saunter, then sit on the wall that separates the garden from Strangford Lough. Mulholland ...now there's a name from the past. Why come out here and tell me about Mulholland? And, what sort of person forgets the name of their favourite doll? 'I'll have a look at Mulholland for you, Susan,' I say, finding it hard to call her Susan. I want to say *wise up* and make her come clean and spoil the façade. 'Oh, be careful, Simon. I'm scared of any man coming near me. He's so possessive. I haven't had a boyfriend for a couple of years. He frightens them all off,' she explains, touching my arm. I hate people touching my arm.

'Look Susan, I'm afraid I have an appointment ...about a story,' I say, thinking on my feet.

'Oh ...I'll go, Simon. Don't let me keep you back. You famous journalists.' I escort her to the car and she talks of catching up on old times. Of course, I agree.

The barn wall takes my weight and I watch the dust rise from the wheels as she disappears over the crest of the lane. I grab a Marlboro and blow smoke at the blue heavens. But Mulholland... why Mulholland? I sigh at the spider making its way across the concrete. Maybe Mulholland's involved in the Andrews Corporation ...could be payback time... but none of this makes sense. She didn't know Peggy-Sue. The real Susan Patterson would've known right away. It can't be Susan ...if she is I'm a fish. It's hard not to be yourself and even harder to be someone you're not.

Chapter 4

Her nose is different. I throw the old black and white photographs on the floor and wait for the wall to enlighten me. My gut says it's not her. Yet, here I am replaying her words and wanting to believe that she is Susan Patterson. I take one last look at the five-year-old girl, standing, in a winter coat outside my home, some thirty years ago. I try to transform her, past ten, puberty, to young adulthood and into my yard a few hours ago. I know it isn't Susan Patterson.

My journey through her life stages has given me a mental picture of the real Susan Patterson. I swap it for the clone. The real Susan Patterson would be similar, yet different. I would've travelled to her present age, watching her expressions, recalling their occurrence from a distant age. With this woman I didn't. There were no triggers powered by her presence. All I had managed to do with the woman was draw a blank. A block. A stranger.

I play with the photographs and shuffle them like a deck of cards. Eventually I replace them in my late parents' room with the others. I will clear this room, bag their clothes and try to put their deaths behind me. Who am I kidding.

I walk from their room to mine and sigh. Everything is everywhere. I'll start here first, let the Susan Patterson thing ferment, connect and gather momentum. I always find a revelation happens when I leave it alone, don't tug, twist, or force it to happen.

Two coffee beakers clink into the black bag. I have a habit of twisting up little balls of paper and flicking them at things, when I'm thinking, working. The floor is covered in miniature paper golf balls. Photocopies of articles connected with the Andrews

Corporation lie everywhere. Drafts of my stories, rendered unprintable, have been ripped, usually in anger, and are discarded with Coke cans and Twix wrappers. Two skyscrapers of dictaphone tapes evolve and grow on the desk next to my faithful word processor. I vacuum with vengeance while my nose clogs, itching with the dust.

 I lean on the windowsill and survey my toil. The place is clean and tidy – perhaps Protestant, if I am to believe the superstition of my culture. My bedroom, cum office looks much bigger and the bookshelves beside my bed are full once more. The entire house takes my wrath with the vacuum. I hate housework, especially in this heat, although I try not to think about it. Iconic images of a can of Harp, its coolness, egg me on.

 I slump down against the barn wall and drink. It's well in the eighties. The fields shimmer in the haze. I listen to the news on *Cool FM* and smile when the Andrews Corporation is mentioned. Hopefully, it won't be the last time. I feel pleased with myself and celebrate with a second can and another Marlboro.

 The heat of the wall oozes into my back and I close my eyes, listening to Mary Coughlan. I pull myself away from thinking about the real Susan Patterson. A vision of Trevor Mulholland crossing my mind takes care of it. Mulholland following someone around makes sense. I finish my beer and go inside. The scent of *alpine forest* hits me immediately. I sniff it in. It doesn't smell like an alpine forest to me …I could invent names for furniture polish.

 The walk through the kitchen is pleasant while my eyes adjust. I have files on Mulholland. The carpets feel spongy once more after the cleaning. I prepare myself for the struggle with the filing cabinet. If I live to be a hundred, I will still hate filing cabinets. I'd kept loads of my old stories tucked away in the innards of this grey, kicked occasionally, thing. I peep into manila folders and quickly locate the fattest one.

 The horror of the bombing is shown by Mandy's picture on the front page. The twisted metal of Tom and Nancy Mulholland's black BMW throws a stark reality on how violently they must have died. I had been in the car park of the Stilster Restaurant when Mandy took this picture. The smell of the aftermath and burning was something I had never forgotten.

 I scan down my own words. The paramilitaries had issued an apology for killing Tom and Nancy Mulholland – their intended target had driven a similar car and frequented the same restaurant.

I flick over other copies in the folder. Some of Mandy's pictures show Trevor Mulholland being helped to the church by friends and relatives. Belfast had come to a standstill on the day of the double funerals. It was one of those events in the Troubles when people were shocked – beyond the normal. Tom Mulholland and his wife, Nancy, had been attending a charity function, before returning to their car which promptly exploded as they drove off.

One of my colleagues had prepared a piece on the lives of the Mulhollands. A family portrait showed Trevor and his sister Mary. A synopsis of their lives followed. Mary was very successful, working as a computer programmer in California. Trevor was written about as the right hand man to his father in the business. Tom and Nancy, the staff reporter had written, were renowned in the social and business world for being upright citizens – proud and Presbyterian.

The picture interests me. Here I go again analysing pictures. Mary and her parents are standing with their shoulders and bodies open to each other, Trevor isn't. He looks out of it. His face is pointing towards the camera, yet his body doesn't want to be there.

I sit back on the bed and take a deep breath. All of Trevor Mulholland's non-verbal behaviour points to the fact he was not part of the family – in spirit at least. I study it several times and keep coming up with the same conclusion.

It all looks so perfect on the outside. They could have been the *Cornflake Family* of twenty years ago. Old Tom looked the part with the expensive suits, slicked-back grey hair and a ruddy complexion. Nancy gave me the impression that she would put up with anything to keep the family together. She's wearing a red dress. Maybe she's saying she's angry ...maybe she's saying I thought happiness would come, along with the money ...maybe they were happy.

I look at Trevor Mulholland again. He convinces me they were not. It's all too perfect. The big outside image and the successful grins look like a mask. I glance to Mary wearing a blue business suit, smiling, minding not one iota about touching shoulders with her parents. Trevor is touching none of them. He stands apart. His eyes remote and glancing to the side. I turn the picture over and flash it back. I see a family of three and one outsider.

Was dear old Trevor trying to run away, separate? People who plant bombs move away. The target nearly always moves towards the bomb – a familiar object – part of their life – their car. It's the one logistical consistency when planting small bombs. I'll bet he knows about the bomb. In a way he is trying to leave this picture, like he no longer belongs there.

I reckon the picture had been taken about four months before the bombing. It would fit. He's guilty already, like a little kid standing back and saying, *it was him!* Functional families all stand together. Trevor is a loner, distant. With his contacts and money he could pay to have them killed. I light a cigarette and blow smoke at his face. So ...you get mummy and daddy out of the way and you have full control of the business. Did daddy not approve of your new methods? Was he holding you back? It's possible.

Quickly, I skim over the condemnations from the politicians. I have heard these since I was a kid. It was one of the rare times in the North that they all agreed. The same old statements were written in different ways to break the boredom. *No stone will be left unturned.* There must be hundreds of police lifting up stones somewhere and everywhere to find *cold-blooded murderers.* And, I smile at the old classic: *Terrorism will never destroy the will of the law-abiding people of Northern Ireland.* As long as our will is okay. These dickheads live on a different planet.

Of course, none of them could resist a go at their favourite enemy. The Prods blamed the Catholics and vice-versa. Ian Paisley blamed the Secretary of State. Nothing new.

I read every paper, spanning from the murders on the 16th of August 1989, to the funeral four days later. *The Irish Scribe* had run a full-page picture of the mourners following the coffins. I was there covering the cortege; the world and its wife was there.

Trevor Mulholland had moved back home after the rumpus and funerals. So he's gone back to the womb. Back to the family home. It's starting to make sense. I scratch my head and stare at the wall behind the desk. He could be a stalker. She said he was. He's a big empty nest and it needs filling. That bit made sense when she said he was following her. He becomes obsessed by a woman and ...surprise, surprise, she gets spooked.

The clone that called gives me the *Fatal Attraction* story and mentions Mulholland. Yet I'll bet she isn't being stalked. She wasn't scared enough. Her words lacked frustration and the uselessness the victim experiences. Her non-verbals weren't congruent, either. And ...she's not the type – too intimidating. Now I'm more confused than ever. Why me? Why come to me and pretend to be someone else? Am I meant to know it isn't her? …or am I a step ahead?

I walk over to the window and gaze into the barley. The woman slipped up. I sat with Susan in that very field, eating raisin buns with our imaginary children. Peggy-Sue went everywhere with Susan, except when she moved to Drumfiddy. It was like a custody settlement between divorced six year-olds. I walk along the short upstairs hall and into the bedroom that was always known in the house as the guestroom. I make for the old teak wardrobe and delve into the bottom, below dresses belonging to my late mother. I flick back shoes and there she is. I pull the scruffy rag doll towards me and smile.

I take Peggy-Sue back to my room and place her on the windowsill. I make a few brief notes from the papers and replace the files in the cabinet. Somebody is playing games. But why involve me? Mulholland is a fruitcake, okay, but surely not such a fruitcake as to leave a trail right to his door. Was he behind all of this? Too many questions are attacking me all at once. I'm hungry and a large pizza appears from the mélange of thoughts swirling around. I call Mandy and blow a kiss to Peggy-Sue. I'll call with Mulholland on the way.

Chapter 5

I have no trouble finding Silcott Avenue. At the time of Tom and Nancy Mulholland's murders, I more or less camped out here. Trevor Mulholland lives in number four. I pull the Toyota in behind a green car and gaze up at his home. Expensive cars line both sides of the road. South Belfast is a desirable address since the Ceasefire. Money would never be a problem to Trevor Mulholland.

A little girl on a black bicycle smiles and rides on, unsteadily. I'm right beside a large sycamore, which shields me from the evening sun and a man cutting his lawn. He gives me the odd glance. I stroll past the house. The barbecues are working overtime in the hot summer. Hedge trimmers and lawnmowers serenade me while I smoke a cigarette. The insects of the evening have awakened, congregating under the trees for their night out.

The house looks rundown, with drawn curtains in every room. The unruly privets, surrounding the grey roughcast, two-storey house, hide the neglected gardens. I lean on a post box at the corner of Silcott Avenue. The house is barely recognisable from the time of the murders. The gardens had been immaculate then, neat borders of pansies, busy lizzies and baskets of begonias, everywhere.

I'll bet I'm looking at the house of someone who is mentally ill. Perhaps sick enough to follow Susan Patterson around, or invent a Susan Patterson. I reckon the inside would be left as a shrine. In a way, we have something in common. It would have been easy for me to stop living after my parents died. Looking at Mulholland's house, I'm glad I didn't.

Closed curtains usually mean paranoia. Alcoholics pull the curtains when they go on binges. Mulholland isn't an alcoholic. He likes to snoop on people. Well ...maybe. It fits. He watches people yet nobody can watch him. The state of the place also says *stay away*. I look at the curtains again and still I'm taken aback.

I walk to the gable wall and down an alley at the rear of the properties. I peer into the hedge and see that the back garden is overgrown and neglected. All the windows have their curtains pulled. Maybe he's stopped trying to hide his illness. He can't any longer. It's pointless. His weird thoughts are open to the world, like this place. I bet the neighbours whisper among themselves, the way some people do, pointing at a person with mental illness. So he murders his parents or gets them killed and they talk to him. They stalk him mentally.

Perhaps he projects it onto someone else. 'Do unto others,' and all that. It's possible. *Why did you do it, Trevor?* mummy maybe asks, from behind closed eyes. A little at first, then, he is frightened to sleep or close his eyes at all. Next, she starts to appear in daylight asking the same question. I amble slowly, working it out, connecting bits.

The large mahogany door opens. The swarthy features of Trevor Mulholland scurry towards the blue Mercedes in the driveway. Because it is the corner house, it's the only one in the entire avenue with a driveway. I squeeze myself closer to the post box. The engine of his car fires first time. The nose of the blue Mercedes appears and the darting head of Trevor Mulholland checks for traffic. He roars to a halt beside me at the corner. I lower my head and fumble for a Marlboro. He's gone.

I quicken my pace and break into a run. I slam the RAV4 into gear and cause a blue Mini to brake sharply as I nip into the traffic flow. The RAV4 is useless for following anyone. It stands out like a sore thumb. In this case a big red sore thumb. Mulholland is moving east. I catch sight of his car at the lights and judge my arrival so I am not too close. Susan Patterson lives in the east of the city, or at least that's what the woman said – Hawthorne Drive.

Trevor Mulholland turns right and travels east on the Newtownards Road. I wait until I'm sure, then I take a maze of side streets. Little streets with cars parked on both sides. I hope I've guessed right. The big yellow cranes in the shipyard help me keep my bearings and I check their position now and then. I should be moving away from them to the right. I bounce over ramps put in to stop speeding cars. People chat at their doors and glance as I pass.

I pull up close to Hawthorne Drive. An elderly gentleman mutters about the fine weather as I lock the Toyota. He makes his way slowly, looking at his anxious legs. I peer around the gable wall and Mulholland's car drives carefully past me. I sprint off, past the newsagents and dry cleaners and turn left into Hawthorne Drive. I'm not sure which house it is. It could even be the apartment block at the end of the terraced street. There are two, white Ford Fiesta's in Hawthorne Drive.

Mulholland drives into the courtyard of the apartment block, through an archway with fancy ironwork, to the large stone building. I reckon it was probably an old warehouse at one time. There are six apartments with little windows. I fiddle with my shoe and peer past an old, rusty car. I would be seen if I moved closer. It's a dead end. The apartment block acts as the cross on a T. He knocks a blood-red door. A white Fiesta sits close by. It has to be Susan Patterson's apartment. He shuffles from foot to foot. He looks slimy in his grey slacks and white polo shirt. My visitor opens the door and Mulholland waltzes in. I get a good look at the woman. It's definitely the woman who called with me. I fall back against the old car and try to comprehend what I have witnessed. The stalker thing is a load of crap ...*so what is it*, bites at my stomach.

I screech to a halt in the majestic driveway of Mandy Drummond's home. She lives in Cultra, an exclusive area between Bangor and Belfast, about a fifteen-minute drive away from Hawthorne Drive. Large mansions look over Belfast Lough, towards Carrickfergus on the other side. Mandy's home is breathtaking, sitting back in the pines – a massive Georgian, box-like house with balconies at the front.

I don't bother knocking and find the white tiles, slick and slippery. 'Goodness, Rogers, have you seen a ghost?' Mandy makes her way downstairs and I give her one of my looks.
'Ach ...Mandy. I don't know what I saw. But then I wasn't meant to,' I reply, shrugging.

She ushers me into the large marble kitchen. There's no mention of the gym yet or any digs about me being conniving. I slump over the marble worktop and glance around. I always stare in Mandy's house. Everything is plush. The kitchen is something else. It's green: green cupboards, white utensils and green marble panelling on every wall and the ceiling.

Mandy pours two juices. She looks relaxed, somewhat casual, with a white shirt flapping loose over her denim shorts. She

places my drink down next to the ashtray and sits on the stool beside me, flicking back her long blonde hair. 'Tell an old dyke what bothers you, Rogers.' Mandy shuffles herself comfortable. She always calls herself an old dyke. Rory doesn't *really* like her, partly because she's English and partly because he shudders to think what lesbians get up to. In the years we've worked together I've yet to meet one of her girlfriends. She's not old – nearly forty-five. I half laugh.
'It wasn't her.'
'Was not who, Rogers?'
'Who she was meant to be …the girl who visited me at Tullydeen. She wasn't Susan Patterson. She pretended she was …I was fooled for a minute but I smelt a rat. And, a rat cropped up in the conversation,' I say. Mandy sips her juice slowly.
'Stop, Rogers. Who is Susan Patterson?'
'Ach …a girl who lived beside me years ago. We were childhood friends. Well, this girl said she was Susan Patterson …but she's not. Well, I don't think she is.'
'Explain the rat appearing, Rogers.'
'Trevor Mulholland. She said Mulholland was following her.'
'You expect me to believe all of this, Rogers. You would stoop to anything. To make your non-appearance more palatable, you concoct this gibberish, dashing in here to woo my sympathy. Well …it won't work, Rogers. You weaseled your way out of the challenge, the way you weasel out of everything.' Mandy was off the stool and almost off her trolley. I knew I would have to listen to this. She has picked a bad time. She never lets anything drop. I nurse my drink and try to ignore her.

She grabs my shirt, taking me by surprise.
'Well …did you?'
'Did I what?' I snap back.
'Did you plan it, Rogers?'
'No, Mandy. I did not plan it.' I'm angry now. I shove her hand off my shirt and slap the worktop.
'I pulled a muscle,' I say. She laughs contemptuously. I give her my gritted teeth look and somewhere it registers.
'I had to listen to a cock and bull story about her being followed. Bloody *Fatal Attraction*. So good old Simon here decides to help her and I go to stalk the stalker. I follow him to the apartment and they greet like lovers and go inside. They've probably ordered a

takeaway and a video.' I grab a Marlboro and stuff it into my mouth.

Mandy has a large grin stretching all over her face. 'Oh Rogers, you are so gallant.' I'd love to wipe the grin off her face. I pull hard on my cigarette and stare at the microwave.

'Do you remember Trevor Mulholland, the accountant? His parents were killed in that bomb at the restaurant,' I manage, after the silence.
'How could I forget,' Mandy answers in a reflecting tone. Her eyes roll towards her forehead and I'm glad to see a sour look cross her face. I know she hates Mulholland. In fact they almost came to blows at the funeral. Mulholland tried to push her away. Nobody pushes Mandy Drummond. 'So he is the pursuer?'
'If there is a ...pursuer,' I say, using her strange choice of word. I would have said *the stalker*, or *the man*. But then I wasn't educated in Surrey. 'Well, what do you think?' I ask.

She has the benefit of looking from the outside. She is also very practical, likes things in black and white, perfect for a photographer. She rubs the base of her glass, trying to put logic to my story. My mind is starting to slow down again.
'What's the name of your doll, Mandy ...your favourite one?' I drop in, quickly.
'Pastel,' she answers, without hesitation although a little bewildered. 'Why, Rogers?'
'Ach ...I was just wondering. Mine was Barney ...a Teddy Bear.'
'How nice for you, Rogers. Shall we eat? I think you should.'

Mandy escorts me towards the door. I stare into space and connect things. The evening is quickly drifting into night across Belfast Lough. We are travelling along its shore towards Bangor. I enjoy watching the moon on the water. I toss a coin: heads I pay. It's tails. Mandy pushes the accelerator pedal to the floor.

Excited teenagers, smelling sweet and sometimes overpowering, pass, making their way to the nightclubs. We dribble past the amblers making our way towards the many fast food bars. Bangor is looking well. As a teenager I came here to stand in the corner of nightclubs until the beer took effect. I could dance then. Next, it was the wall along the seafront and I cursed the dodgy sausages.

The old seafront is a large car park now, leading to the trendy Marina. New hotels watch over the sea, familiar buildings have received a facelift or been converted. I gaze around while

Mandy buys the pizza. The gentle breeze makes the evening pleasant.

We stroll along and find a bench, close to the boats.
'Perhaps Mulholland assumed you would smell a rat,' Mandy offers as we sit. I'm glad she said that. She rips the lid off the pizza box and hands it to me. The heat and fragrance of the food escapes. I'm so hungry.
'Should I go up the garden path, Mandy?'
'Like a teddy bear, Rogers – a conniving teddy bear. One who weasels out of commitments.'

I let her have her little joke. It's Mandy's way of saying it doesn't matter – forget it. I think of Mulholland, Barney and Peggy-Sue, and the woman who is pretending to be Susan Patterson. I've got an urge to meet the real Susan Patterson wherever she is. …But maybe the woman is Susan Patterson, I remind myself. Mandy shuffles a slice of pizza towards me. I burn my fingers: she laughs and I wonder if it's an omen.

Chapter 6

Mandy's in the process of dressing. I've been up for hours. The morning news picked up upon the Andrews Corporation story. Not much else had happened, news wise.

    I've made a few possible connections and put my holidays on hold. I sip coffee on the veranda leading from my room. I call it the lemon room. It's my second home, with a big bouncy bed and an en-suite.

    Mandy appears, her blonde hair pulled and plaited tightly from her face. She's wearing black and grey clown trousers and a yellow blouse. She's an unhappy clown. 'Morning,' I say. She simply replies with a shrug, coming to join me at the table. I pour her a cup of coffee and she slumps over it like a drunk at the bar.
'Sleep well?'
'So-so, Rogers. Shut up.'

    I brave her mood and mention her pictures that made the news. She shrugs again and cuddles her coffee. I don't want to leave the morning sun, dripping in from the tall pines with the birds in good voice.

    I drop Mandy off at Hawthorne Drive. Mulholland's car is still parked in the same position. The white Fiesta sits close to the blood red door. 'Snap anything that moves,' I say. It's out before I can stop it.
'Rogers ...I am a photographer. I take pictures. You resort to gibberish trying to captivate my work. A task beyond you.' Mandy is awake.

    I make it to the Belfast General Hospital and find a parking space. I was born in this hospital. Some ten years later I had my appendix removed here and was rushed to Accident and Emergency in a deep sleep, eight years after that. A shiver crosses my back, walking towards the sliding doors. It turns out Susan Patterson used to work here before moving to Jersey. Janet, the receptionist, peroxide pretty except for the roots gives me a postcard Susan Patterson sent from there. Corbière Lighthouse is on the picture side and the scrawl on the back mentions the usual things and her boyfriend, Mervyn. He works in Spain, Janet informed me.

    I use the mobile in the Toyota. Mandy has snapped the location and bribed her way into a young lady's home. I mention the postcard and the guy called Mervyn, working in Spain. I listen for a pause, but there is none. I'm paranoid. I drive to Tullydeen, pack a few things and grab my dictaphone and laptop.

    So this is Drumfiddy – Drumfiddy, Co. Antrim. I haven't missed much. It looks a little like Tullydeen, only with a chip shop and an Orange Hall. I pass under the arch spanning the road. King William of Orange looks down in triumph, with the backdrop of the River Boyne. Scotland looms on the horizon, shimmering across the Irish Sea.

    A couple of fishing boats prepare for the tide, and the ruddy men pay careful attention to my presence, rising from their stooped position. The large sheds of Patterson Engineering unfold from the fields, past the harbour and the white houses. Red, white and blue kerbstones and graffiti with a large Red Hand of Ulster on a gable wall declare loyalty to God and the Queen. I don't imagine there are many Seamus's or Bridget's in this part of the world. This is Ian Paisley country where names like Billy or Elizabeth dominate. I'll bet the seagulls are even Protestants and certainly not homosexual, well, openly at least.

    I park in customer parking and walk stiffly towards reception. It's a small grey brick building, a bit like a porch on the front of the massive corrugated sheds. I meet one of those receptionists, as stubborn as hell. Maybe it was she who painted the red hand on the harbour wall? Pearl Patterson is not available, she tells me, scanning my indignity from head to toe. I set my card on the counter and her hooked nose could easily lift it.

'Ach ...if she's not here then could you tell me where she lives?' I ask, leaning on the counter. How dare you, her big rosy face seems to say without words. I drum on the desk.

'Mrs Patterson does not like people calling at her home. I am not allowed to give out her address or private telephone number to any

Tom, Dick or Harry,' she states, trying to sound important. Maybe if Dick called at *her* home he could humour her. She returns to her typing. I glance around. It's a beautiful reception, with soft sofas and a coffee machine, immaculately clean.

'Please telephone Pearl Patterson and tell her I'm waiting,' I say, sternly. She glances up from her word processor with disdain. I slump down on the soft sofa and flick through the *Ulster Tatler* and *Northern Woman*. The receptionist from hell picks up the phone and mumbles. I smile in victory.

Pearl Patterson walks from the mahogany door, dressed immaculately in a blue business suit with a white blouse peeking out. She has stunning legs. I try to picture the real Pearl Patterson from my childhood. Is this one a fake, too? Her warm smile and short blonde hair seem right.

'Remember me?' I say, throwing the magazine down. She stops and both of her hands cover her mouth.
'Simon? …Tullydeen Simon? Oh my goodness, Simon. It's *that*, Simon Rogers. After all this time.' Pearl Patterson hugs me like I'm the edge of a cliff. Her hazel eyes dance, waltzing with her words. I'm sure it's her.
'Sandra, fix us some coffee, please,' she says, eagerly. We walk into her office. An antique, oak desk sits by the window. I aim for the sofa beside the wall opposite. Pearl hangs up her jacket on the matching coat stand. She has a fine figure and is about five eight, to the undertaker's eye.
'You've done well for yourself,' I manage. She smiles and moves around to sit on the front of her desk. I can't help but look at her legs. 'How's Susan?'
'Oh, she's fine. I wanted her to give up nursing and help me out in the business, you know. Peter died back in eighty-three,' she informs me, twiddling her fingers. I glance at the photos on the walls: men shaking hands with Pearl, obviously, contract signings or something like that.
'So what brings you to the grand domain of Drumfiddy?'
'Mind if I smoke?'
'No …feel free. I smoke like a train, you know.' Sandra enters with the coffee and plain biscuits. I give her a little grin. She ignores me. Pearl pours and joins me on the settee.

We drizzle with small talk over coffee. It is like a replay of my meeting with her supposed daughter. She grabs my knee occasionally and I normally hate people touching my body, yet with Pearl it's different. I pick things from my childhood only she could know about and we laugh. I stub out my butt and take a deep breath. 'Penny for them,' she says. I try to work out Pearl's age. She must be middle fifties, yet she looks younger and very attractive. Her spiky hair adds to the high cheekbones and her sensual mouth.

'Susan came to visit me a few days ago, much like we're doing now,' I bolt out, clearing my throat. She eases back, slightly. 'She couldn't have ...she's in Jersey, working.' She grabs her cigarettes and a shake develops in her hands.
'Somebody's playing games, Pearl,' I add softly. Pearl walks around the office, folding her arms across her cleavage. 'Susan's in Jersey,' she says again, fanning out her hand. 'I talked to her last night ...on the phone, you know. She's working at St. Tanons, near Gorey.'
'Yeah, so I believe,' I say. 'Does she have an apartment in Hawthorne Drive?'
'Yes, why?' she answers quickly. I look down at the plush green carpet.
'Sit down, Pearl.'
'What's going on?' she asks, holding her hands. I tell her the saga of the woman passing herself off as her daughter. I deliberately leave out the name of Trevor Mulholland for the moment. Her skin is soft and sunburnt, like the clone who had been out to dupe me. A drill somewhere in the factory squeals, causing me to wince now and then. Pearl lies back on the sofa. She is baffled.
'It's so many years, Simon. How did you know it wasn't Susan?'
'How did you know I was Simon Rogers?' I bounce back. Pearl thinks and nods a yes. I watch her movements. These were mannerisms stored in my mind from a distant age. Now that I am looking at them again I recall more from those days: her placing me on her knee; my drawing that she put up on the kitchen door – little flashes.
'Well, Simon, you haven't changed, you know,' she says. I give her a frown and she laughs.
'Ach ...Pearl, I won't pee on your sofa now,' I jest. I love her laugh.
'You won't? Thank goodness. It's just little things, you know.'
'What, me peeing?'
'No,' she says with a mocking slap. 'Little things about you, you know.'

'I'm glad you said that. I couldn't connect the woman with Susan,' I explain. She sighs and pulls her lips into a straight line. We have more coffee. 'Does the name Trevor Mulholland mean anything to you?'

'Yes, he's my accountant. Has been from day one. His father was very good to us starting up.' She pauses. 'Has he something to do with this?' Her voice is soft and subtle. She doesn't hold that near-Scottish accent associated with this part of the world.

'Might have,' I say. 'The Susan who said she was being stalked, said Trevor Mulholland was the stalker,' I finish. Pearl gives a little laugh, more from disbelief and bewilderment than out of humour. I shake my head and chance a biscuit. We both sit in silence. Pearl exhales loudly now and then.

'What do you think's going on?' she asks.

'Pearl ...I haven't a clue,' I say. 'It could be me they're after or you and Susan.' She studies me for a moment before letting me go. 'You keep saying *they*, you know. Why do you do that?' Her words are always slow and deliberate.

'Good question,' I shrug. 'It has to be more than one person. Well ...I think Mulholland is involved. It's just my gut. I've no proof, but I did a big story on the Andrew Corporation and my instinct keeps coming back to them. I think Mulholland might be involved with the Andrews Corporation. He might be a director or something.'

'I read about that,' she intervenes. 'I didn't even know it was you ...my little Simon. Well ...you're not so little any more. Look at the size of those shoulders.' I feel my face burning as Pearl grabs me, eyeing me from head to toe.

'Ach ...Pearl, you're embarrassing me,' I say, clutching my hands, the way a kid does when the neighbours are in. I can almost see down her throat when she laughs.

'I called at the hospital and they said Susan had a boyfriend called Mervyn.'

'They're engaged,' she corrects. 'I have yet to meet him, Simon. Apparently he works in Spain doing some type of computer work, too high tech for me,' she dismisses.

'Whereabouts in Spain?' I ask. I'm wanting her to say Malaga. I'm leaning forward, like a gambler waiting for the dice to rest.

'I don't know,' she shrugs. She fixes her skirt and swipes at a piece of fluff. I let my shoulders ease again and sit back.

'Susan and I don't exactly see eye to eye, you know. Her dad and her were so close. We've had troubles,' she concedes. I am sure she was going to say more, then decided against it. Pearl moves over to her desk and grabs a large blue diary. 'Here's a photo of Susan. Was that her ...the girl, you know?' Pearl's eyes are apprehensive and so beautiful.

'It wasn't Susan who visited me,' I say confidently. I watch the relief on her mother's face.

This is really my childhood friend. The other woman had the same colouring, yet the real Susan Patterson looks stunning. I study the picture. It had been taken at the beach, Portrush. Pearl is busy dialling a number. I am lost in Tullydeen, playing on the rocks and having picnics. The connections come: chasing her with a mackerel; having to feed that stupid doll and the day we looked up the atlas to find Drumfiddy.

'There's someone here who would like to speak to you,' Pearl says, waving me over to the phone.

'Peggy-Sue's pregnant. It was Barney. I'll get onto the Child Support Agency. '

'Simon! Simon Rogers.' I can't get a word in edgewise, yet Susan answers all of my questions. Pearl lights me a cigarette and sits closely.

'I'm coming over to visit you.' A spur of the moment decision, which I manage to utter in between her string of excited questions. Pearl taps my shoulder.

'Tell her I'm coming too,' she whispers, with the most beautiful lips I've ever seen.

Chapter 7

I follow Pearl's white Toyota Celica, past the harbour and back to the main Belfast to Coleraine Road. Before today, it had been the closest I had come to Drumfiddy. Pearl nips across the road, into a lane leading to an old farmhouse. A new conservatory had been built and a blue van sits close by. I park beside a red, rusty cement mixer next to some barns.

'Please excuse the mess. I'm renovating.' I tiptoe past the concrete blocks, to what appears to be the popular entrance. The kitchen is in the middle of being re-plastered. 'Find a seat in there.' She points towards a door at the far end of the large kitchen. 'I won't be long.'

I make my way into the new conservatory. It's full of furniture, from the other rooms. A workman chases after Pearl and they have a brief discussion. Somebody, somewhere above me hammers nails into floorboards. I squeeze myself over to the large windows past what I believe is the new wicker furniture for this place. Sheen sheep are grazing at what is left of the field.

What will I tell Rory? I know he'll listen to all the details, in his usual manner, be polite to Pearl Patterson, with his mumbling smile, and probably see something I've missed. I pick up a photo of Susan and her late father, sitting at the kitchen table. Their smiles are alike and both have similar colouring. I recall Peter Patterson as a kind man. Susan looks like him, with the same dark complexion.

'There we are,' Pearl says. I almost drop the picture.

'Sorry,' she smiles. 'That was one of the last pictures taken of Susan and her father, you know.'

I replace it. 'How did she handle the death?'

'She didn't. Susan was twenty-one, then, and a pain in the bloody arse, to put it mildly. You talked to her on the phone. You just have to listen with Susan. She does all the talking, you know,' Pearl states, reflecting. 'Why do you ask?'
'Ach ...I was just wondering,' I say, trying to close the subject. 'Love the blouse.'

Mulholland would've known the family history, probably documented it like figures, every little detail. Accountants are meticulous. He would coach the clone.
'Will I do?' she asks, fanning out her arms. 'Ach ...I'll take the bad look off you,' I jest back, eyeing her jeans and white gypsy blouse. A tiny blush crawls over her cheeks.

I have a load of questions I want to ask, however, I bite my tongue. We settle on Pearl's Celica. I grab my laptop and stuff, and park the RAV4 in the old barn. 'You drive,' she says. It takes me a little while to get used to the car's lower driving position. I can't see as much.

I find myself taking sly glances at Pearl. Her profile is stunning. Here I am, like a teenager fantasising about an older woman. It's like being back at school with Mrs Brown, the English teacher. Everybody fantasised about her.
'Penny for them?' Pearl asks.
'Ach ...I was just wondering about things,' I reply. She smirks and lets her fingers float in the breeze from the open window. I pass my first tractor and love the power under my foot. She *would* drive a Celica. It's her.

'Why would Mulholland be involved?' Pearl asks, out of the blue.
'Don't think he's trying to swindle me? I brought some figures with me if they're any help.' She shuffles around in her seat and gives a little sigh. I had thought about the possibility. Patterson Engineering looks to be doing nicely.
'It could always be possible. Are you doing well, or is there anything strange in the books?' I inquire.
'No,' Pearl answers, quickly, sort of disappointed. The possibility of her having a fling with old Tom Mulholland has crossed my mind. However, I don't bring it up. Maybe Trevor is getting revenge for his deceased mother? It's a long shot.

We drive across the Lagan Bridge. 'It's so handy,' she observes. Pearl gazes at the new buildings being erected since the Ceasefire. 'Oh, it's so good to be away from Drumfiddy, you know.

Running a business is not all it's cracked up to be. You miss out on so many things, Simon.' I love the way she says Simon. The way her cheeks move and the way it rolls off her lips. I glance over at her and she catches me. 'Yeah ..I suppose so,' I manage, amazed I didn't mumble.

The sun is still baking Belfast. Pearl is enjoying being driven around. Pigeons jaywalk in Oxford Street around the brown legs of the shoppers. Exposed bodies carry bags and music blares from cars with every window open. 'The city's really returning to life, you know.' She glances at me like a mother proud of her child. 'Yeah ...the nightlife's all back and there's a good atmosphere around,' I add. 'This is us up here.' I point to the large glass building in Manford St.

The car park of *The Irish Scribe* gives us some desirable shade. 'Welcome to the world of media, Pearl.'
We climb the stairs and the smell of ink and grease oozes from the door leading to the presses. 'It churns out sixty thousand copies an hour. Ach ...Rory will probably give you a tour,' I smile, shaking my head. I escort Pearl through a yellow door and along the claustrophobic hallway to the newsroom.

It's modern and open plan. Pam Lavery looks up from her keyboard and smiles a hello. Junior reporters dash, harassed, checking columns of print, quickly, hoping to make bedtime. Deadline is seven. Pearl's taking everything in and I stand back.

Rory spots me. Mandy is sitting, dangling her legs over a chair in his greenhouse. He hates me calling it his greenhouse. The click of keyboards and processing paper appears to captivate Pearl. 'It's massive. There must be so much work goes into a paper, you know,' she states, absentmindedly.

'Ach ...it just looks worse than it is, Pearl. What these ones are working on will be printed tonight. Then, in the morning people will read it. The next day somebody will be eating fish and chips out of it.' I pause. 'They used to clean their arse with it as well,' I whisper into her ear. She lets out a little chuckle and gives me a mischievous slap.

I do the introductions. Rory positions a chair for Pearl. Mandy hands me the prints she had taken at Hawthorne Drive. I glare at Trevor Mulholland, kissing the brunette goodbye. 'The door was obtrusive. However, she is in focus, Rogers,' Mandy explains, handing me a blow-up of the woman. It is definitely the woman that pretended to be Susan Patterson.

'Good work, Mandy.' She twitches her nose as if it's no big deal. Secretly, she's always pleased when her work's praised.

'What is next, Rogers?'

'I need you to keep snapping these two.' She nods and throws me a bit by her compliance. 'Here, this's the real Susan Patterson,' I say quickly, passing her the print.

'Much prettier, Rogers.'

Rory finishes fussing over Pearl Patterson, with a quick rundown on the history of *The Irish Scribe*. I *overhear* him mention a tour. He pats his thinning fair hair as usual and sits on his desk.

He listens intently to my tale, jotting down the occasional note. I show him the two Susan Patterson's and he stops to congratulate Pearl on having such a beautiful daughter. Pearl looks at me, slightly blushing. I am delighted to see Rory Hamilton baffled. He fiddles with his gold-rimmed spectacles and places them gently on the desk. Mandy is studying the surfer on the calendar, from the paper manufacturers. Pearl hands Rory the figures she had brought with her.

'Do ye mind if I get one of our experts to take a look at these, Mass Patterson?'

'Be my guest,' Pearl says confidently. Mandy rolls her eyes. I almost laugh.

Rory escorts Pearl through the newsroom, pointing at various things and stopping with people he wants to introduce her to. 'I'll be lucky to catch the flight,' I say.

'Which flight …your fancy? Goodness Rogers, you are into grandmothers, I see.'

I ignore her sarcasm and stick to the facts. 'I'm going to interview the real Susan Patterson, in Jersey.'

'How nice, Rogers. I take it mother is going also.'

'Yes.' I wait for more of Mandy's subtle digs. However, they only appear in her grin. I don't rise to the bait.

I take the opportunity to make a list of things I need checked out. A list of bankruptcies from Mulholland's firm tops the list along with a police check on the girl posing as Susan Patterson. They both need to be observed. Mandy will take care of that. Trevor Mulholland in the family portrait grabs my thoughts. Is it the murder of his parents? I want to tackle Mulholland and ask questions, but that would be stupid.

'I shall observe, Mandy.'

'Sorry.'

'Observe,' I say again. 'What's up?'
'Nothing, Rogers.' She pulls her body together and stands. 'Perhaps you will call before your flight.' She disappears from the office before I have time to answer. I watch her stroll across the newsroom. She's in one of her moods. For a long time I used to think I'd offended her in some way. It's just her. She goes like that, yet she tries to make me feel as if it's my fault.

Rory and Pearl eventually appear again. I've read the other papers and their coverage of the Andrews story. It's big news, a lucky break. The time of the release was perfect, nothing else of any importance had happened. I was competing against the weather forecast and the imminent hosepipe ban. Other reporters had latched onto it. They ran pictures of company representatives reading prepared statements on the steps of the Andrews Corporation in Belfast. According to several reports *The Irish Scribe* is being sued. Talk's cheap. It takes money to buy drink.

'Can you sort this out, Rory?' I say, handing him the list.
'Look at this, Mass Patterson. Always working. It's work- work-work with him, Mass Patterson.'
'Oh he's like that, Mr Hamilton, you know.' Pearl says, grabbing my neck and laughing.
'It's just, Rory, Mass Patterson. Just call me Rory.'
'What do you think of his greenhouse?' I ask, trying to keep my face straight. Rory is touchy and very proud of his office. He's a little pissed off though he tries to hide it.
'I'll send you a little something from Patterson Engineering, Rory. I think it will look well in here,' Pearl says, with something in mind.
'What is it …a watering can?' I interrupt.
'Never you mind,' she replies, with a mocking scold. Rory watches us like a game of tennis.

Chapter 8

'Fancy a pizza?'
'Why not.' The heat in Royal Avenue is almost unbearable.
I order salami, pepperoni sausage and extra mushrooms. Pearl wanders off to window shop. It gives me time to look at her. I stand transfixed. She sways gently with her carefree stride. She's spotted something she likes in Marks & Spencers. Her ankles are crossed as she gently contemplates the garment. Several men glance at her as they stroll past.

We've sort of hit it off. ...But, maybe she's just being polite. If I tried to kiss her she would probably say you are a nice fella, but I just want to be your friend. Then all the rejection hits home and you even look fatter and uglier in the mirror ...and the defamatory voices arrive. *Who would fancy you? You're just a big lig*. I don't want to be a *nice fella* or *a friend*.
'Hey Simon. Wakey-wakey.'
'Sorry Mario. Much is it?'
'Ten pounds to you, Simon. To anyone else ...eight pounds. You famous now ...famouser than old Mario. Keep chasing those Andrews bums,' he salutes.
'Keep ripping people off, Mario, and I'll do a piece on you,' I push back. 'I'll put your ugly oul face on the front page.'
'Only scare the kids, Simon. Enjoy,' he yells, smiling.

I juggle the bottle of Coke and the fifteen-inch pizza. I see the bus, but I can beat it. The draught of the vehicle sways my shirt. The driver blasts the horn. Everybody's looking.
'It's meant to be old ladies who can't cross the road on their own, you know,' Pearl giggles.

'He speeded up when he saw me. They always do that,' I explain, still puffing. 'Here we go,' I say, in the best traditions of Belfast.

Pearl grabs the Coke and we walk to the benches around the City Hall. People are enjoying the afternoon sunshine on the manicured lawns. We take a bench in the shade. I hear a long blast on a car horn. An ambulance is going somewhere close by, probably on its way to the Royal.

We ignore our parents' advice and talk about everything while our mouths are full. Her legs are crossed in a casual manner. She wipes some tomato puree off my chin, ever so tenderly, with a Mario's napkin. When she's concentrating, her chin moves slightly to the side and her tongue rests on her bottom lip. I sit like a little boy and don't mind having my face cleaned. I glance down at her blouse and the valley it makes outlining her breasts. The hint of her *Chanel No. 5* drifts over me, just the right amount. The clone that came to visit me wore the same perfume. I want to kiss her, but I hold back.

We collect the plane tickets from Belfast City Airport. It's the ten-thirty flight into Gatwick, with a transfer to Jersey. Then we cruise around the city, past Van Morrison's birthplace, past the murals, Loyalist murals, declaring an intention to defend Ulster. We stop at Charles Hurst, the Toyota showroom on the Boucher Road. We take a test drive in a new Toyota Celica. Pearl can't decide on the colour. Michelle works out a deal for me to change the RAV4 while Nigel chats to Pearl about colours and things. Pearl looks over now and then and smiles.

We eventually arrive in Hawthorne Drive. Pearl tells me she had bought the apartment for Susan a few years back with insurance money following Peter's death. Mulholland had been involved in the negotiation, of course. I cruise along the Newtownards Road. The cranes in the shipyard stand tall and yellow in the sunshine. I drive south, towards Silcott Avenue, past Ormeau Park and take a right. We drive slowly past Mulholland's rundown home. His blue Mercedes is in the driveway. 'Bit of a mess,' I say. She appears quite shocked. Shocked enough to confide in me how she doesn't like him. Pearl speaks fondly of the late Tom Mulholland and how she doubts if she would be where she is today without his expertise and friendship. I want to ask if she had an affair with him, but I don't.

We saunter through Ormeau Park. The trees loaded with leaves give us some shade. She points at the rose-beds. I'd noticed some at her home. I talk her out of walking up to Susan's apartment and asking what's going on. We stop and study two golfers across the fence. 'He should take up bowls,' she whispers. A Labrador called Tara gives us the sniff over and refuses to return to her master. Pearl makes a fuss of the dog. Tara is reluctantly, dragged off by her human friend – at the second attempt.

'Do you have a dog, Simon?'

'No. You?'

'No ...not now. I always had, you know, Labradors. I love Labradors.' She seems to have forgotten about Mulholland and the apartment. Things were getting a bit tense, just before the dog arrived.

'What about the police?' she asks, looking up at the tall beech.

'No, not yet, Pearl. Anyway, Mulholland will have it all tied up. Rory and us have a guy in the police, he sort of works for the paper. Drops us stuff ...things like that. I'm getting the girl checked out so we have to wait,' I explain.

'Is that legal?' she asks, with a mocking glint.

'Ach ...Pearl, is it right to ask a donkey to hee-haw?'

We reach Tullydeen. I reintroduce Mary Ginty to Pearl and leave them to chat. The old bitch looks quite happy. Her best friend must've died. I wander outside and sit on the windowsill. The old wobbly shelves and her crooked glances are too much for me. The smell of cow dung floats across the air. This is reality country style. Tommy Dickson's tractor has left a pile of dung like a small mountain, outside the shop. The tyre marks are visible in yellow and various shades of brown. They're in a straight line, which is unusual for Tommy.

'Nice country air,' I joke, as Pearl comes outside. She creases up her face, pushing out a tiny whimper.

'That'll clear your lungs, you know.'

'Did you buy anything?'

'Ehmm. Some chocolate and a rundown on you,' Pearl smiles. She grabs my shoulders and playfully nips them.

'Ach ...she loves me alright,' I respond. 'She won't sell *The Irish Scribe* because the word Irish is in it.'

'I heard all about it,' Pearl giggles. 'He's a Fenian lover working for that oul thing and wearing them oul jeans and white gutties. I'm surprised he hasn't grown a beard like that oul Gerry Adams. He always was a bad looking article,' Pearl mimics.

'Who, me or Gerry?' I ask.

'Oh, I'd say both of you, you know.'

I'm glad I cleaned the house. It must've been a premonition. I show Pearl to the guestroom and give her a refresher tour of the house. I find fresh sheets and a clean duvet cover and leave her to settle in. I phone Mandy, nothing has changed. Her mood is vague, rebuffing my attempts to dribble around it.

Rory phones to say he has the list of bankruptcies. He emails it. A few large businesses had gone into liquidation following the murder of Mulholland's parents. Thompson's Foundry and Fast Frank's – a chain of chip shops. A host of other small firms bit the dust, mostly caused by the ever-present recession, Rory believed. He suggests I look at Thompson's and Fast Frank's in his scribbled note. Patterson Engineering is in the same locality. I sigh and fire the printout towards the kitchen table.

So Mulholland sends a clone to befriend me and possibly make me visit Drumfiddy. Nice to see you and all that stuff. …That would be stupid. Why take the chance? …It's too obvious. I grab a Harp from the fridge and slump down on the chair. I doodle on a notepad. I think I was meant to know it wasn't Susan Patterson. Mulholland planned it that way. Did he know I followed him to the apartment? So in his mind he's stalking me. Wrong Simon. The girl mentioned him. Damn ...I am meant to know he's in the picture. So I've done what he wants me to do, like the obedient dog. If he is involved in his parents' murder maybe he wants to lead me to the killers? I think of the house, the condition it has fallen into. Maybe the weight of guilt is too much.

I draw a little fire on the pad to represent the bombing. Next, Mulholland as a matchstick man, with some terrorists organising the act. It was supposed to be mistaken identity ...no mistake. I make a cross for the funerals and a pound sign for him taking control of the entire accountancy firm. I draw arrows pointing downwards for firms going bankrupt followed by the word *years*.

So, he plans the bombing and is held to ransom by his action? ...By whom? I look back at the matchstick men. It had to be the people who planted the bomb. Perhaps the guilt appears when he closes his eyes. I stare at the window. Pearl is fumbling above my head, probably placing things to her liking.

The envelope of photographs Mandy had taken might cast some light. Mulholland is ill, pain is written all over his face. The pulled curtains flash across my mind. It's a defence ...the neglected gardens say: *keep away*. People look at neglected gardens. He wants them to look at the garden, not him. Don't look in ...you might not like what you see, or you might see my secret. He bounces awake at nights hearing the bomb exploding ...perhaps he watched it go off.

Over the years it doesn't go away ...gets worse. People give him a wide berth because of what happened to his family ...feel sorry for him. It probably helped for a while, now, nothing only death will erase the nightmare.

People confess the strangest things if they think they're going to die. The years, in which they hid their shame or guilt from the outside world, appear to mean nothing any more. Their regrets and innermost shame usually pour out in preparation for the next world ...or whatever. Mulholland wants out. Death is out. Maybe there's a big fire waiting for him. His actions, being ticked off in the big book. *Why did you have me killed, Trevor?* mummy maybe asks.

He's trying to make some amends. Killers usually see the faces of their victims, in the dark hours. Mulholland becomes frightened. Mummy and daddy pop up in daylight as well as the dark. There's no escape. He pulls the curtains so they can't enter. Can't see him. Can't question. Yet they do. I bet they do.

'Haven't had much of a chance to wear these, you know. What do you think?'
'I think Trevor Mulholland killed his parents and he's leading me or us to the killers. The ones who planted the bomb,' I say, turning around. Pearl's mouth falls open and she leans on the doorframe. I take a sip of my beer and let her settle and think about how crazy that sounded. Then, it was meant to sound crazy, otherwise it couldn't have been pulled off. Fact is stranger than fiction, I remind myself. She joins me at the table, touching my shoulders on the way past. 'You look wonderful. Want a beer?' I grab two more Harps from the fridge and she is studying my symbolic thoughts on the pad.
'What does all this mean?' she asks.
'There are always many sides to a story and at least two sides to a human being. One is what we want the world to see, the other is what we keep hidden, or try to keep hidden, usually not on purpose. That's the one that fascinates me – the unconscious. It is always

communicating through body language or choice of words. It leaks out in many forms. Those drawings are an attempt to enter Trevor Mulholland's secret world. To think like him and operate the way he does. I could be wrong. Some people think it's a load of crap. I don't think so. That's what led me to study Psychology, Pearl,' I explain, taking a long swig.

'You're a psychologist?'

'Ach ...I'm supposed to be.'

'Goodness,' she replies, raising her tin of beer.

'Love the shorts,' I say. She sort of gives me that look, which doesn't say, *you're a nice fella* or *I just want to be your friend.*

We drink more beer and I search for the wine I had placed in some cupboard during my mad cleaning coup. I find it eventually, beside the broom in the tall cupboard close to the door. I place it in the fridge and we go walking towards her old home. I carry a supply of beer, dangling by the plastic. We sing *My Aunt Jane,* sitting around the ruins of her old cottage. Pearl's words are starting to slur and her face is getting rouged.

I tell her about the broken walls. How no one had ever lived in their cottage after they left Tullydeen. Gradually it fell apart, storms taking their tuppence worth. That sort of thing. She reckons I'm sitting on what used to be the kitchen wall. Pearl points to the various rooms. She's sitting where the stove was, she figures. She rests her left leg straight out on the old mortar. Her right one dangles down.

The barley slithers around with its hypnotic whisper, visualising the presence of the gentle breeze. She throws her head back and lets the wind tickle her neck. The beer allows me to take longer looks at her thighs. My eyes are constantly drifting along her contours. She asks about women in my life. I laugh and briefly mention the divorce. She apologises. I throw her another beer and we sit and remember and rule the world a bit. She grabs my shoulder occasionally, and I want to hold her. She knows I want to.

'Tell me about Thompson's Foundry,' I say, forcing myself to do so. My shorts feel sticky, twitching, as flurries of sexual imagery flash before my eyes. She gives a little cough and holds my stare. I want to say I don't give an iota about Thompson's Foundry.

'I'm fond of Billy Thompson, you know,' she utters, in her soft, deliberate voice. 'In fact, when he went bust, I offered to help him out. Rumours circulate around the place. Poor Billy,' she says. Pearl

places her can on the wall and watches the swallows skim past. 'Billy Thompson couldn't believe how he went bust, you know,' she continues. 'He's started a taxi business in Coleraine now, doing well. Hard worker, Billy, same as his father.'
'Do you think Mulholland helped him go out of business, Pearl?'
'Yes. Billy was supposed to have raped a girl. Rubbish if you ask me. It really, really annoyed his father, you know. It never came to court or reached the rumour stage. Brian Thompson, his father, told me all about it, poor man. Billy was a bit of a wild fella growing up, getting drunk, but he wasn't a rapist, you know,' she explains, with certainty.
'How do you know?'
'I'm a woman.'
'Think it was blackmail?'
'It could've been. Brian died then and although I don't know for sure, I bet he paid whoever it was off.' I sit back. Pearl has obviously discussed this with herself many times and wondered.
'Did he say who it was?' I ask.
'No ...I got the feeling he didn't know. Don't ask me why,' she says, flicking out her arm.
'Did you ever hear anything about Fast Frank?' I ask.
'No,' she answers, quickly. 'But I know one thing, with the profit on food, how could a chain of chip shops go broke? It's the best business to be in, you know. Fast Frank's chips were lovely. He had good locations. I often wondered what happened to him,' she says, shaking her head.

    Pearl pushes herself off the wall. She ambles around the various rooms and perhaps her memories. I watch her buttocks wobble and the way her beige shorts hug them. I sigh and gaze away towards the barley. I light another Marlboro and she walks back into what was her kitchen.

'Fast Frank isn't so fast anymore, you know.' She stops and giggles into her hands.
'What's up?' I ask.
'He had his left leg amputated. It's not funny, you know, but I just have this picture of him hopping around quickly on one leg and asking if you want salt and vinegar on your chips.' She bursts out laughing and staggers over to me.
'No more beer for you, my girl,' I laugh, pointing a patriarchal finger. I feel her press against my chest, her heat. She takes my

cigarette and inhales deeply. I place my arms around her and she snuggles her head into my neck.

'Tullydeen is so beautiful, you know. I missed this place.'

'Ach ...Pearl, there's not much to miss,' I laugh. She grabs my can and takes a mouthful. I look at her long eyelashes and she sets the can down. 'You're shaking, you know.'

'Yes ...I'm shaking, you know,' I mimic. She pokes my ribs and we giggle. Her hair feels so soft on my fingers and she gives a little groan that makes my shorts twitch. If I live to be a hundred, I will never hear a sexier groan. Her long fingers rub gently around the back of my hand. She pulls me off the wall and I let her take me to wherever she has decided upon. We pick our way through the ruins of the cottage. Pearl stops and dangles my arms in unison with hers.

'What's wrong?' I ask.

'Ssssh,' she utters softly, gently running the back of her hand across my cheeks. I pull her tightly to my body and all of my boundaries imagined or otherwise merge and melt.

Pearl releases herself from our embrace. Her mind wants to connect things. I wait for that line about being a *nice fella* and the big *but* before *just friends*. I'm sort of geared for rejection. Pearl strolls over to me and looks straight into my eyes. Her finger is soft and soothing, as she runs it around my lips, then down the bridge of my nose. Her warm breath collides with my face. Her pupils, watching every movement mine make. She gives that little groan again, slinking slowly to her knees.

Chapter 9

I replace the receiver and struggle out of bed. Pearl is fast asleep, blowing bubbles at the pillow. I sit on the toilet, smoking. Eventually I saunter into the kitchen and flick on the light. I'm not angry at being wakened at this un-Godly hour. Mandy sounded excited on the phone and as usual wanted to play her little game: Guess who's in the picture. It must be good. I fill the kettle and wait for the email. I'm too relaxed for 3.00am, too awake.

If I live to be a hundred, Pearl's little groan will always get me going. I gaze into the darkness of Tullydeen, watching my reflection in the window. Sometimes it becomes hazy, unfocused. The kettle tries to draw my attention, like a spoiled brat wanting sweets at the checkout. I yawn, yawn away the satisfaction of sex. It's gone …my fantasy. A new one is being built, scurrying testosterone, rallying to the call. I feel strong and peaceful. I'd held it in check from the first sight of her legs, walking towards me in reception. The way she wiped my chin, cleaning me with gentle dabs with a Mario's napkin. Her legs dangling on the broken walls of her cottage. The cottage they had left all those years ago to set up home in Drumfiddy.

Pearl is sophisticated. I can visualise her strolling along the boulevards of Paris in the October winds, soaking up the colours, stopping to look in the windows, crossing her ankles and contemplating. The smell of coffee in the wind, mingling with the floating leaves in the midst of the autumn holocaust. I don't want to move from my reflection in the window. I see my image come back into focus, the white T-shirt and my shoulders, which she had paid careful attention to. Pearl's nails had left their mark on them. I remember the email, the electronic intrusion. …Sometimes it is. Even in Tullydeen, there is no escape.

A man with fair hair that had been cropped looks from the page. I recognise the door as Hawthorne Drive. His mean eyes and his heavyweight physique, stride on the photograph. I grab the other pages and scrape my feet over to the table. More shots of Trevor Mulholland and the girl follow, then a quick note from Mandy. The new face is a man called Tommy Johnston. It doesn't ring a bell. I read on and Mandy informs me he is a Loyalist paramilitary, very much sought after in the underworld for his special talents. Private contracts are his forte.

Mandy has already checked them out with Barnsey, our police snout. Barnsey had no luck on the girl, matching her picture with their files. It means she's clean. Well …until now. She's not important. A few quid was probably dangled in front of her nose. Mulholland would've kept her in the dark.

Johnston …Tommy Johnston. …His name is coming back. I'd heard rumours about this renegade. I yawn and stretch and remember the kettle is boiling. I make a strong coffee and return. I study his face some more and fiddle a Marlboro from the pack. I'm sure I have never seen him before. I read Mandy's scrawl, which includes a brief life history. Johnston had been born and raised in Ballytogert, a Loyalist stronghold just north of Belfast. He had become involved in paramilitary activity following his father's murder by the IRA in 1979. His mother had moved to Antrim to start a new life. According to the intelligence, Tommy Johnston did not. Barnsey believed he had been responsible for numerous murders yet they couldn't pin any of them on Johnston. Witness wouldn't testify …what's new.

I skip over some words to the bit Mandy had underlined. *Tommy Johnston is believed to be the top bomb maker for the Loyalist paramilitaries. A bitter feud in 1985 made him flee the country and set up shop in Spain, Malaga.* I exhale loudly and my ears begin to feel a little numb. I draw heavily on my cigarette and my heart's going twenty to the dozen.

I gather my thoughts and return to the pages. Mandy's postscript is interesting. She had put the words *self-employed*, in speech marks. Tommy Johnston is a self-employed terrorist. His cause being the fattest wallet. Interpol had kept an eye on him for many years. Now and then, they feed his whereabouts to the RUC. They have no hard evidence of Johnston's terrorist involvement.

Johnston's too smart. Now he's back in Belfast and nothing can be done about it. I check his picture once more. It's the door at Hawthorne Drive. He's definitely here.

A cobweb I had missed around the fluorescent light moves gently, mesmerising me. The Andrews Corporation, Malaga and the white villas, hover in my spinning thoughts. I try to relax my shoulders. They've gone tense. So what happens? I blow smoke at the cobweb and can't think. I push back the chair and reach for the phone. Indecision makes me stop. 'Self-employed,' I mutter.

I open the door and enter the coming dawn. An anorexic moon watches over me. Is there a bomb under the Celica? Pull yourself together, I scold myself. I think Mulholland is trying to lead me to the killers. Keep going up the garden path. …But why me? The Troubles and politics aren't my areas. …That's Big Paul's field. It bores me. Looking at dodgy nursing homes and exposing them is my forte, or stopping people selling kids dangerous toys. This isn't my stuff.

I walk into the garden past the barns. My eyes are adjusting. The sea crackles, trying to calm me. 'I'm not a hero,' I say, shaking my head. I leap over the wall and land on some buttercups. The black rocks loom like death and my thoughts. 'Calm down, Simon, for God's sake.' I light another Marlboro and sigh to the heavens. The shingle takes my footing and I stumble. Somehow I manage to get my hand out to break the fall. The noise disturbs a few rabbits or what I think are rabbits close to the wall. I turn quickly to look at where the rustle came from. There's no silhouette of a gunman standing. I breathe again.

If Tommy Johnston is after me, employed by the Andrews Corporation, that means Mulholland is in on it. So much for making amends. My profile of Mulholland had been wrong. Why else would Johnston come here? He goes to Hawthorne Drive, probably gets a file from Trevor Mulholland and a rundown of the house from the girl. He has all he needs to know. I push the word *coincidence* to the fore, which gives me a little hope. It's either two different things or one big mess.

The story on the Andrews Corporation had gone bigger and better than I ever imagined. The financial experts hired by *The Irish Scribe* were inundated with useless savings policies from angry people, worried. Is there something I've missed? Many people live in Malaga. A piece of rationality washes over me. It starts the tide and I struggle to my feet. The cigarette butt traces through the dawn to the water and dies.

Mulholland must've known about the story. He probably does work for the Andrews Corporation. There was no trace to him in any of the documents I received. There wouldn't be ...would there, I shrug. So he recommends Johnston to take care of me. It's possible ...more than possible. Tom and Nancy Mulholland were killed in '89 after Johnston went self-employed. But it doesn't add up. Why would Mulholland let the girl mention his name, if he was behind it all? ...It's crazy.

I think of Mulholland's house and the state of it. He's showing me the killer. Why? I'm convinced he still wants to get away from the guilt. So ...I get a tip off about the Andrews Corporation ...word spreads ...the guys in Malaga want it stopped. Mulholland says he knows someone, and bingo, he kills two birds with the one stone. ...Am I supposed to write a story naming Johnston as the killer of the Mulhollands? It would be big. Johnston goes to jail or slips the police ...Mulholland relieves his guilt a little and when Johnston's released from questioning he kills Mulholland for grassing. Mulholland gets his peace, dead, ...a positive tick in his sick mind. ...Where does that leave me? Johnston goes back to Malaga to lift his cheque. But why wait until the story is running? Johnston should've popped me before it ever made the streets. It's too late now. I sigh and it connects. Simple ...Mulholland fed them bum information ...changed the dates ...maybe told them it would run next month or something. So I get a chance to see the killer of his parents, point him out, and we both die. Why Susan Patterson? What's she in all of this? I fire a stone at the rocks and it ricochets, clattering into the clover. Nothing's what it seems. I can't make the connection ...except for the apartment and Mulholland being Patterson Engineering's accountant. There must be more.

My mind has had enough. I watch the animals of the night preparing for daybreak. Their shift is over with a good day's sleep ahead. I can hear for miles in the stillness. Calls and communication between cows swoop from beyond the village. It will soon be milking time and faithful guardians will awaken and tend to their chores, placing caps at acute angles on itchy scalps. Dungarees, stained and smelly, pulled and fastened while staggering to the parlours, where technology quickens and empties the vagrants from the fields.

I could've been part of it. I should have stayed where I am. Yet it all beckoned in those days. I hate farming. I hated it then and

I hate it now. I hate wanting to farm now. I hate being scared, looking for the security of the womb. I've no welcoming arms to kiss my cut better. I freeze. A shadow catches my eye.
'Are you okay?' What is *okay,* I want to ask.
'Ach ...I was just taking a dander,' I reply. I approach Pearl. She's wrapped in my sweater. We hug. I feel her pelvis fuse into me, the warmth of her neck on my lips.
'Mandy phoned ...couldn't get back to sleep again,' I offer.
'Let me cook you breakfast.'

Chapter 10

We make the last call for the flight to Gatwick. I have to buy newspapers, which always pisses me off. I have an office full of free newspapers a few miles away in the centre of Belfast. It's like paying to go to work. The stewardess smiles as we take a few quick puffs before we are forced to surrender our anti-social habit into the ashtray provided.

'If this plane's going down, I'm lighting up,' I tell her on my way past. 'I'll join you, sir.'

Pearl sits by the window. I show her the email from Mandy and the picture of Tommy Johnston. Her look tells me she has never seen him before. 'I packed Peggy-Sue,' I say. She laughs and returns to the message.

I sort of forgot about meeting the real Susan Patterson. I'll play it safe. Jesus ...Pearl's her mother. I glance over at her profile, her petite nose. Her stunning looks. I have the eye of the beholder. How could she ever have a daughter the same age as me? ...My old school friend. They could pass as sisters. The *Chanel No. 5* drifts from Pearl's lemon blouse. I peck her ear and listen to her give that little groan again, pouting her lips in the process. If I live to be a hundred, that will always get me going. She hands me the message.

'Gets stranger by the minute, you know.'

'Oh by the way, what about rooms? I reckoned I would stay at the Clontarret in St. Helier. Are you staying with Susan? I don't want to be in the way,' I rattle out.

'Me stay with Susan ...you must be joking,' she pauses and laughs. 'I'm psyching myself up not to have a row with her ...not to take the bait, you know. We're fine on the phone, Simon. Face to face is different.' She giggles and moves her lips towards my ear. 'A good ride relieves the tension, you know.' I smile and nudge her shoulder gently.

'The Clontarret it is then,' I say, swiping my hands, like cymbals.

We read the newspapers. It's bloody annoying having to buy newspapers. I start with Mary Ginty's favourite, *The Newsletter*, and sift through their piece on the Andrews story. Rory will be doing the same right now, checking no one has overstepped the mark and misquoted us. Pictures of angry shareholders, picketing the Andrews building in Belfast, have made most of the morning editions. *The Irish News* leads with that too. I caught a few stares on the plane when we boarded and whispers about me being 'the reporter fella.' It's running like a locomotive. Insurance bosses are to discuss it at their general meeting in a few days. Loads of calls and policies have continued to arrive at *The Irish Scribe* to be checked.

It's hard to believe nothing else has happened in four days. The North is quiet, only the heat wave and imminent hosepipe ban challenges the Andrews story. That's unusual, too. I read of the continuing punishment beatings in West Belfast. A foiled bank robbery in South Belfast. And, of course the farmers, complaining. The Met office is clouding them with doom with no end to the sunshine.

We wait at the carousel and watch the little door. Customs men watch us. We have a smoke and suddenly the bags appear. Our bags come out first and together. I feel a little nervous. Susan is supposed to be waiting. We pass the peripheral glance of the clean-shaven Customs man. It's even warmer in Jersey. Couriers mingle and I shoot glances for a tall brunette. 'There she is,' Pearl says. I hear the rattle of trolleys coming behind me, as I watch Susan coming towards us, smiling. Pearl and Susan hug. I pull the trolley to the side to allow the impatient to begin their holidays. My mouth is a little dry. Susan is talking quickly and then turns to me.

I move away from the trolley. I think about cracking a joke but one won't come. She's different from her picture and my imagination. Much taller and thinner, too thin. She doesn't look like Pearl at all.

'Did you bring Peggy-Sue? I suppose you did. You will love Jersey. It's beautiful. Have you been here before? Look at you, you are so handsome,' she rattles out. I try to answer. There isn't time. She has curly hair, long and frizzy. Pearl makes eyes behind her and waits.

'So you're a nurse, then.'
'Uh-ha. Tell me all about you. It's so long, Simon. It's thirty-two years. All that time. Can you believe it? No. I can't. We're getting old. Then age is a state of mind.' Susan's off again. I manage to nod. 'Mum says you're a psychologist. Well! You must come into the hospital and I'll introduce you to some of ours. No wonder you can afford to stay at the Clontarret. Old money bags,' she says, poking my ribs. She grabs the luggage trolley. 'Let's go. The car's outside. Did you have a good flight? I hear there is a heat wave at home.'
Pearl lets her pass with the trolley and waits for me. She has that, I-did-warn-you smile on her face.

Susan is already into the Jersey afternoon by the time we reach the sliding doors. Taxi drivers shout out for employment.
'Wait until you see her drive,' Pearl smiles from the side of her mouth.
'Is she always like this?'
'No ...never usually this calm.'
'What?'
'Remember what I said about a good ride ...you'll need it too, you know.'
Our bags were in the red Ford Escort before we arrived at the car.
'Will I ...?'
'No-no-no, Simon, it's alright. I'll take it back. You're on your holidays. Relax. Take it easy. Enjoy the sun,' she rattles out, aiming for the trolley park. I look at Pearl.
'We'd better get in, you know. She'll be at the hotel before she notices we're missing,' Pearl says, sarcastically. I smile and enjoy the heat and the joke. Susan is on her way back.
'Not allowed to smoke either, you know.'
'Sssh, she's here.'

Susan jumps into the driver's seat and wrestles with the seat belt. 'Well, it's great to see you ...just great. It's so warm. Then it's always warm here. Not like home. Bit of a novelty there. Sometimes it's hazy here in the morning. Then the sun comes up. The shops are open late at night, you'll be able to browse. Perfume's cheap. No tax,' she says, glancing in the mirror. We're not even out of the car park yet. I nod like a donkey in the back seat.

Granite cottages with masses of flowers blooming from their pinkish walls roll past. Susan is onto business in Drumfiddy, occasionally watching the road, between looks at her mother. I pray we reach the Promenade. I can't wait to get my jeans off. Jersey is too hot for jeans. What will she say if she finds out about Pearl and me? Probably a lot, I muse. We bypass St. Aubin and descend. I'm hitting the floor with my feet, braking at least fifty yards before Susan remembers to. When she hits the brakes we all roll forward and the whole car shudders until she finds the right gear.

I haven't been in Jersey for about four years. The Prom is packed. Bodies relax in the sun. On the descent it had become a goal just to make it to the Prom in one piece. Jet skis cut the water and the castle sits proud. I watch the interaction between mother and daughter. They tolerate each other. Susan talks. Pearl listens.

'The Clontarret is a nice hotel. We have conferences there. Very nice. The staff are helpful. You been in Jersey before? It's lovely. Bit like Ireland. Lovely and green. Sits in a gulf-stream or something. I won't be able to stop. I tried to swap my shift. Couldn't do it. I have to get some sleep. I finish in the morning. I'll arrange a nice restaurant. Yes ...that would be nice.' I nod and think of a ride.

Susan beats the porter to the boot and has our luggage out and is busy explaining to him. Her long one-piece red dress sways with her words. 'I'm so sorry I can't stay. You know how it is. Well ...you will get settled in. There's a lovely little bar just up the road. What's it called? Oh ...'
'We'll be fine, you know,' Pearl intervenes. Susan clasps her hands and smiles.
'I can't wait to have a chat, Susan. Thanks for meeting us,' I say, putting my arms around her and smothering another outburst. Her body is shaking. I move away and Pearl says her goodbye. The swarthy porter points towards reception. I go into my luggage and fumble around. 'Oh Susan, you're going to be a grandmother,' I say reaching Peggy-Sue through the driver's window. Her eyes settle on the rag doll and she cuddles her just the way she used to. It's hard to believe that she would be lost for words. She looks at me. Then looks again. Then drives off.

I had stayed here before. The plush foyer is on two levels. The reception is to the right as I walk in. A porter's desk sits to the left. Sofas and tables are placed in little groups. Piped music rains down. I pass the bar to the right. I recall the layout. I will be able to navigate my way around St. Helier from here. The receptionist is Irish and bubbly. We're in room 127. 'That's the biggest bed I've ever seen, you know.' The net curtains flap around and we have a view of the castle and the Promenade. Two soft chairs and a coffee table sit by the window. An en-suite is off to the left, by the room door.

'Ach ...this'll do, I suppose.' I nose dive onto the bed's cream throw-over and stretch out.

'Was it worth the wait ...all those years?' Pearl laughs.

'She totally different from what I expected. Ach ...I knew what she looked like but I pictured her to be calm and easy-going, like you,' I say carefully. I don't want to be too critical. She is her daughter and I don't like people criticising Grace. Pearl leans on a long desk opposite the bed and laughs.

'She's a pain in the bloody arse, you know. She never shuts up. Never listens. Never sees anyone's opinion except her own. And, I'm glad she never took up my offer to help me out in the business,' she finishes, laughing.

'Fancy a coffee?' I ask.

'I do, you know.' I crawl across the bed and flick the switch on the kettle. I unfasten my jeans and sigh.

'It's too warm for jeans,' I add, throwing them at a chair. I can't be bothered to unpack my grip at the moment. The door knocks. 'Get that, Pearl.'

She gives me a look, she's already unpacking stuff into the wardrobe.

'Room Service, Madam.' She stands back and the brown suits walk in with champagne and chocolates. I lie with my legs crossed and my hands behind my head. She looks to me for an explanation. I shrug.

'I'll see you later ...I've no cash,' I explain to the tallest Portuguese. They fuss over the placement of the ice bucket and jibber away in their native tongue. Smiles flash from their faces on their exit.

'What's all this?'

'Ach ...Pearl, this's better than coffee.' I grab the bottle and pour Pearl a glass. 'Madam,' I mimic. She appears a little emotional and another expression drifts across her face. It seems every time I look at her I notice something different. Our glasses clink. 'To us, Pearl.' She watches me as she sips.

'You think Susan is involved in all of this,' she says. I swallow my mouthful.

'Ach ...Pearl.'

'I don't believe you, you know. I think it's because of the apartment. You think she's involved in all of this.'

'No I don't.'

'Hummh,' she shrugs. Pearl spins around at the en-suite door. Another part of Pearl Patterson is surfacing. Her face has gone surly. 'You're lying.' I swallow hard and try to comprehend her statement. 'You used me to get to her. You arrive in Drumfiddy all concerned and all along you suspected her and probably me. I bet you planned it all, you know.' Pearl walks towards me spitting the words. All the serenity I associate with her has gone.

'I feel like a fool. Now all this. Champagne and chocolates,' she states, fanning out her hand. 'Did you forget a vital piece of information? Oh ...it's all right, champagne and chocolates will open her mouth and her legs. You used me to get to Susan. All you want is a story,' she tapers off.

I sit on the bed and she wanders around the room. Her hands are shaking. She lights a cigarette and walks to the window. It takes two to have an argument. I suppose it does look like that. I think Susan is involved. It's her apartment. Yet meeting her sort of finished that off. Certainly, I want to ask her things about Hawthorne Drive. Another glass of champagne helps and I ignore Pearl. A good dose of no notice is best. Any talk or intentions I put forward, she will use against me.

She sighs and looks over to me. 'Many women find you attractive, you know.' I don't answer. 'I saw them look at you on the flight. You're tall and handsome and clever and genuine. Women fall for that. They hate posers, well, most do, you know. I want to believe this is for me. Then I think of the girl opposite us on the plane, the one with the bobbed hair. She fancied you.' Pearl pauses and sighs in resignation. 'When you get your story I will become obsolete, you know. I'm the wrong side of fifty. I'm not stupid. I suppose that makes it easier for you. I suppose you think I'm glad of a good ride and the affections of a younger man. You'll be in the pub telling your mates how we did it and laughing. Buy her champagne and chocolates and she's easy,' Pearl says, with a hint of resignation. She spins around. 'Well, I've news for you Simon. I'm not some boring, old woman that needs you. I'm independent and I don't like being used.' She turns back and looks out at the castle. 'I don't like phoneys or posers, you know,' she spins around again. 'What ...?'

'Ach ...Pearl lighten up,' I say with a pair of her knickers on my head. I move my pupils towards my nose. Grace always giggles at this one. Pearl wants to laugh and I grab a handful of ice cubes from the bucket and throw them at her.

'Did you ever hear of trust?' I ask. She tries to interrupt and from somewhere she pulls a little giggle. 'Good fit these,' I say, taking them off my head. 'See you haven't washed them,' I add, exhaling loudly.

'Stop that,' she laughs with a little blush.

She smiles in the silence and picks up some of the ice cubes and puts them back in the bucket while wiping her wet hand along my cheek.

'You're right about me being clever and all that handsome stuff,' I smirk, walking around, putting on a posh voice. However, the lady you referred to was most likely a lesbian and the two men she was with were gay also. I suppose you didn't happen to notice the way they lifted their glasses or pick up upon how they sat. The woman opened her legs, resembling a male posture, whereas the men sat, with legs tucked in like a mermaid, hence a more feminine position. I will let you know when a woman fancies me,' I finish. I grab her blouse and she appears confused.

'When someone fancies you they'll usually ignore you and talk to the person with you. Now and then they will take sly glances when you are not expected to notice. The way I did with you in the car. You caught me. I blushed. We flirted. The woman did that with you.'

'I did catch you looking at me in the car, you know. You did blush.'

'Blush ...I nearly crapped myself. I'm shy, believe it or not.'

'Did you know I fancied you?' she asks.

'Ach ...Pearl. I sort of. Well ...I wasn't sure. No.'

'I thought you were never going to kiss me, you know.'

'Ach ...Pearl, I'm shy and I did.'

'Aye you did after a bit of prompting,' she smiles.

Pearl reaches for the bottle of champagne and fills both of our glasses. She's relaxed again.

'Is all that stuff right?'

'Trust me.'

'I had to say it, you know. I speak my mind. I look in the mirror and see wrinkles around my eyes ...you're still young, Simon. I feel like a dizzy schoolgirl, but the mirror brings back reality. I don't want to be hurt, Simon.'

'I'm not *that* young. Wise up.'

I sip my drink and decide to voice my thoughts. It's the truth. 'When you walked out to meet me from your office yesterday, I almost couldn't stand. I just thought you were the most beautiful woman I'd ever seen. Call me a romantic, but I always believed I'd look at a woman and she'd look at me and we'd fall madly in love with each other. Anyway, you've sexy legs. Jesus everything about you is sexy. I fought hard not to be a mumbling idiot yesterday,' I laugh. 'If two people look at a forest one might see the beauty of the trees and one might see the litter on the ground. It's still a forest, Pearl. Keep looking at the beauty of the trees.'

I light two cigarettes and hand her one. She takes a quick puff before stubbing it out. Pearl pouts her lips and has that impish look on her face.
'Ahh that's freezing. Stop it. It's bloody freezing. I'm soaking.'
'If you're romantic you won't mind'
'Pick on someone your own age.'
'That's so romantic. Are you *still* shy?'
'Yes.'
'Are you sure?'
'No.'

Chapter 11

My conscience speaks to me. It says, *you told a lie*. It nibbles at me in the en-suite. I shower quickly, bypass a shave and don my faithful blue shorts. A lucky dip into my grip pulls out a white T-shirt. Pearl's blowing bubbles again, lying face down. I stop to admire her naked body, momentarily. Gently I pull the sheet over her back. She turns, mumbling, and her breasts fall to the side. Her rib cage takes over where they leave off. I tiptoe to the window and push it further open. The room is stuffy. The lingering cigarette smoke and alcohol seem to have added to the humidity since my shower. I scribble a note to explain my actions and on my clean pair of heels, slip from the room.

A complimentary *Daily Telegraph* hangs on the outside of the door in a plastic bag. I unfold it and quickly flick over the first few pages. The Andrews building is shown with the RUC holding back an angry, *wanting-to-know* mob. Not the typical yobbos, rather ordinary people who had worked hard to invest their money with the company. Should I write another piece? A ten-car pile up on the M6 has taken the lead. The picture is shocking, burning vehicles and emergency crews.

I need a car. One journey with Susan was enough. Some might say a sign or vision from God. I don't want to die in a high speed, fast-talking crash. I think if I arrived at the Pearly Gates all mangled, God might ask, *Why do you think I got you a Barclaycard and surrounded you with car rental firms?* I check with reception. Rory hasn't phoned or faxed. I cross to the wide Promenade and stroll to clear the cobwebs. The pathway over to the Castle is visible with the receding sea. I watch a large ferry, moving along towards the harbour. St. Helier appears to be coming awake.

I sit on the wall and allow the early sun to cascade over me. It's already warm, pushing its rays into my back. I smoke and study the statue of Queen Victoria, count the windows at the front of the hotel and give up when my eyes jump the second time. I reckon we will stay until tomorrow. Maybe longer. ...I'll play it by ear. I love the smell of salt water. It's home from home. I push with my hands and it lands me onto my feet, ready to try the many car rental signs. The roads are picking up pace. The financiers and business people are making their way to work. They all look so sophisticated and fashionable. Some of them watch me, peering through bent arms waiting at the traffic lights.

A middle aged guy in a beige suit talks me into keeping the car for a week. I pay by Barclaycard and he gives me a quick rundown on the controls of the blue Ford Escort. The Islanders have a relaxed way with them. In all my visits to Jersey I can't recall meeting one obnoxious local. I take the coast road to Gorey. It's narrow and twists with no escape at the sides. Granite walls glisten, beckoning the wing mirrors. Little things about the island float in: the parishes all named after saints, the ledges on the chimneys for witches to rest, and the most beautiful yoghurt in the world.

The castle in Gorey never fails to take my breath away. It sits strong and magnificent, looking down on the houses and harbour, like a big grey mother, cuddling her kids. I take a left turn up a huge hill. The car is nice to drive. The famous cattle graze in the fields. Honey is for sale, advertised from small home-made signs dangling from gateways.

St Tanon's Hospital sits in the middle of the country. It's impressive. A large grey stone building set back with what looks like a village green in front. I drive slowly as the sign asks, over the ramps. Petunias grab my nose with their dispersing scent. The heat is sucking at my sweat already. I had expected Susan to be working at a general hospital – this is psychiatric. Several patrons walk around, smoking intensely. They watch me with wary eyes. I had served my placement in a psychiatric hospital as part of my psychology degree. I feel quite at home.

The reception is beautifully cool and I announce myself. The receptionist is Irish, too, with Irish auburn hair. I take a seat next to the sliding doors and wait. Squeaky feet scurry along and then appear into view.

'Morning, Simon. You're up early. Where's mum? I suppose she's still sleeping. It's a lovely morning.' I nod. At least she isn't driving.
'Can we have a chat?' I manage to get in.
'Yes, wait for me. I finish in a few moments. We can walk around the reservoir. You'd like that,' she rattles off, disappearing.
I'm exhausted already. How will I ever get her pinned down? I saunter outside and light up. Cigarette butts are everywhere. I look at things I would normally not look at: the pointing of the building, the crack in the pane of glass. I listen to the lark and watch an old man shuffle across the lawns, all stooped over. I wonder what he hasn't forgiven himself for? I recall my old professor telling me that most of the wards in mental institutions could be vacated if people could forgive themselves. Guilt and shame are killers, he always said.

A lady rocks on a bench, clutching her handbag and mumbling to herself. I stroll across and sit down beside her. 'Morning,' I say. She doesn't answer. The woman glances, fearful glances and continues to chant about how it isn't her fault. 'My husband thinks I don't know,' she tells the trees. I feel calm and relaxed and spread my shoulders back against the bench.
'I saw them,' she says, through tatty grey hair. I look into the pain in her folded face. Her greyish eyes look too small, a sure give away she's been doped for conformity.

Footsteps stampede behind me. It's Susan. I smile at the woman beside me and rise from the bench. 'I'm Gladys,' she says, gripping her bag. 'I'm Simon,' I say gently. Somewhere she summons enough courage to look at my eyes, passing self-loathing, her torment and being branded Mentally Ill. I reckon she's in her early sixties yet, she looks as if she's well over seventy.
'Isn't it awful when no one listens, Gladys. They'd rather tell you how to live your life,' I add, walking off.

Susan's champing at the bit. Her whole body's swaying.
'What are you doing talking to her? She's such a nuisance. Never does anything she's meant to. Follows you everywhere. The reservoir is down here. Let's go,' she rants.
I don't believe what I'm hearing. I stop. Susan is at least ten yards in front of me before she realises I've stopped. I'm angry, angered by her attitude.
'Come on then. It's this way,' she coaxes. I stoop down and untie my laces very slowly. I feel her walking towards me, her impatience. I look up at her narrow face, browned by the Jersey sun.

'I'm just tying my laces.' I wait as long as possible until she is a little less hyper.

We take the trampled track by some trees. 'I need to talk to you Susan,' I say calmly. She's off again, about two paces in front. 'Talk away. You will love this reservoir, all the trees. There's a walk around it,' she gabbles. I pray for patience. The trees throw their image onto the water. It's perfectly calm in the morning sun. A few rowing boats sit here and there, most likely used by fishermen. 'Can we take a seat, Susan?'

Her long white uniform sways with her sudden stop. Susan looks at me and for once doesn't say a word. I reckon she's about six-foot. There's an inscription screwed to the backrest of the bench where I sit down, which I can't be bothered to read at the moment. I pat a Marlboro on the pack and dangle it between my lips. 'Yes I smoke, Susan.

'But you shouldn't. It's bad. Daddy smoked and look what happened to him. The same will happen to you. It's nice here. I knew you'd like it. Not as nice as Tullydeen though,' she shrugs coming to sit down. I hate anyone patronising me, yet I let it go.

'Look Susan, someone is cloning you back in Belfast. They're living in your apartment and they even came to see me and pass themselves off as you.'

'I know.'

It hits me like a punch. 'You know? When did you know?' This is getting crazier by the minute.

'Look Simon, just keep out of it. I'm doing an old friend a favour. Look at the swans. Aren't they beautiful.' She walks over to the water's edge. She's enjoying the element of surprise. There's a cocky gait to her. 'Is that why you and mum came to Jersey? To tell me something I already knew. Sit me down and hold my hand. Look at the swans, Simon. Do you like swans? There's no swans in Tullydeen,' she says fidgeting around. I fight back the urge to grab her, shock her out of the *holier than thou* mode. I watch a bee and count to ten. There are swans in Tullydeen.

'How's Trevor Mulholland connected in this?' I bawl out. It draws back a little of her cockiness at least. Her face and shoulders stiffen.

'Simon, just forget about it, please. Let's walk. I have to get some sleep. You've had your sleep. I had to work all night. We meet after all this time and all you can do is ask me stupid questions. Just let it drop.'

'No way,' I say sternly. 'I want to know what's going on. You could be in big trouble.' She laughs it off.

I run after her and grab her arm. 'One of the most wanted terrorists in the world was seen in your apartment with Trevor Mulholland and the girl passing herself off as you. You'd be better talking to me than the police. It's only a matter of time.' I stop short of mentioning the bombing of Tom and Nancy Mulholland.

'Let go of me. Let's walk. It's nothing. I'm getting married soon. I wish I could live in Jersey,' she says, abruptly. Susan Patterson folds her arms tightly across her chest. She played the trump card and revelled in its surprise. I try to remember what I've said in the heat of the moment. Have I said too much? ...No.

We reach a dam in silence, except for the ideas racing in my brain. 'Do you sympathize with the Loyalists?' She doesn't answer. 'Susan, for Christ sake, I'm your friend ...I'm only trying to help.' My plea seems to register with her. She sighs, but her posture remains dominant.

'I know we were friends, Simon. And, if you are still my friend you will let it drop. I'm a big girl now. Mummy is a pain. She started all of this. She is always interfering. I suppose she phoned you. That's what it is. Yes,' she says, working herself into a frenzy.

'What about your mum ...does she know?'

'You never give up, do you. What do you know? You know nothing. You poke your nose into my business and cause trouble. Just piss off. Yes. Just piss off.' Susan runs along the edge of the dam, back towards the hospital. I slap the wall.

Ducks shout at each other in the water below me, head butting the surface for food. I wish I was a duck. She knew. Between the trees, I spot Susan Patterson still running. ...It makes sense she was bound to know. I set off at my own pace. It's time to get back to the hotel anyway. Pearl will probably be up. I labour up the little inclines on the path and almost stumble on a rut, like a dry riverbed running across the path. Had she got caught up in the Loyalist thing in Drumfiddy? It's definitely possible.

I arrive back at the hotel in a daze and I throw the keys to the doorman. 'Room 127,' I say, remembering a tip. I have two messages. One is from Rory, the other from Mandy. I prepare a fax for Rory. Nothing has changed in Belfast, according to him. Mulholland has been to the house and Mandy watched from her 210mm. Barnsey hadn't traced the girl yet. Tommy Johnston is in residence at Hawthorne Drive. I read her P.S. She wants some *Opium* perfume brought back. I crumple the paper and miss the bin.

I hate myself for doing what I am doing. I scribble out the name of Susan Patterson and fire it into the ashtray on the glass table. I look to the ceiling and the guests mingling around reception for courage. I re-write the name of Susan Patterson. What do I really know about her anyway? All I have is a little girl who has grown into whoever: a hyper pest. I jot it down on the fax too. It's strange that Barnsey didn't pull her file at the beginning. It's not like him. Maybe he did and is waiting until we ask.

I mention the possibility of Tommy Johnston and Susan attending the same schools. My brain is tired. I don't mention she knew about the clone in her apartment. The receptionist takes my fax and I look at the world clocks on the wall. People in New York will be in the final throes of sleep and it's lunchtime in Paris. I want to tell Pearl first. I don't like having a guilty conscience. I did lie when she asked about suspecting Susan. Well... a bit. It had crossed my mind then. Now I'm sure she's involved.

Pearl answers my knock. 'Paper, Madam,' I mimic, grabbing the freebie from the door. She has really spiked up her hair, using some gel. It looks cool.
'I thought you were lost, you know,' she smiles, nudging me. I meet her kiss and pull her close. 'Sleep well?' She gives a raunchy giggle and that little groan again. We separate and I stare at her beautiful cream top with a peach rose blasted across her chest. Her striped leggings in matching colours are already giving me thoughts.
'You get the car?'
'Aye. Will I order breakfast?'
'No fry for me,' she says, quickly. 'Something light, you know. You choose.' She continues doing whatever women do in front of mirrors. I order two continental breakfasts with coffee. I slump into a chair and watch her put the finishing touches to her eyes.

I know she likes *Chanel No. 5*. It's all the little things. What sort of music does she like? ...Her favourite meal? I feel impatient to know all these things. Does she eat *Jelly Babies* or *Clove Rock*? I've a sweet tooth once I start. Can she eat one sweet and keep the rest for later? ...I can never do that. I love setting the bag between my legs while I'm driving and stuffing my face until they're done.
'What will we do today?' she asks. I don't answer and her eyebrows prompt me for an answer.
'Maybe go for a swim at St. Quens, the tide should be in about three,' I say, checking over my shoulder. The telephone rings and

we both look at it. I pick it up and the girl in reception tells me of another fax.

'A fax has arrived,' I convey. 'Be back in a minute.'

It's worse than I had expected. The schools drew a blank. However, Susan Patterson was captured on intelligence snaps with Tommy Johnston in Malaga. Barnsey hadn't access to the shots but he had painted the picture, Rory had written. However, Susan Patterson has no criminal record or convictions apart from her link with Tommy Johnston. Sadness swoops over me like a rapid shore mist. Interpol had been aware of Susan Patterson since the early eighties. Rory reckoned they maybe met because she was a nurse. He had a theory that Tommy Johnston had been injured at some time and she had been brought in to tend his wounds. ...Maybe under threat of death by his cronies. Or, out of a sense of cause. 'It makes sense, Rory,' I mutter.

I scribble out the fact Susan Patterson knew about the clone and that her apartment was being used. *Do not tell Barnsey this information*, I write with big lines around it. I know Rory will catch my drift. Although the paper has Barnsey in its pocket we still don't trust him. He's useful, but that's as far as it goes. I'll bet he knew all about Susan Patterson before I arrived in Jersey.

People chat in the foyer. Some sort of business grouping has arrived. I can trust Rory, Big Paul and Matt Brown. I pause. Yeah ...I'd trust *them* with my life, not Barnsey, ...definitely not Barnsey. Why can he not trace the girl? I reckon he could if he wanted. All that crap about not having clearance to the files.

'It's getting to be a habit,' I jest with the receptionist, handing her the fax.

I rap impatiently on the room door. Pearl looks concerned. The smells of fresh coffee and fresh bread drifts over. I hand her the fax and walk to the table and sit where she has prepared my place. I pour both coffees and glance to read her reaction.

'Oh my God.' She lets her arm dangle by her side.

'You never met her future husband, did you?' Pearl shakes her head.

'Only the ring, you know. She was wearing it yesterday.'

'Does she go on many holidays?' I ask. Pearl sort of shuffles around. 'Aaaah ...one or two a year, I think. ...Spain,' she utters in resignation.

The coffee is welcome and I let my legs fall outward as I relax on the chair. I just don't want to think about anything. I'm angry with myself for messing up the meeting with Susan.

'People always broke my trust, you know. That's why I had a go at you yesterday ...about the champagne and chocolates. Now it's happened again,' she concedes. Pearl sits on the floor beside the chair. I rub the nape of her neck. She places her arms under her head, on my knee and rocks gently.

'Can it get much worse, Simon?'

'No. Not if you tell me everything you can about Susan. It's thirty odd years since you left Tullydeen. A lot can happen in that time,' I sigh.

'Emmh ...you've grown into a man, you know.'

'Aye ...and I want to keep growing,' I mutter. Pearl's eye catches and holds my drift.

Chapter 12

Corbière Lighthouse, it's ironic that I'm standing looking at it. It was depicted on the postcard Janet gave me when I called at the Belfast General. This time it's for real and my reality doesn't reflect the weather. I feel dull and dismal, Jersey and the lighthouse are basking in the sun. The water foams at the mouth, paying homage at its feet. Cameras click, with cherished loved ones, standing on the rocks. Around the fire at Christmas or in the aftermath of grief families might recall this day, look at the snaps and remember the gulls squealing. They'll probably laugh at the fashions of yesteryear. Was I really that thin back then? How I miss him. Little tinges of guilt, the rows, the little things, surfacing, piercing. A cold injection, flowing into the heart of loneliness. It's the unfinished again. If only. If only. If only my parents could have seen this. They never made it to Jersey. They always wanted to. The unfinished remained so, following their deaths. I should've brought a camera.

Pearl has worn her shades. 'Will we take a seat down here?' I ask, pointing. If I live to be a hundred I will never forget the picture of the first time Pearl wore shades. We managed a light breakfast and just drove, saying little, letting the cliffs and castles and strands and hanging baskets massage our souls. Sometimes there are no words. Sometimes I like to be still and open my mind, relax, let the waste out and give the mud time to settle.

We're sitting on top of one of the old German fortresses and the gulls are bigger than they are in Tullydeen.
'What do you need to know, Simon?'
'Just talk me through her life, anything.' I pause. 'I want to tape

this, okay?' She smiles a yes.

I want to wrap her up and carry her off into the sunset with the waves licking my feet. Pour oils upon her and pamper her and fight off the dragon, piercing its heart with my sword. I'm male and macho and powerless to relieve her of the torment. Both of us are hostages. Some giant finger pinpointed us from the masses. I should be researching how some old people get beaten up in nursing homes. Pearl should be in Drumfiddy, ordering steel or signing contracts. Yet the leveller has raised its ugly head, the sleeping giant in the Nationalist North or Loyalist Ulster – The Troubles.

'Penny for them?'
'Ach ...I was just wondering.' She pecks my cheek and twitches her nose as she laughs. 'Are you ready?' I ask.
'I suppose so. Well ...when we left Tullydeen things were strange. Settling in, you know. Peter worked hard and used the money his parents had given us.' She pauses, smiling. I mirror her gesture. 'Peter was a brilliant engineer. He hit upon a design to strengthen kids' pushchairs. That was the break we needed, you know. Tom Mulholland was our accountant and he found some money to help finance the building of our present site. It was so exciting, Simon.' She pauses and wriggles around.
'What about Susan?'
'Oh she fared well in Drumfiddy ...in school and with the locals.'
'What about paramilitaries or Loyalists ...did she bother with them?'
'The Troubles were in full flight, everyone in Drumfiddy was very loyal to the Queen. The IRA murdered some people in the village, two UDR men, then Willie Morrow, the butcher. It made everyone bitter, you know.' Pearl stops and looks at a young boy chasing a gull.

Why did she stop when she appeared to be fluent? It's that look again, her lips appear to put on the brakes, her eyes shoot a tiny glance at me, to see if I've noticed. The little blush in her cheeks gives it away, crawling onto her nose. She sighs. 'Susan joined The Drumfiddy Defenders ...the flute band.' She laughs and grits her teeth. 'Peter or me didn't want her to join it, you know. Everybody knew who the paramilitaries were and they were all in the band. Her teenage years were hell. She started drinking, spending her time running about with that lot. What could I do?'

she asks, pushing out her hands.

'Most of them worked for us. Decent people, unless you were a Catholic,' she explains.

I release the record button on the tape and touch her shoulder. She points to a gang of black, bobbing bodies trying to catch the waves on surfboards. 'I'd love to try that, you know.'

Pearl lights two cigarettes and hands me one.

'Do these guys still work for you?' I ask.

'Some do ...some were lifted, a couple were shot and some retired. I have a workforce of fifty including myself. I would say six or seven still work there. But, that's not counting the sons of those people. They're good workers and very loyal to me. Over the past few years all this legislation has come in about fair employment.' Her tone is getting angry. 'I haven't a single Catholic on the payroll. It's impossible in Drumfiddy, you know. They've threatened to close me down because I don't employ Catholics. Huh,' she gasps. 'Maybe it works in Belfast but it would never work in Drumfiddy. I've nothing against Catholics, but whoever thought up the idea should spend some time in places like Drumfiddy. Feelings run deep. I wouldn't employ a Catholic simply because I would fear for their safety. If something happened to them I'd feel responsible. I've told those civil servants that. But it's useless, you know,' she explains, puffing out her words in smoke. 'I'm thinking of retiring. The red tape is getting too much. I've fought it off simply because of the people needing to earn a living, but they want me to open a factory in a Catholic area. It's the only option the government's given me. I'm too old,' she smiles.

'Ach ...Pearl, I suppose you're right,' I say, casually, taking the wrath of her look. I grab her arm and we walk down the hill towards the lighthouse.

We let some of the salt air and sun drift over us. The one makes the other pleasant. 'So Susan became a nurse,' I say.

'I was glad. Got her out of Drumfiddy. I'm the wicked witch. Peter and her were close, you know.'

'Was he involved in any paramilitary stuff?'

'Peter ...no.' She finds it amusing. 'You could give Peter a welder and some metal and he was as happy as Larry.' Pearl smiles at the sea and turns to me.

'When he died ...Susan turned on me,' she says quickly. 'Well ... you've seen what's she like. There were rows and more rows. She blamed it all on me because he smoked, you know. Okay, he

smoked, but all of us will die whether we smoke or not.'
'What about boyfriends ...did she have many?' I ask.
'In Drumfiddy she went out with several of the local lads. One week wonders, that sort of thing. When she started nursing I don't really know. She never talked about them. Trevor Mulholland used to dote on her.' She pauses again. 'He had started with Tom in the business. She never liked him though.' Pearl grabs her shades and pulls them off.

The majesty of her beautiful eyes, bite into my soul as they move over my face for my thoughts. I'm holding my bottom lip and pulling it wondering about Mulholland.
'Maybe they met in Belfast, Pearl. The clone said Trevor Mulholland followed her ...stalked her. I think Mulholland sent the clone of Susan not because she was directly involved, but because of the romantic link to Tommy Johnston. Let's say Mulholland had a thing about Susan. He might follow her. He would see her with Tommy Johnston.'
'You think this Tommy Johnston blew up Tom Mulholland?'
'Yes.' Things are starting to connect. I sit down on the dusty ground. 'Let's say Trevor Mulholland is following Susan and he gets caught,' I begin slowly. 'Tommy Johnston will know when he's being followed. Jesus ...it's in his job description. Bingo ...Mulholland and Johnston meet. Trevor Mulholland is useful, so Johnston doesn't kill him. It's only an idea,' I shrug.
'Could be that, you know.' Pearl digests my thoughts. I struggle to my feet and walk toward the ice cream van, up the hill a bit. I have been watching the queue getting smaller. I hate queuing.
'Hang on,' Pearl shouts after me. 'If this mysterious boyfriend of Susan's turns out to be Johnston and we know they have met ...what will happen to her?' Pearl's face is coaxing me to tell her Susan will live happily ever after. I can't lie. I just don't know how much Susan Patterson is involved in all of this.
'Well the best thing that can happen is that he jilts her at the church,' I say. 'Do you think this Mervyn is Johnston, Pearl?'
'Yeah ...the church ...Mervyn. I do, you know.'
'Ice cream?'
She gives a yes with a wave of her hand.

I can't get my mind away from Patterson Engineering. All that metal just waiting to be made into guns. ...Would Pearl know? Nothing looked out of place in the books. I remember her saying that much. Maybe the boys at the paper will find something in the figures. It's bound to be. You have paramilitaries, a welder, metal and whatever else it takes, and if they're not, why not? I take the yellow ice creams and fumble out a Jersey five-pound note. I have Jersey bank notes that I'd been given years ago. I had collected foreign notes as a child. I used to take them out of a leather wallet and imagine I was on the other side of the world.

We stroll around licking the ice cream. Pearl sighs now and then. I want to ask about the possibility of making guns in the factory. Maybe she's thinking about it.

'What happens now, Simon?' she eventually asks.

'Ach ...Pearl, I don't know. I think Mulholland is pointing out Johnston. I still believe he was behind the bombing of his parents. He probably thought he could live with it, what with all the money that would come his way. He could only see the power of complete control, I think. Nothing's what it seems. There's a price to be paid. Not a financial one ...more a personal one. He's ill. Nobody can keep repressing that sort of guilt without something giving,' I hypothesise. 'He's a pig,' she fumes, trying to hide the venom of her outburst. A tiny blush rushes to her face. 'Anyone that would kill their parents, isn't up to much,' she throws out. Her arms are crossed and I bet there's something more. 'I suppose I am meant to be understanding like a psychologist. Well, I'm not. My daughter is involved in this, you know. And ...if Mulholland is using her too, I will kill him,' she spits at me.

'Using her too? Is he using you?' I ask, quickly.

'Stop twisting my words, Simon. Just stop it.' Pearl walks over to the edge of the rocks and peers down into the water. She slipped up. *Using her too* is playing in my ears and mind. Her unconscious is communicating. Her defence mechanisms had dropped slightly. *Using her*. How could Trevor Mulholland have used Pearl? ...Maybe the factory for making guns. No ...it's more than that. ...More personal. Maybe Mulholland blackmailed her about old Tom? ...Maybe he walked in on them or something. I watch her standing at the cliff. She knows she let something slip and that I grabbed it like a wicket-keeper diving for a bad edge, flying low and hopefully escaping his gloves. Pearl knows I caught the ball. She's out. But not yet, I decide. I stroll over to her and rub her neck. 'Don't worry, it'll work out,' I say. I hate people saying that to me, but here I am turning into the person I hate.

'She is in big trouble, Simon. Big, big, trouble.'

'Ach ...Pearl, we'll take it as it comes. Johnston's in Belfast under surveillance. If anybody's going to get it ...well it's me. I'm the number one target. Not Susan,' I add, feeling a sudden panic.

'The Andrews Corporation. Do you really think it's them? It could just be a coincidence. Maybe Mulholland set this up for you to get the story, you know.' Pearl's face is deadly serious and sincere.

'I wish. But they're bound to be involved. Why would Johnston come from Spain? Jesus ...Susan isn't even in Belfast. It could've been a lovers' rendezvous. It's not ...she's here. Malaga was where the front men for the Andrews Corporation lived, in the villas, where Mandy took the pictures. No ...it's no coincidence, Pearl.'

She contemplates this strutting around.

'What about Billy Thompson – did he have paramilitary connections?' I ask.

'Billy ...probably. Billy is very loyal. Hates Catholics. I don't know for sure but I'd say so,' Pearl states, reaching for my hand. She rubs the back of my fingers.

'Did Billy Thompson and Susan know each other?'

'Yes. Since they were kids. Since we moved to Drumfiddy. The Thompsons would be over at our place quite a lot, you know.'

'Did Billy and Susan ever go out together?' I ask. I'm ready for any connection about the alleged rape that she might ask. And, I will lie.

'No. Well ...not as far as I know,' Pearl answers. 'Why?'

'Ach ...I was just wondering. Trying to build a picture,' I rationalise. I avoid her eyes and look at the outline of Guernsey in the haze.

I've no proof but one of the tiny logic fingers in my stomach keeps tapping the wall of my gut when I think about Susan Patterson and the alleged rape against Billy Thompson. If Susan had a grudge against Billy Thompson, Mulholland or Johnston maybe fixed it for her. Maybe it was a misguided love for her father. If Billy Thompson and his father went out of business, Patterson Engineering would prosper in her mind's eye, at least.

'It's time to get back, Simon. My dear daughter will be arriving at the hotel soon,' Pearl states with little enthusiasm.

Chapter 13

I order a prawn cocktail, followed by a huge steak, chips and mushrooms. A builder's dinner as it's sometimes called in Belfast. I coax myself to play it cool and not force the issue. Susan orders plaice, no starter. Pearl wants garlic mackerel, then the same as me.

All the waiters at the Clontarret seem to be Portuguese. I look over the Prom from our table at the window. It's nicely spaced out. No one else is close to us. I can't stand eating in restaurants with no elbow room. The air freshener they use is giving my nose the come-on. I pass the cigarettes around to annoy Susan. Pearl takes one and both of us smoke. I don't know if Susan will mention my visit to the hospital. I deliberately didn't mention it to Pearl.

Susan shuffles her chair side on. She's very edgy, hasn't stopped fidgeting since we sat down. Maybe she didn't sleep well. I hope not. Susan's finding the silence hard to cope with. She's put my life on the line for whatever reason and I choose to think it was out of love for her intended marriage partner and ignorance to the consequences.

Again, Susan tugs at the tablecloth and it's really pissing me off. There is a fold in it that doesn't please her. 'Did you see some of the sights? They're lovely. The weather's really good again,' she babbles on. Pearl looks at me over the wine menu.
'Choose one yet?' I ask. Susan looks at both of us. 'No ...think I'll have something soft, you know. We drank enough wine last night,' Pearl says, reaching to slap the fresh air.
'Ach ...we solved a few problems ...ruled the world a bit,' I laugh, playing along. I attract the waiter and look expectantly at them.
'What are you having?'

'Sparkling water for me. I have to drive. Can't drink and drive. Water will be fine.' Susan eventually shuts up.
'I'll have a double Scotch,' Pearl says.
'Beer please ...lager.'

I excuse myself and make for reception, as Pearl was asking how work at the hospital was going for Susan. I stop short and admire a landscape of St. Aubin with the full tide and small boats sitting in the harbour. I glance over at them. Susan is gabbling away about something. Pearl nods now and then. They don't resemble mother and daughter. Susan's wearing the same long, red dress she wore when she picked us up at the airport. She's far too thin. Pearl is more rounded and looks like a million dollars. I love womanly women.

At reception another fax has arrived for me. Barnsey wants to lift Tommy Johnston. I bypass the lift and take the stairs to our room. I curse the key and manage after several attempts to unlock the door. I grab the receiver and follow the instruction stuck to the telephone on how to make calls.
'I've bad news for yee,' Rory says, right away. 'The RUC has lifted Tommy Johnston and the girl.'
'Shit,' I yell into his ear.
'He'll be out in an hour or two,' Rory sympathises.
'Damn right he'll be out in an hour or two and real mad. What's Barnsey at?'
'Don't talk to me about Barnsey. I'm sick of him. He reckons he's got enough on Johnston to keep him for a while.' Rory pauses and swallows.
'What's up, Rory?' What wonderful news is he going to tell me now? 'They have lifted Trevor Mulholland as well,' he speaks slowly.
I can't believe it. That's all I need. I let the phone dangle between my legs. They'd be camping outside the police station soon and I'm in Jersey. Rory's *Hellos* rattle off my knees.
'Yeah I'm still here,' I say quickly. 'Who's covering the arrests, Rory?'
'I'm sending Big Paul, he's away now. What's with you, Simon?'
'Nothing ...we'll catch the flight. What are they charging Mulholland with?' I ask quickly.
'Don't know. Big Paul will have it all. I want both of ye on this. What time will ye be home?' he finishes.
'Ach ...I don't know. I'll phone the airport ...get a flight,' I stammer out, thinking. 'I'll ring when I arrive.'

The receptionist puts me through to British European. I book two seats on the 8.30pm flight into Gatwick. For a moment I almost booked an extra seat. So Barnsey goes for the glory. ...It could only be for the murders of Tom and Nancy Mulholland. This will blow the Andrews story off the pages. I lean on the desk like a drunk about to throw up. I push the control on the TV and keep pressing until *Sky News* appears. Johnston's face is shown followed by Mulholland. *More details will follow*, the anchor girl says. Bloody Barnsey. Anybody that sells themselves for a set of golf clubs and a few quid is always worth watching. He's something to do with this. He lifts Johnston. Why would he do that? I sigh. To let him know something is up. To hide any involvement which might be thrown at him. If Johnston thinks Mulholland has confessed ...then he's a dead man. Dead men can't tell tales.

I shove what clothes I had unpacked into the grip. I check my watch several times. It's only 5.30pm, three hours. I kick the en-suite door and turn on the cold water. Sweat is trickling down my forehead. My face is ruddy from the sun and everything else. The water laps around my neck. 'Bloody hotel water is never cold,' I mutter into the towel. A quick comb of my hair helps hide my harassed appearance and I try to prepare for the dining room again. I take a few deep breaths and grit my teeth.

I step casually toward the table. It's bad timing. Susan darts past me, clutching her napkin. I spin, watching her rush past the paintings on the wall. Pearl knocks back her Scotch.
'What's up?' I ask, with open arms. Pearl sighs aloud. 'Miss Goody Two Shoes doesn't approve of you and me, you know. She can run around with a terrorist but I can't share a room with you,' she fumes.
I rub my neck. 'Let's go.' I attend her chair and run my fingers across her back, a sort of, you'll be all right. I call the waiter and slip him a tip and have the meal redirected to room 127.
'Something's up,' I whisper, walking.
'Tell me?'
'They've arrested Mulholland, the girl and ...Tommy Johnston.'
'Oh ...is that all?' Pearl replies, with a wicked grin. 'At least you'll be safe for awhile. I threw a wobbler with her, you know. I said too much. She almost died when I mentioned Johnston ...her mysterious future husband. Some Mervyn, huh.'
'It doesn't matter, Pearl. Don't tell her he's been lifted,' I urge. She links onto my arm.

'What did they lift them on?' she asks.
'Good question. Bloody good question,' I say, sarcastically. 'I booked us on the 8.30pm out of here. Maybe you want to stay ...spend some time with Susan,' I add, which sounds stupid. She gives me that look.
'My life's with you,' she says without warning. Her face tries to pull back the words. She gears herself for rejection, building walls, bracing herself. I stop. I feel a shake in my entire body.
'Am I rushing things?' she asks. I want to keep her hanging but it's not fair.
'Do you like Jelly Babies or Clove Rock?'
'Clove Rock.'
Her face relaxes, puzzled. 'I have to know these things. I'd hate to bring home something you didn't like,' I say with an emphasis on the home. She hugs me tightly. 'It's early days yet, you know.' She pauses. 'I'm falling in love with you, Simon.'
'Only falling? ...I've landed,' I say, feeling her excitement squeeze tightly around me.

'Youse make me sick. Look at youse. You silly old fool.' Susan is rushing towards us, her face twisted in rage. I parry a left handed slap as we untangle from our embrace. Pearl stumbles slightly. I grab Susan's hand and spin her into my body.
'Lets talk in the room ...not here, Susan,' I whisper calmly.
'Leave go of me. I never want to see youse again. Just stay away from me. She hates me. I always knew she hated me. And you,' she breathes heavily and scans my body. 'You must get some sort of kick out of frustrated, old women. She couldn't wait until my dad died to get screwed all over the country. You ask her. She's a ...' Pearl connects with her cheek and the slap of flesh takes the momentum out of Susan's outburst.

I grab Pearl by the arm and pull her towards the lift, half expecting an assault from behind. Pearl is ashen and shaking. I fight to get saliva in my mouth. We reach the room and collapse on the bed. 'I better pack,' she manages following a cigarette, in silence. I nod and hear the dinner arriving outside the room. I open the door and Susan is standing with my prawn cocktail. I manage to get a hand up to stop the glass hitting my face. It rebounds off the door and spins into the room. The prawns are all over me. I lunge forward and pull her into the room. Pearl runs to help and she bites Susan's hand, which releases her grip on the silver knife.

Susan is no match for her mother. Pearl has her tied in an arm lock and is pulling against any movement Susan makes.

'I'll let you go if you can act like an adult, Susan,' Pearl says calmly. I close the door and watch. Susan tries to push her face off the maroon carpet. 'I want an answer, Susan,' Pearl states, sternly.

'Okay.'

Pearl moves her legs off her daughter's body. It's an expert hold. She must've done martial arts or something. Susan shakes her dress and pushes her hair from her face.

'We're leaving Jersey,' Pearl begins, walking over to her. 'I don't want to fight with you Susan. I don't want to part on bad terms. Shut up,' her mother spits, reading her face. For once, Susan Patterson is lost for words. 'We ...I came here with Simon thinking I could help you. You are getting yourself into big trouble. You lied to me about your engagement. I know who the man is. It's your life, Susan, but be warned, think long and hard before you do something that could cost you everything.' Pearl finishes her speech.

Susan is rocking with impatience and cockiness. 'I don't need your advice, mother. I am thirty-eight ...the same age as Simon. Then you know all about men ...you've had plenty yourself.' I grab Pearl as she lunges for her once more. Both of us are covered in prawns, like little pinkish slugs eating our clothes.

'Youse make me sick,' Susan taunts, at her face.

'Get out. Get out,' Pearl shouts.

'Don't worry, I'm going. Make sure you pack all your naughty knickers, Mummy. Trevor loved those,' she ends, laughing.

I can't control Pearl's legs. She hits me with a donkey kick and I drop my hold. She has knocked me off balance and spins me through the air. My back connects with the coffee table and cups bounce everywhere. Susan is sprawling against the door. Pearl's standing over her. Shit. I struggle up and dive at Pearl's ankles. She kicks violently. Susan spits on us and kicks my back.

'Just go back to Northern Ireland,' Susan blasts. 'Don't think you'll be the only one, Simon. She lets anyone screw her. Trevor Mulholland, yeah, Trevor Mulholland. You'd have to be hard up to let Mulholland into your knickers. She likes her picture taken while she's doing it. And then there's the newsagent. I suppose she got a free newspaper for that one. She must have a thing about newspapers. You work for a paper. You're an old whore, M-O-T-H-

E-R,' Susan spells out at Pearl's face.

'I'll kill you,' Pearl seethes, trying to break free of me. 'Get out.'

I scramble over Pearl and run down the corridor after Susan. 'Susan, stop.' She keeps dashing along the lemon corridor past the cleaner and the trays left out for room service. 'They've arrested Mulholland and your friend Johnston.' It gets her attention. She stops, almost bowling herself over by her own momentum. I catch up with her.

'You fool. Just go home. Leave me alone. Mind your own business,' she screams.

'My life's at stake,' I shout back. 'Your beloved Johnston is over to kill me, I think. ...You know, from Malaga. A nice little job to pay for the wedding expenses.' Her eyes connect with my words. It's something. She has obviously been given a different story. Susan Patterson half stumbles and saves herself with a palm onto the wall. 'Leave me alone. Just go back home. Just leave me alone,' she screams again, taking the stairs.

My hands are on my hips gasping for breath. She knew I worked for a newspaper. I didn't tell her. Pearl's standing in the hall behind me. 'She's gone,' I say. 'What's all this about Trevor Mulholland. Is it true?'

'Yes.'

I slide down the wall and watch the Portuguese cleaner try to comprehend what is going on.

'It's not what you think, you know.'

'Oh, so you're the expert on thinking,' I snarl. I push myself up and nudge her shoulder. 'Nothing's what it seems,' I say, strutting off to the room. I can't bring myself to think of her and Mulholland having sex. A young upstart is just that when he complains about the rumpus. Just perfect. He lands on the carpet and I close the door of Room 131. I hate smart asses like him that can't mind their own business. 'Great therapy,' I yell. My knuckles are sore.

I grab a towel from the en-suite and wipe off the sticky gunge. I fire my T-shirt into the bath. Pearl stands at the door.

'I did have an affair with another man. ...Trevor Mulholland took pictures of us and then blackmailed me. The pay off was to have sex with him. Have you got a cigarette?' she finishes.

'Have I got a cigarette? You're one cold bitch. Casually you mention it with a cigarette ...a bloody cigarette. Now I suppose you'll say you were going to tell me. You were waiting for the right moment. Just ...piss off,' I scream, cleaning my legs.

Pearl leans on the doorframe using her elbow as a rest. I feel her stare and my anger is ebbing. 'They're beside the bed,' I say.
'What?'
'My cigarettes.'
She walks off and I check my watch. It's almost seven. I drop my pants and reach for the shower. Maybe it will beat some sense into my body. I don't want to know about the blackmail, if it was blackmail ...I visualise her and Mulholland. I push my face into the jets and bang the wall.

She looks at me with a strong will. I stand dripping. No wonder she's run a business and become successful. I feel like an employee on the carpet for bad time keeping.
'Remember that lecture that you gave about trust. Now it's time to trust me, you know. I am not a whore. Yes, I had flings sometimes, only for sex following Peter's death, not before. And ...Mulholland well ...the bastard took pictures of me with a man. He threatened to show them to Susan or drop the photos somewhere, *like Belfast*, to use his words.'

Pearl walks into the en-suite and I drop the towel. The walls are spinning. I want to follow her and ask her for all the details, make it hurt a little more. The fragrance from the brazil-nut shampoo wafts around. She's in the shower. I grunt and sway around looking at the mess on the wall and the luggage. I just want to walk out and drive and drive. It doesn't matter where. I can't. I can only drive to the airport. I hear Susan's words replay in my mind. We need to get ready.

Pearl finishes her shower and tiptoes over the mess at the door. Her contours are sticking to the towel. My jeans are tight and uncomfortable already.
'I'm leaving at seven thirty,' I say. 'If you want a lift, be ready.'
My Barclaycard pays the bill. Then, I strut into the bar and have a double Smirnoff and Coke. She better be ready in five minutes or else I'm going. Two more doubles bite the dust trying to quench the nomadic murmurs in my mind. One bottle of Coke does all three. 'I'm off,' I smile to the barman.
'Say hello to Belfast for me, sir.'
'I will, Billy.' Everybody's Irish or Portuguese here. My throat is on fire but it won't last. I exit the lift and the effects are starting to arrive. It's usually my sense of smell that goes first and I

sniff more than usual when I drink spirits. The cleaner is removing the marks my hands and the prawn sauce made on the walls. I throw a tenner down by her bucket and walk on.

Pearl's zipping her bag and stops when I enter.
'What's wrong?' I ask sharply.
'Nothing.'
'Are you getting the cold?' she ventures, with a wicked grin. I try to hold my angry, no nonsense look. Her smile washes it away.
'Do you want a tissue?'
'No. I'm gonna sniff all the way home. Here's the keys…you drive. I'm sorry.'

Chapter 14

Different airport same country. The infamous Belfast *now* greets us. I had phoned from Gatwick. Big Paul said he would pick us up at Aldergrove. The late night travellers scurry the way intermittent rain does. We have to wait for luggage.
'How's your bum for love bites?' Paul Morgan howls across Arrivals. He stands, smiling, complete with black, curly hair, which was longer than I had expected it to be.
'Big man,' I smile, meeting his hand in greeting. 'This is Pearl, Pearl Patterson.'
'Bout ye, Pearl. Keeping all right?'
'Not too bad, Paul. It's nice to meet you, you know. Simon really-really talks about you all the time.'
'Huh ...that'll be the day, like,' Paul smiles, his dark suit flapping around as he sways back and forth on his heels.

I grab the bags and Paul rushes to grab a free trolley. We had made up on the plane. I'm still drunk ...well almost. The sour taste is left and the shiver. I'm at the apologising stage, although I could murder a drink.

Paul drives. Most people aren't happy with their body image, so the researchers say, because tall people want to look smaller and small people want to look bigger. Pearl and I are cramped in the back of an orange Yugo.
'When are you gonna get a decent car?' I jest.
'Stop griping, mate. With all them joyriders about, like. You must be joking, mate. Nobody steals this, like.'
'What about Mulholland and Johnston?' I ask. Paul looks in the mirror. He's normally straight, yet now he's all crouched over.

'My da says it's gonna hit the fan, mate. He was raging at that gipe Barnsey, like. Did you enjoy Jersey, Pearl?'
'Lovely, Paul. I wish we'd had more time there.'
'Maybe yer man there will stick an oul ring on your finger and ye can go for your honeymoon, like. ...I wanta see that, like,' he laughs.

A calm has fallen over the newsroom, deadline has past and the pages have gone. The place looks lonely, only Rory and the night desk crew shuffle around. The drone of production simmers in the distance, rattling off copies of tomorrow morning's edition.

'Any word on the girl yet?' I ask, entering his greenhouse.
'Hello, Mass Patterson,' Rory says.
'Not a thing, Simon. Now don't be getting yourself all excited with Barnsey, Simon.'
'Excited, Rory? Huh. Why could he not wait?'
Rory is busy fussing over Pearl again. I read the proof of the story being printed in the morning edition.
'They found a gun on Johnston, might be able to pin a murder on him, mate,' Paul adds. He knows I'm pissed off.
'I'm going on with my own piece,' I say. 'That all right with you, Rory?'
'Fine, Simon. Oh ...the Andrews' boys are taking a suit against ye. This came for ye ...don't worry, we're picking up the tab,' he says, handing me the fat envelope. I go to take it yet he holds on. It makes me look at him. His eye barely moves. Paul's leaning on the filing cabinet and gives me a knowing glance.
'Hey Da, how come you're paying his legal fees and you never think of buying a drink, like? You're a miserable oul shite.'
'Away with ye, Paul,' he tuts. 'Sure you're not safe in bars in this place ...despite the ceasefire. Isn't that right, Mass Patterson?'
'You have a point, Rory,' Pearl laughs.
'Well, maybe you'll stick your hand in your pocket when these two get married, like. You better start saving Da,' Paul says, with a straight face. I cut him a look. Pearl smiles and tries to suppress it as best she can. Rory has his head turning looking at us in a robotic motion.
'I'll drop these two off at the City, Da. Right Da, get a tenner out for the car park,' Big Paul says, cracking his fingers.
'Where would I get a tenner? ...You shouldn't be carrying big sums of cash round with ye.'

'See, Pearl. Only way to get a tenner out of him is to threaten to tell oul Maureen he's back on the sugar. He's more scared of oul Maureen than being kneecapped.'

'Bring me a receipt, well,' he says, making a big fuss of digging in his pocket.

We catch the late news on the way. Trevor Mulholland has been tucked into his cell for the night. Johnston too, the anchorman says. Shouting journalists harass their lawyers from the police station steps. *No Comment*, their war cry. It's one of those stories that will grow and grow. Everybody knew what had happened to Trevor Mulholland's parents. Most of Ireland has a soft spot for him, but now all that might change.

'We missed the boat, Pearl,' I say, dejectedly. She blows a sigh and rubs my leg.

'It's not over yet, you know. You have a head start.'

A wicked grin etches out at me. She's right. The rest of them will be running around chasing their tails, wasting their time outside the courthouse, waiting to hear Mulholland's reaction to his arrest. They'll be digging into Tommy Johnston's past and throwing matchsticks in the air. Barnsey had been responsible for the arrest and despite all his faults he'll give us the first shot at it. 'Yeah ...good point,' I eventually answer.

'What do you think, Paul?'

'My da thinks Mulholland'll go down, mate.'

Pearl walks towards the terminal. 'I'll pay for the car,' she says.

'Get the receipt.'

Paul stands with his hands in his pocket and waits. 'See that envelope he gave ye, like. It's stuff from Mulholland's house. Didn't want to say much, like.' Paul rattles out, quickly. He fidgets from foot to foot, his brown eyes darting around for eavesdroppers.

'Look Simon, mate ...there's pictures of Pearl in there with a man.'

'How'd you get them?'

'In the house, like.'

'Yer man was away to jail and all the other dicks stayed at the cop shop ...so I nipped up to Silcott Avenue, like. You wanta see that hole, like. Cobwebs everywhere ...it's stinking, mate.'

I look at the envelope in my hand and grip it firmly.

'Am I being sued?'

'No.'

What else did you get? Anything about Johnston? Anything about the Andrews Corporation?' I rattle out.

'Neah. I took pictures of the hole.'
'Look at the files she left with Rory. Look for steal ...maybe more than would be needed to make the normal things, Paul.'
He smiles and sways around. 'It's in the envelope, mate. They make iron furniture, whatever the hell that looks like. It's ...'
'Guns,' I interrupt.
'Aye. My da says she probably doesn't know, like. Barnsey checked out the names on the payroll. Didn't have to, mate. They were common knowledge, like. Apparently the cops knew about Patterson Engineering or the work force ...some of them anyway, mate,' he explains.
'What are you doing the morrow?' I say, seeing Pearl walk back.
'I'm on the jailbirds. My da says you've to keep digging.' Paul turns and smiles at Pearl. 'Bloody pain in the hole having to go away in there to pay the car park.'
'It's okay, Paul. There's your receipt.'

Paul folds himself into the orange Yugo and sticks a long arm out in salute.
'That's some car, you know,' Pearl muses.
'Something else.'

We tiptoe through the kitchen in Drumfiddy, its walls still damp with fresh plaster. Electrical wires hang awaiting connection of wall lamps. The bedroom is finished and welcoming. Glass tables and wrought ironwork is the theme in black and white. I stop and survey it. Even at this late hour it's worth taking time to digest.
'Do you like it?'
'I love it,' I say. 'Never seen furniture like that before.'
'I design it all myself, you know. It's made in the factory. I've a lot of orders coming in for it. Our web site's inundated.'

Twice in an hour I've been told different. I took for granted that an engineering firm would make industrial parts. The white satin duvet cover ripples with my weight as I belly flop into it. It's lovely and cool. Pearl laughs.
'I'll leave early in the morning,' I say. 'I want to check out Fast Frank and Billy Thompson.'
'Say hello to Billy for me,' Pearl adds. 'He's in Coleraine. Do you know where the Leisure Centre is?' I nod, recalling the layout of the town. 'Well, if you park in the car park there, his taxi business is just up a bit on the left, you know.'

Pearl is undressing. I smoke. I watch. She places her necklace on the black iron dressing table and unfastens her jeans.

'How do you keep fit?' I ask.
'Oh ...I swim regularly and as a younger woman I did a lot of Judo. It's hard to beat swimming, you know ...tones the body. Why?'
'Ach ...I was just wondering. I'd like to lose some weight. I'm eating too much.'
'How do you feel now?' she asks, looking at me from the mirror. I know she's talking about her and Mulholland and the pictures. My gut gives a jump, reminding me of the envelope in the room.
'You are honest with me, Pearl. I hate the thought of another man being with you.' I sigh. 'It's not my business.'

She removes her lemon blouse. Pearl turns and sits on the dressing table. 'What's your fantasy?' she asks, taking me by surprise. All of a sudden the words seem to have stuck below my tongue and no matter how much I poke and prod for them they won't come. My ears seem to have the sea rushing through them like they did when I fought with Mary Ginty, all those years ago in Tullydeen.
'What would you most like to do?' she asks again.
'Hey, I'm the psychologist here.'
'You always do that, you know. Laugh or crack a joke when you're nervous,' she replies. She has that wicked grin on her face. 'Are you going to tell me?' Pearl doesn't wait for an answer. I shuffle around onto my side. 'Well, I'll tell you mine, then. Ever since I saw you in the office I wanted to throw you down on the desk and kiss you all over. Then, I want you to massage me all over and make love to me.' She pauses. She smiles. Her honesty doesn't cost her a thought.
'You'll have to stop beating about the bush, Pearl, and say what you mean,' I mimic in my best W.C. Fields voice.
'See, you're doing it again, you know. Cracking a joke. So what's yours then?'
'I ...would like that, too,' I say, nipping my nail into the palm of my hand. Pearl walks over and crawls onto the bed beside me.
'You're telling me fibs, Simon Rogers.'
I concede and hug her. 'Just give me time. Pauline was unfaithful to me,' I say, not sure why it came out. 'I pushed it away, then my parents died ...now it's all starting to affect me. I swore I would never trust another woman. I'd decided to go out and have sex now and then and to hell with the rest of it.' I pause and sigh. 'I couldn't go through with it. I'm not that type. Then all this with Mulholland cropped up today ...well it just brought it all back, Pearl.'

'Would I have known your ex-wife? Did she come from Tullydeen?'
'No, she's the Bitch from Belfast,' I say, in a scary voice.
'I will never be unfaithful to you, Simon. It's not my style.' Pearl pushes back my hair and runs her finger down the bridge of my nose. My hands trace down her back and I squeeze her buttocks. She gives that little groan again and pecks at my nose. I think of her on the office desk and the hunger I had at the old cottage.
'Penny for them,' she whispers.

In one movement I roll onto Pearl. My tongue passes the satin, it passes the row, it passes the pictures and into trust and the warmth of the woman I've fallen in love with. Her fingers grab the iron headboard and I hear her surrender with all her might.

Chapter 15

Coughing my lungs out in the dawn is something I do. The flight from Jersey has interfered with my sinuses as well. It's hard to navigate around a strange room in bad light. Eventually I find the envelope and make my way towards the bathroom. It's finished in gold and white. It's large with white tiles and the odd gold one here and there. I park on the dark toilet seat and listen for a moment. I feel like a kid sneaking a midnight feast.

Mulholland and Johnston were probably sleeping in their cells. It would be interesting to know. I remember reading research from America where a psychologist studied patterns of behaviour of people arrested for serious crimes. The guilty were calm, I recall. The innocent paced the cell. They'll be sleeping, glad to ease the burden of guilt — Mulholland anyway. I rip the envelope and look through the smoke.

I pull the prints out that Big Paul had found in Mulholland's house. Plus the one's he had taken of the inside of the place. Paul was right. It's a real hole. Next there are six pictures all showing Pearl with a tall, grey-haired man. I wince and the August heat turns into a winter wind, eating my T-shirt and into my bones. The butt of the cigarette cushions my teeth. I spend little time on the pictures. The letter from Rory helps to drag away my attention. The man pictured is a respectable newsagent from Portrush – except for the odd fling. I'd never seen him before. He had no paramilitary connections.

Rory changes the topic to the books Pearl had left with him. Bob Duncan, a financial wizard who guides the finances of the Irish

Scribe, reckons the incoming amounts of metal and the outgoing net profits do not match up. The overall profits would be too high. It's well done, Rory states. Bob Duncan had been very impressed by the way it was hidden. 'Bit like the wind, you know it's there, yet you can't see it,' Rory has plucked from the sky. I smile. He writes differently to how he talks.

Why, bothers me. I know Mulholland blackmailed her because of the photos, but she had sex with him. Both of them. Why? She's not the type of woman to give into demands. So Mulholland takes the photos, shows them to Pearl and demands the payoff of sex. I'm fighting hard to keep this outside myself. Mulholland shows the prints to Susan anyway. So Pearl's off the hook. But she still keeps Trevor Mulholland on to do the books. After all that? …No way. I lose it with a vision of Mulholland fondling Pearl. My teeth are digging into my bottom lip. I stare at the bidet as my mind murmurs. There must be more.

I read over Rory's letter again. My brain's tired yet alert, too alert for sleep. Dawn's seeping through the window. I creep back into the bedroom and find my jeans and shoes. Pearl's blowing bubbles. I make my way downstairs slowly. The damp smell of new plaster guides me. I take the Celica and drive off along the lane. Rabbits are caught out, but I give them time to move. I take a right and drive towards Portrush.

The Atlantic springs into view and I always gasp at the sight of the golden beaches. A wonder of the world is just down the road a bit. I pass the sign for the Giant's Causeway – Ireland's first patio. A Japanese sun waters, firing up for the later hours. I park at the East Strand and shuffle onto the beach. The envelope fits nicely under my arm and my hands are delved deep into my pockets. The wind is soothing and warm, blowing mini blizzards around my ankles.

I made sand castles here under the watchful eye of my father. The big waves used to cover me. I loved diving into them. My folks applauded, acknowledging my bravado. I want them to applaud now. But they can't. They're dead. My throat needs them to clap. I check over my shoulder. No one is here. It's just the tall dunes and me. I suck air through my teeth, trying not to cry.

All those holidays are hounding me. Flashing past. The dodgem rides and my dad banging into the other cars. Mum waited with ice cream. Their time: their love. It's all gone. I think of Grace, making me ham sandwiches. I want to hold her now. Tears smart my cheeks. Why did I come here? ...Why? All this crap: terrorists and Mulholland's clone. All I want is to be a boy again with hindsight. I stop beside a jellyfish, stranded from the receding sea. The waves roll land ward, talking and sitting down. I've never brought Grace here. A surge of certainty tells me I will. I know I will. My shoulders straighten and I breathe in the happy times they gave me. I grab the envelope and fire it across the sand. I sniff and wipe my eyes and visualise me, the little boy, diving into the waves. I applaud him. He dives again. I wait anxiously to see his head appear.

'That's fun,' I yell to him. I was lucky to have fun. God ...I wanted the same for Grace. It wasn't to be. ...Her and *good old Tom* from the bank. Now she's sorry. What bloody use is sorry?

The little boy runs to me from the waves. I'm my dad. My mother talks excitedly, telling him that he was wonderful. I hug him in the towel and love him the way I love Grace. His eyes are beaming. Happiness oozes from his tiny, rosy cheeks. For a moment he looks like Grace and I know he loves me. I sigh over at the guesthouses across the bay. I look at my mother and her contented smile leaks out. 'I was lucky,' I say softly. 'Thank you,' I whisper to my God and the sea.

It's all gone. I pick up the envelope and trudge through the soft sand to the beginning of the dunes. Mulholland has something on you, Pearl, something worse than a few pictures. You probably knew he'd show them to Susan. I struggle to light a cigarette in the wind. It's almost 7.00am. The guesthouses across the bay will be preparing an Ulster Fry. I could murder one myself and decide to walk back. I stop. The word *murder* tackles me again. Did she murder someone? ...Nah. It would have to be that bad to let Mulholland have sex with her ...even after Susan knew. She still kept Mulholland on to do the books. A chill develops in my spine and crawls along my ribcage. It says: *you're getting warmer*.

A road sweeper sweeps, in the centre of Portrush, past the shutters on the shops. I pull up outside the newsagents and take a deep breath. I stride confidently over the threshold past the drinks' cooler to the counter. I pick up *The Irish Scribe* and wonder what she saw in him.

Pearl is smoking when I return. 'There's something here for you,' I say, handing her the shots. She freezes and looks at me. 'Here's the paper,' I say, throwing it down on the bed. She walks to the window. 'Paul found them in Mulholland's house,' I explain.

Pearl nods, miles away.

'He's a newsagent in Portrush,' she says, turning to face me. I look at the paper and she twigs. She looks at the ceiling with closed eyes. 'What has Mulholland got on you, Pearl?' You let him have sex with you and he shows the pictures to Susan anyway. So they lose their power. You can tell Mulholland to get out of your life, yet you don't. His firm still does your books and ...'

'Shut up, please. Please shut up,' she shouts. She rubs her hair violently and shakes.

'Tell me,' I say calmly, sitting on the bed. 'We're back to trust, Pearl.'

'I can't,' she concedes. She swipes at tears, using the arm of her cream blouse.

'Maybe you can't ...but I can,' I add, watching her twist and parry my notion. 'I think you murdered Peter,' I say quickly.

Her head falls forward and she knows that I know. I move over to her and she sobs into my chest.

'It was an accident,' she mumbles and suddenly a different picture emerges. 'I'll have to phone the office. I can't go in like this.' Pearl straightens herself and blows her nose. 'There, that's better.' She dials the number and talks quickly to Sandra. It's my turn to stare out of the window. She's still talking.

 A blue van makes its way up the lane. The bloody workmen. Soon they'll be hammering and banging about. It's not the ideal place to confess innermost secrets. She finishes the call and looks at me. 'The workmen,' I say, nodding towards the lane.

'Let's go somewhere, Simon. Somewhere away from Drumfiddy.' Pearl is undressing and flinging her business suit over the chair. A workman is stamping around downstairs. She pulls on her jeans and a black T-shirt. She checks her make up and flicks at her hair. I gaze at the headboard. She stops and smiles. 'Penny for them.'

 We drive along the Coleraine Road. The traffic is heavy and I pull the RAV4 into a lay-by.

'So what happened?' I ask. Pearl sits silent for a moment and stares out of the window. I doubt if she sees the traffic.

'We had a row in the factory one night about money. Peter had made some stupid errors on pricing, you know. I called Trevor Mulholland and while we waited for him to arrive both of us started. I can be a real bitch, you know. Peter had been ill for some time. He wasn't himself.' She stops and fumbles for her hanky. 'Well ...it got out of hand, Simon. I remember Peter's face turning a greyish colour. I should've stopped. Why did I not stop? I didn't,' she shouts, regretfully. 'I kept getting madder and madder. We were by the lathes. I picked up a sample of a heavy-duty hinge Peter had worked on and threw it at him. It hit him on the side of the head. Trevor Mulholland arrived and Peter was lying on the floor by the lathe.' Pearl stops and turns her head toward the sunroof. She gives something similar to a dry cry and smothers her face in the handkerchief. I don't intrude. It would be too easy to say, *it'll be all right,* or touch her. How can it be all right? I hate people touching me.

'I was ranting and raving and hysterical and he phoned an ambulance. I killed him,' she says, softly looking at me.
'Were the police involved?'
'No. The post-mortem showed a heart attack.'
'What about the blow to the head?'
'It showed he had fallen against something sharp on the way down. Mulholland kept the hinge. He stalked me, Simon, mentioning it to make me have sex with him. Showing the photos to Susan with the other guy was a warning. A warning of what it meant to step out of line. He said he would go to the police and get the case reopened. I thought I'd go to my grave with this, you know.'
'That's taken some courage to admit, Pearl.' She half laughs.
'We're back to trust, you know. That's how Mulholland and Tommy Johnston came in to being. You're right, Simon. They killed Tom and Nancy Mulholland. They used my business to make guns and I couldn't do a thing. They laundered money from their schemes. And, I bet the same happened to Fast Frank's Diners. Mulholland gets something and uses it. He could control the outside image to keep the red tape in order. Look what happened to Billy Thompson. Billy would have fought it like we all did, but Mulholland is really, really smart. He destroyed Billy Thompson, you know. You have to take his offer,' Pearl finishes, opening the door.

I keep my distance. Her shoulders are hunched and she walks more from memory than purpose.
'He's going down, Pearl ...but you're not,' I say, determinedly. She spins around with venom and pain written all over her face.
'He made me his whore, Simon. How can you even talk to a murdering whore?' I grab her and push her head into my neck.
'I might see it differently. Maybe it was the survivor in you who made you do his will. Kept you alive until the right time, or the right

person came along,' I say, holding her tight. 'What you have been through is abuse. It's no different from a child being sexually abused by their father. Only the victim dies, Pearl. The survivors live physically, perhaps for years, maybe driven into alcoholism or suicide attempts by their shame and guilt. We'll work through it when you're ready. The first step is to stop blaming yourself. You hit Peter on the head ...it didn't kill him.'
'I did. I killed him,' she says, pushing herself off my chest. 'If I hadn't shouted and lost my temper he would've been alive.'
'Come on, let's go. I have an idea.' I grab her hand, pulling her reluctantly towards the Toyota.

'Liz, is that you?' I ask, watching Pearl from the corner of my eye. 'Tell me... if I hit somebody on the head with something heavy while they're having a heart attack, would you lot know if I killed him, or the heart attack killed him, ' I explain on the phone.
Pearl swipes at her hair and gazes at the traffic. Liz starts into her multi-syllable monologue. 'Stop ...talk in English. Yes or no?' I interrupt. Pearl turns my way. I'm relieved to hear Liz say, yes.
'I've just won a tenner, Liz. Talk to you soon.'

'What's all that about?' Pearl frowns. The jury has found you not guilty ...or at least the expert witness has,' I say happily. Professor Elizabeth McFarland is by far the top of her tree. She's out of her tree to do that job,' I laugh.
'Who is she ...a coroner?'
'Yes, as well as being an expert in criminal psychology. She's an all rounder. She knows how people die and what it must feel like,' I joke. Pearl slaps my arm. 'You didn't kill him. But if you're not happy I'll take you to meet her. You'd like her.'
'I suppose she's examined you,' Pearl says, sarcastically.
'No ...we were students together ...that's all.'
'That's all?'
'Yeah ...students.'
'Huh,' Pearl sighs, contemptuously.
'Ach ...Pearl.'

Chapter 16

Mulholland's out. Paul phoned. I flick on the radio and catch the ten o'clock news. Barnsey is giving a statement to the press about how Trevor Mulholland had assisted the police with their inquiries. Pearl looks at me. Tommy Johnston remains behind bars. The station gives a recap on Tom and Nancy Mulholland's murders and supports the notion that Johnston will be charged with the mistaken identity car bombing. 'Some mistake,' I mutter.

'It makes Mulholland sound like a hero, you know. Helping with their inquiries, helped kill them would be more to the point,' Pearl says angrily.

'This's a load of crap. I can't see them pinning the bombing on Johnston. He's too smart for that.'

I stare into space, something I do from time to time. 'In a way it's a good thing they've released Mulholland,' I say. 'It gives us a shot at him. First we'll start with the one legged wonder,' I say getting out of the RAV4.

Fast Frank's in the garden, watering his *naumachia* and weighing me up at the same time. I think about Pearl's vision of him hopping about on one leg, asking if I want salt and vinegar. I suppress my smile. He has two legs at the moment. One is probably wooden, or whatever wooden legs are made of these days.

For someone who's supposedly bankrupt he appears to have managed well. He lives in a large bungalow with perfect lawns along the Portrush to Portstewart Road.

'Frank Bole?' I ask, walking up the driveway.

'Aye, who wants to know?' he utters, from beneath his straw hat.

I'm right up to him now. He moves a little gingerly. The shade of his hat shows a huge, red nose that rest in the middle of a poker face. I imagine he has a droll sense of humour.
'Simon Rogers, from *The Irish Scribe*,' I announce, pushing out my hand.
'What do you want?'
'I'd like to talk to you about Trevor Mulholland.' His face grins in contempt and his hoarseness spits onto the lawn just past my feet.
'It won't take long.'
'This way,' he grunts, turning his short legs. I follow him and we take a paved path at the side of his bungalow.
'You're the boy that caught them boys ...them boys stealing the money. Aye ...them boys stealing the money.'
'Yeah,' I say casually, not wanting to sound smug. Fast Frank isn't so fast anymore as he labours in front of me. He has a bad chest as well. His white shirt and brown slacks have seen better days and looser fits. The false leg kicks out more than his right one making him look as if he is walking with one foot on the pavement and one on the road.

    We end up in a large back garden, complete with a long greenhouse full of tomatoes at the bottom.
'Take a seat there, son. Take a seat, son. Sit down there,' he says, pointing to the patio. Fast Frank goes inside and returns with two glasses of red liquid. 'Great stuff, this. You'll have to try this. Great stuff, son. Great stuff, son,' he smirks, from under his hat. He shuffles into the chair opposite me and places his hat down next to the ashtray. He's still sizing me up.
'What's this?' I ask.
'Homemade wine. Aye ...homemade wine, son.' He coughs.
I take a sip. 'It's good.'
I can't tell one wine from another anyway. Can't be bothered with the people who talk about vintages and all that crap. I have a simple philosophy about wine: just drink enough of it and get drunk, no matter what colour it is.

'So what brings you to this neck of the woods, son? You're a brave bit from Belfast way up here. Aye, way up here, son,' he says, looking at my cigarettes. I reach him one and he rolls it around in his yellowed fingers.
'Trevor Mulholland did your books. I think you were swindled.' Fast Frank gives me the impression he wouldn't appreciate small

talk or pissing about. He doesn't answer while he rubs one of his chins. His face is crooked, sort of to one side, as if he grew up in an easterly wind. I hold his gaze and light my cigarette.

'You're a shrewd man, son. Aye, a shrewd man, son. If you can take down an outfit like them boys in the town, you must have guts, son. Aye, guts.' He stops and we both sip the wine. 'Mulholland'll get what he deserves,' he throws in, quickly. 'Get what he deserves, son. Aye, he'll get it, son.' Fast Frank taps the cigarette once more and lights it.

'Maybe you can help give him what he deserves,' I slip in. He coughs and slaps the table. I'm not sure if he's playing for time or baiting my naivete. He takes a sip of his wine again and smacks his lips loudly.

'Take a look around you, son. Just take a look, son. Take a look at me. I worked hard all of my life. Aye, all of my life, son. Weekends ...long hours to build up the business. For what? For what, son? For bad circulation and one leg. Aye, one leg, son. You want me to fight Mulholland? Listen son, in a few years I'll be dead. Chippin' spuds in the big chip shop. Aye.' Fast Frank pauses and looks around, reflecting. 'I'd enough stashed by. Mulholland did me a favour when he told me I was bankrupt. Boys he did. Aye, he did, son. Don't you fall into the trap of working all hours. This isn't a dress rehearsal, son. Nah ...this is the real thing, son. The real thing, son.' He sits back and his words carry conviction.

'Nice looking tomatoes, Frank,' I say after the silence. I've thrown him. He follows my gaze to the greenhouse. 'What are they ...*Aisla Craigs*?' I rise from the table and walk slowly onto the lawn, peering into the mass of plants. I love the smell of home grown tomatoes. He shuffles down behind me.

'I'd wild trouble with greenfly this year. Wild trouble, son. Ate to bits son. Aye,' he croaks out.

'Stick a few marigolds in around the base of them,' I say confidently, turning to look at him.

'Marigolds?' he grunts. His face is like a jigsaw. I can see him asking himself what a reporter like me would be doing growing tomatoes. 'Yeah ...marigolds. They keep the greenfly away.' I knew all the hours I'd spent watering and looking after my parents' tomatoes would come in handy some day. I used to hate it.

He shuffles past me and shows me some of his best tomatoes. Their scent is beautiful. They are so different to the supermarket's scentless and tasteless varieties.

'Look at this leaf ...ate to bits, aye. Marigolds, you say? Marigolds.' He gives a little chuckle and coughs.

We walk back to the patio. 'Finish your wine, Frank. Nice to meet you,' I say walking off.

'Hang on a minute, son. Just hang on. Aye.' He disappears into the kitchen and I hear him fumble about. 'There you are, son. There you are now. Take them with ye. And good luck. Aye, good luck, son,' he says, reaching me a bottle of the wine and a plastic bag full of his tomatoes.

'Thanks.' I figure it's his way of saying, maybe a younger man will help you. 'I'll not trouble you, Frank.'

'Aye ...I know you won't, son. I know you won't, son,' he replies quickly, shaking my hand. A sadness seems to zoom across him. Maybe it's the powerlessness of how he's been stitched up.

'You get the boys. You're the boy to get the boys. Aye, you're the boy. You're halfway there, son. Halfway there.'

I feel as if I'm half asleep and somebody is saying the house is on fire and for a second you go back to sleep until it registers.

'The Andrews Corporation?' I snap back.

'Aye, them boys. A wee bird told me you were tipped off. Tipped off about them boys, son. Aye.' Fast Frank develops a cough and I smile. Every time I tried to trace the caller about the Andrews Corporation it led to a dead end. No one else knows – only Rory and Mandy. So Fast Frank's fortune had floundered off the coast of Malaga.

'Was it you who phoned the newsroom?' I ask.

His cough appears to get worse, yet his knowing eyes give me a confirming glance.

'I'll be damned,' I say, happily, patting his back. I kiss the bottle of wine and waltz back to the RAV4.

'He wants you to measure him up for an iron leg. Sent these as a deposit.' I throw the bag onto Pearl's lap. 'Home made wine.'

She lifts her mood enough to smile. How could she be anything else but distressed, raking all that stuff up again? I curse myself and get in.

'It's all one big pile of shit. I received an anonymous tip from a caller asking for me at the very beginning of this Andrews thing. We could never find him. Guess who it was?'

'Fast Frank,' Pearl answers, taking my cue.

Chapter 17

We cruise into Portstewart in the middle of the holiday season. Every sort of accent floats around us. The beach is busy, so we park along the seafront.
'Want a Coke?'
'Coke's fine.'
I dart across the road and buy the drinks. Kids pass by, being pulled by stressed parents promising to bring them back after lunch. It doesn't look like much of a holiday for them. I think about how I will handle Billy Thompson.
'Can we walk, Simon?'
'Aye. One quick call and I'll be with you.' I phone Rory and he picks up on the second ring. I tell him about Fast Frank. He'll chew it over and put it together. That's the way he works.

Pearl has stopped at a playground, watching the kids. I take a mouthful of Coke and stroll towards her. She sips slowly.
'Rory sends his regards,' I say.
'Huh. I'll never be able to face him again, you know.'
'Again is only until this evening. We've to go to Belfast. He wants a meeting ...Paul and Mandy and me. You can't run, Pearl,' I state, rubbing her shoulders.
'But they saw the pictures of me, Simon.'
'So did I. I haven't shunned you.'
'That's different,' she hisses.
'Ach ...Pearl, these are my friends. They don't laugh at me ...maybe with me. They won't laugh at you. They're fine people. They wouldn't be in the job they do if they weren't fine people. I've seen

Rory Hamilton drop stories because he's frightened he might drive someone over the edge. We get a bad press as journalists, raking up the dirt and all that. It's different with the Andrews Corporation ...it was premeditated. We eat them alive then,' I explain, walking off.

'Simon.' Pearl is running to catch up. She opens her arms and almost knocks me off my feet. 'I'll face them,' she says. We clink our cans.
'You will have mood swings,' I say on the beach. 'It's part of recovery. Some of the time you will blame yourself. Then the new way of thinking will take over. This happens because you have lanced the boil ...so to speak. All the repressed feelings start to come out. In other words, you feel your feelings. Some days you'll want to kill yourself, Pearl. Others, it will be the feeling of freedom. A good tip is to stop the thought at the beginning, refuse to think about it. Don't let the negative take root. For example, don't start to put yourself down. If and when you do, stop thinking about it. It can't grow unless you give it power. A plant needs water. When you feel down, force yourself to talk to someone. It'll be hard, but you have to do it.' I place my arms around her and hold her tightly.
'I'm frightened, Simon.'
'Come on.'

I look for a quiet place on the beach.
'This is your mind,' I explain, drawing a big bucket in the sand, with my finger. 'All throughout our lives we take in hurt. Things people say. Like you're getting fat or I hate you. So, gradually the bucket fills up with resentment and emotional pain. Any form of sexual abuse and manipulation like you have suffered fills it up very quickly. What isn't filled up we fill with guilt and shame. Then suicide attempts happen, with powerlessness and the vicious circle continuing. Every time you talk honestly to another human being you are lowering the water in the bucket. As you do this, new ideas will come, different perspectives.' I pause and smile.
'Know the truth and it shall set you free,' she says, looking at the sand.
'Yeah ...that's about it in a nutshell,' I say lying down.
'What made you become a psychologist?' she asks, leaning on my chest.
'Confusion. I was useless at reading people, naive. At school I was teased because I was fat. People seemed to gain my trust and then

break it. It made me hypersensitive. At the age of eighteen, I tried to commit suicide. Then, I woke up in hospital and was sent to a psychiatric hospital or the *mental,* as it's affectionately known in these parts. Everybody was telling me how lucky I was not to die. I didn't feel lucky. Once again I had to face everything. My folks couldn't cope. Questions, questions and more questions,' I explain with a shrug. 'My ma seemed more worried about what people in the church would think.'

'In those days it was drugs for depression. Although I was lucky,' I say in reflection. Pearl gently rubs my chest. 'In walked a young psychologist and she wanted to try some treatment with me. I'd heard of the shocks and other things. I was shit scared. I asked her if it was the shocks. She laughed. She said it was counselling. Just me talking, her listening. We hit it off. She was like a breath of fresh air, Pearl. Other psychologists and psychiatrists had more or less treated me with contempt. She didn't pity me. She treated me like a human being. I spent six weeks in hospital and attended weekly therapy at her home. A few years later I entered that hospital as a psychology student, on placement, working with her. This society drives people into repression. It's all screwed up with religion.'
'It is, you know. She sounds like a marvellous woman.'
'Ach ...she is, Pearl.' I smile and she appears curious.
'Did you fall in love with her, Simon?'
'Naw ...more admiration,' I explain.
She grabs my shirt. 'Point her out ...I'll pull her hair out,' she jests, laughing.
'It was Liz on the phone. The woman I asked about the hinge.'
Pearl catches my drift and flings her head back.
'I would kill for you Simon, you know,' she utters slowly, with determination. We kiss and I massage her hair.
'I'm tired,' I say, feeling her nod against my chest. 'How do you think I'll get on with Billy Thompson, Pearl?'
'Tell Billy you know me. I'll come in with you if you want.'
'No ...I'll see him on my own first,' I state quickly.
'Why do you not want me there?' Pearl pokes my ribs, wanting an answer.
'Ach ...Pearl, it would look bad you holding my hand. That's all,' I reply.
   Coleraine is a little quieter, mostly locals. I follow Pearl's directions while she waits in the Toyota. It's a dirty, grimy place.

Not Coleraine. Billy Thompson's taxi office. Cigarette burns dot the red bench seats and UVF is scrawled on the walls.

'Where to, mate?' the tattooed guy asks.

'Nowhere.' His face creases and his gelled back hair glares at me. 'I'm Simon Rogers from *The Irish Scribe*. ...You Billy Thompson?'

'Don't talk to reporters, asshole,' he smacks out from behind the mesh.

'Pearl Patterson said you'd talk to me.'

He stops and shouts angrily into the radio. 'Bloody drivers,' he snaps at me. 'Pearl Patterson, heh.' He looks me up and down and sets the baseball bat back against his desk. 'How do you know Pearl Patterson, heh?'

I walk over to the mesh and hold his stare.

'I'm after Mulholland, Billy. I'm gonna put him away. She thought you were swindled and so do I.' It gets his attention. He unlocks the wire door and nods for me to come through. Billy is probably mid-thirties, yet he is an awesome figure. He's as hard as nails. His biceps bulge from the hems of his black T-shirt and his stomach is as tight as a drum. Billy Thompson pulls up a plastic chair and turns down the radio a bit. The spearmint from his chewing gum drifts around. He leans over the back of the chair and rests his chin on his arms.

'What did Pearl tell you?'

'She told me many things, Billy.' He's wondering if I know about the rape thing. His eyes seem to fill with shame.

'Tell me why you went bankrupt?' He laughs, showing a missing front tooth. I shiver, thinking of anyone brave enough to do such a thing.

'Everything went down like a ton of shite, heh. Our business was good. We were big and could handle rough times. I got up one morning and Mulholland was in the office early saying tthe bank had contacted him, heh. That was it,' he says, raising his arms.

'How much did you pay out to keep the alleged rape charge quiet, Billy?'

His face goes ashen as if he'd been hit by Tyson. He tries to speak, but the words won't come out. I feel like Tyson, now, moving in for the kill. 'I need the name of the girl, Billy. With that I might be able to get your funds back,' I jab, punching it into his mind. His head sinks into his arms. A tiny bald spot looks up at me.

'I didn't do it, heh,' he manages.

'I only need the name, Billy.'
'Can't do that, heh,' he says surely, shaking his head.
　　　I stand tall over him. He looks up at me. I'm intimidating him. A few minutes previously, I didn't think anyone could threaten Billy Thompson, never mind me.
'Give me the name, Billy.'
'I can't, heh.'
'Why not? Without it I can't help you. We're talking big money here. If Mulholland intentionally put you out of business you will receive compensation. All you got to do is give me the name.'
　　　He jumps up and squares up to me. 'You reporters. Who the hell do you think you are coming in here and messing with the past, heh?' He grabs me and his force bangs me off the wall. I manage to lock his arm and swing him around. Where I get the strength, I don't know. I'm glaring down at him pinned against the wall.
'Okay, no name, Billy. One last question and I'm gone.' I had him by the chest in a fist grip like a vice.
'Did Mulholland bankrupt you?' He looks down at my hand. His anger is receding. I let him go and stand back. I don't think he'll lunge at me. I breathe heavily.
'Aye ...did that. It was all planned, heh. It was the rape charge and there's no name,' he says, softly and slowly. I walk over to my seat again. The reality of pinning Billy Thompson against a wall is starting to dawn on me.
'Thanks Billy ...for your time.'
'You get him, heh,' he says, pointing his finger. 'I can't ...my hands are tied, heh.'
'Who tied them?' He looks at the graffiti on the wall. I follow his eyes.
'The UVF?'
He nods. 'And the rest, heh. It's not about Fenians and Prods any more, it's about money and patches.'
'So you went to do him and got warned off?'
'Like I said, heh ...my hands are tied.' Billy Thompson stands, lean and firm in the shady darkness of his taxi office. I let myself out of the mesh cage and the rattling door clinks back and forth.
'I'll tell Pearl you were asking for her, Billy.'
I spin around where the daylight from the street falls in.
'Oh, by the way, Susan sends her regards.'
I watch my words float through the air, waiting to register. I feel

like Tyson again, when he lands the knockout punch, knowing there is no way back for his opponent. I didn't need to be a psychologist to see the impact. It rocks Billy Thompson, tattoos and all.

Chapter 18

She looked frightened. She looked guilty. She planned it. Maybe to get even or put the Thompsons out of business. Billy had found out and gone after her and Mulholland. That would've been a sight for sore eyes. Then, Mulholland calls in the other paramilitaries a la Johnston, and Billy can only huff and puff. Sweet little Susan's rape rumour is quelled by quid, a fair few quid no doubt.

I side-step a woman pushing twins and cross the car park to the Toyota. Pearl's gone. A piece of paper rests on the seat. I read her brief note and smile: *Gone shopping*.
I grab one of Fast Frank's tomatoes and rummage around for the sachets of salt that I'd thrown into the glove compartment of the RAV 4. I could supply Burger King with sauces and salt. The tomatoes are orgasmic. What sort of person could eat a tomato without salt? Probably a sociologist, I ponder. They'd be worried about their arteries narrowing, and as usual they'd blame society for putting the salt on the tomato.

'I've some lovely clothes for you,' Pearl says. It takes a minute to register. I'd dozed off. She is standing at the door of the Toyota, her hands hidden by bags.
'For me?'
'Yes. How did it go with Billy?'
'Went well ...sends his regards.'
Pearl hands me the bags and I peer inside like an excited kid on Christmas morning. 'Chinos?'
'Yes. Then, I thought the shirt would go with the Chinos. Then, I

thought the black pants would go well under the Chinos.' Pearl leans over me laughing and snuggling close.

'Ach ...Pearl. Thank you. I'm all embarrassed, now.'

'Take me back to my desk,' she says suggestively. 'I've some paperwork to finish before we go to Belfast.'

'Jump in.'

She gives that little groan again.

We drive hand and hand to Patterson Engineering. I slump into the sofa, point to the desk and grab my crotch. She almost laughs while she makes a few phone calls. So much has happened since I sat here the first time.

'I have a proposition for you,' I say, as she is walking over to me.

'God, I love you.' She holds my face and kisses me. 'Sorry ...what's this proposition?'

'It's not the desk' I say light-heartedly. She fakes a frown. 'Well ...not just yet, anyway.' I take a deep breath. 'How would you feel about visiting Mulholland? Sort of a call to inquire about his welfare. I need to see him, get inside the house. He won't let me in but if you go...'

'He might think a ride's on the cards,' she finishes. She stands with her hands on her hips.

'So that's your fantasy ...watching,' she smiles. Pearl's in a great mood.

'No, it's not my fantasy. However, I will fulfil my fantasy if you could help me,' I add.

'It's done,' she snaps.

'Done ...just like that?'

'Yes. I trust you Simon. Today when you were with Billy Thompson I made up my mind not to let this beat me, you know. Pearl Morrow, I said, you are made of stout stuff. It's time you stopped crying and got on with it. I also made a decision to trust you, follow up on your offer of help. And, besides all that, you are a ride and I love you.'

'What's the Morrow?'

'My maiden name.'

'Ach ...Pearl, I don't know if I can help anyone with a name like Morrow. Patterson's bad enough,' I joke.

'Well you have the power to change it, you know,' she hammers back.

'Wait until you experience my fantasy. You mightn't ...'

'Come here.'

'No …we're late …not that late, yet.'

Silcott Avenue is eating dinner. The lull, following a hard day at the office. Soon people will be on the move again, going to wherever they go. I expected some press to be hanging about, yet we cannot see any. Rory peers all around. He's nervous and it took some convincing. Big Paul had done the trick with his banter. Paul has that type of face that makes it hard to say no. A white Toyota Celica drives into the avenue. 'That's her. Mass Patterson,' Rory says, banging the wheel.

I watch her progress and leave the car. Big Paul is standing, trying not to look like Big Paul. Two bodyguards are at Mulholland's door looking bored. I pass the post box and go down the alleyway. I peer through the privet hedge into the wilderness of long grass. There's nobody around. Cars cruise on the Ormeau Road, in the distance. There's nothing to my right. It seems mad. I think of the goons and them getting a hold of me. The bathroom window opens. Pearl has made it inside.

I kick gently at the hedge and wait to see if I am noticed. There are houses behind me. Christy Moore is blaring out from somewhere to my left and the smell of dinner surrounds me. People relax when they eat, I tell myself. Best time to attack. I make it through the hedge and scamper, doubled over to below what seems to be the kitchen window. Quickly, I refresh myself with the lay out from Big Paul's pictures.

My foot kicks off the wall and I hold onto the drainpipe for dear life. The little ledge above the kitchen window takes my weight and it's easy from there. Whoever designed these houses hadn't figured on the increase in crime. I cross a flat piece of roof to a window and listen for Pearl's voice. Noises and voices are coming from the same floor. Dirty curtains, which are supposed to be white-net, protect me from the stagnant whiff of urine that almost makes me want to heave. My lace catches on the ledge and I curse it free. The toilet acts as a step.

The place seems alive with every germ possible. It's almost unbearable. I hold my breath and gently push down on the door handle. Mulholland is standing close to Pearl. He seems transfixed and wanting to have his pay off. She side-steps his outstretched arm. 'Have you any oils?' I hear her ask.

She walks towards me. The bathroom door. Mulholland is shuffling after her. He can't believe his luck. All the times he forced her to have sex with him, but she was never this willing. Now it's different. She's come to him.

'Th-th-there should be some in the bathroom,' he stammers out, pointing to the door. I know no one else is downstairs because her bag is sitting in the bath. Big Paul will be harassing the guards, flashing his press pass, demanding an interview and pissing off the goons.

Come on, Pearl. Tell him to get the oil. Right on cue she does. I stick to the wall, behind the door. He's off guard and on a promise.

'Peek-A-Boo,' I say, kicking the door closed. Mulholland jumps and spins around. He doesn't see the punch. His teeth bite my knuckles and he lands on the toilet seat.

The dark holes he possesses for eyes stare at me. A little blood trickles from his mouth. His shirt rips as I pull him into the hall. The element of surprise is working. Pearl is removing the tape from her blouse. Mulholland cowers, waiting to be hit again.

'Right Mulholland ...listen to me. Your future hinges on a hinge, if you'll pardon the pun,' I snarl. He tries to speak and I smack him on the nose.

'You don't like being out of control, do you? Well, get the hinge and it's all yours again.'

'It's in th-the safe.'

'Where's the safe? Point.' I grab his hair and pull him along the red carpet, into the next dirty room.

'Get out the window, Pearl,' I yell. She looks at me and I wave an angry arm. 'Go on.'

'Open the safe, Mulholland.' His stubble hides behind his shielding arms, waiting for another blow. God I want to hit him all right but I need the hinge. Instead, I push him past the bed and the filth lying on the floor. Crumbs and dirty plates are everywhere. He moves a painting in the lamplight. His drawn curtains are working against him again. His goons are a few feet below, yet he can't see them.

'Hurry up.'

The door clicks open and I hold him firmly by the scruff of the neck. If he's going to bolt it will be now. I'm ready.

'Lift it out.' He tries to stall by looking at me. I watch his legs and make sure he can't donkey kick me.

'Lift it out.' He reaches inside the safe. It's in a plastic bag, like a freezer bag with a wire tie at the top. The grey metal hinge sways with its weight.

'Bring it slowly to the door of the safe and drop it on the floor.' He does as I ask. I wait. His clothes smell of the house.

'Kneel,' I snap. 'Face the wall. I know all about the hinge. We have you on tape now.'

He hesitates and my knee forces him off balance.

'Hands behind your head.' They arrive with precise timing. I still hold his neck and reach for the hinge. His body trembles, sending shock waves up my arm. My fingers lock around the metal hinge.

'Don't turn around.'

'Mu-mummy said you would help. Isn't that right, Mummy? Mummy,' he yells at the cornice. I watch him. His hands. Everything.

'How's daddy?'

'Daddy's bad. Bad-bad-bad. It's his fault. He took her with him. Go away daddy. No I won't shut up. You're bad. Sorry mummy. No ...I won't shut up, mummy. No.' Trevor Mulholland seethes at the images or voices on the wall.

'So Johnston helped?' I ask softly.

'Ssssh. Mummy doesn't like that word. He's bad,' Mulholland begins sobbing and moves his hands off his head. He bangs the wall and I grab him. I look into his face, a face of skin and bone and torment.

'You planned it, Trevor. Now it's time to pay the piper,' I say.

'No mummy,' he says, avoiding my stare. He glances at the corner of the wall once more.

'Mummy says I was naughty,' he utters calmly. His face sways gently as if he is listening to soothing music. Suddenly, it changes. The skin around his mouth tightens.

'You're bad. Bad-bad-bad,' Mulholland screams. 'I'm glad-glad you're dead. You took mummy. You t-took mummy. I told you not to. See, see, mummy. See, see.' He's rocking now, clutching his arms.

'Calm down,' I say, shaking him. 'Why's Johnston here, Trevor? Is he here for me? To kill me?' I ask quickly, checking no one has come into the house. He grins at me.

'Yes. You hit the jackpot. Didn't he, mummy.'

'You want me to finger Johnston?'

'Johnston is bad. Susan Patterson is bad. They are all bad. They killed mummy. It doesn't matter about him. He is bad. No I won't stop m-mummy. You're bad, Daddy, bad-bad-bad.'

I push him against the wall and my heart is pumping in my ears. I have the hinge. I have more than the hinge.

'P-please kill me,' he stammers.

'I'm not gonna kill you. I want answers.'

Mulholland gives a tiny snigger and just for a second I want to kill him. My life's on the line and he's laughing.

'Why did you send the clone?'

'I thought you would enjoy that. Mummy said you would. M-mummy likes you.'

'Answer the question, Mulholland.' I glance around, listening for sounds. I'm taking a big risk staying this long.

'You are doing well. I have do-done better. I ...mummy and me have got them all.'

'What do you mean?' I ask, shaking his shirt. Mulholland's body is limp. He's messing with my head.

'What do you mean? Did you bankrupt Fast Frank and Billy Thompson?' I pause. My temper is taking the bait. Mulholland ignores my question. His head tries to turn around and he's muttering to someone or something. I can't make it out.

'M-m-m-mummy isn't dead. She's here. See, see,' he seethes, gasping like a sick child.

'I don't see, Trevor. Looks like you've lost out on everything. You killed your mother ...she isn't here. It's your guilt that makes her talk to you. She's dead. You killed her.'

'Please kill me-please kill me,' Mulholland pleads.

'No. I would love to. But the price is too great. You know all about that.'

'It had to b-b-be done. He got in the way.'

'Who's he?'

'D-d-d-daddy. No I won't stop, mummy. He's bad. Bad-bad-bad.'

'Is that why you were arrested?'

Mulholland giggles. 'We've got them a-all. Th-th-they knew Johnston was naughty. Didn't they, mummy. Now they are trying t-t-t-to work out what to do. I picked you,' Mulholland says, turning to look at me.

'Picked me for what?'

'M-m-m-mummy always liked you. M-m-m-mummy always said you were a nice journalist. M-m-m-mummy didn't know what I did. I told her I was naughty. I told her what I ha-ha-had done. Mad days jump in dogs pay holidays were but for help getting daddy bad some dogs sad,' Mulholland chants. I grab his body and hold him.

Sadly, I've seen too much of this. The dreaded word salad that a person with schizophrenia lapses into.
'Have you any medicine?' He shakes his head. Some cognitive function remains. I place him against the wall and he continues to mutter.

I sprint from the room. The stairs are clear. The goons are still outside. Pearl has taken her bag from the bath. I jump from the kitchen roof and roll over as I land in the overgrown wilderness. The hedge scrapes white lines onto my forearms. My body's alert. Paul's in the passenger seat, tapping the dashboard at the top of the alleyway. Rory has the engine ticking over and revs it as he sees me getting closer.
'You took your time. Them boys wouldn't let me interview yer man, like,' Big Paul laughs.
'Where's Pearl?'
'Probably at the City Hall by now, mate. What happened?' Paul asks. I sigh in the back seat and let my head roll from side to side. Rory takes a left off the Ravenhill Road. A trickle of blood oozes from my knuckles. I pull out the hinge and stare at it.
'I think they arrested Johnston to put him in the picture,' I say regaining my breath. 'Mulholland lapsed into a schizophrenic state. The cops knew about Johnston and the bomb. They had to.'
'You reckon Barnsey lifted that gipe Johnston to sneak all the latest?' Paul asks, turning around. 'I'd love to mill him if he did. What do you reckon, Da? That gipe Barnsey is in on this. Did you get the hinge? Jesus ...I'm taking Barnsey out the night. Said we'd go for a drink.' Big Paul's questions and thoughts always arrive in torrents.
'Barnsey is worth watching. What else did Mulholland say?' Rory asks.
'Nothing that made any sense, Rory. He's in bad shape. Hearing voices and seeing things. His ma. He definitely knew about the bomb. Said his mum wasn't meant to be there.'
'That figures.'
'I'll have a go at Barnsey the night,' Big Paul seethes.
'If you're going out way him the night don't let on that ye know anything, Paul.'
'Hey Da, wise up. Do you tell oul Maureen you're slipping a wee spoonful of sugar into your tea again? No. Do ya? Ehhh?' Big Paul turns and winks at me.
'That's fussing women. There's more things to worry about in this

place than a wee drop of sugar. If you're out at the house don't be mentioning it. It would be bad for her arthritis,' Rory says, through his mumbling smile.

We stroll into Nugents. Pearl is waiting, sitting at a table. I notice the look of relief on her face. Barnsey's at the bar. A good dig on the mouth would do him no harm, either. I know he's up to his neck in this. My stomach says so. Mulholland more or less said so. We walk sideways to the table to join Pearl. Barnsey spies us, but Rory cuts him off. Barnsey watches us around Rory's shoulder. They walk to the bar under Rory's simple persuasion of an outstretched arm.

'Get them in, Da,' Big Paul shouts, catching everyone's attention.
'It's over,' I whisper to Pearl. 'Feel my jeans.'
'Emmh ...lovely and hard,' she teases, kissing my lips.
'See the guy with Rory ...that's our snout in the police. 'Mr Slippery,' I whisper. A waitress arrives at the table with beers for the boys and wine for Pearl.
'Well, to all of us, like. I'm glad to see you're looking after him, Pearl. Here's to you, too, love,' Paul says, raising his pint.
'Cheers' rings back from us.
'It's a pity Mandy isn't here,' I say.
'Sod's law, mate. She's still stuck in that oul stakeout thing, like. Here they come,' Big Paul says, turning. For a second I brace myself for Mulholland and the goons. It was only Rory and Barnsey walking towards the table.
'Bout ye, Barnsey. How's your bum for love bites, like?' Big Paul yells at the top of his voice. Nobody takes any notice. Most of them know, Paul. Rory pushes past him and sits down beside Pearl.
'Any news, Barnsey?' I ask.
His wrinkled face points to Rory. 'He'll fill you in on it,' he replies. Rory does the introductions and we sip and smoke. Barnsey's small, stocky frame and cauliflower face never add up to his gentle voice.
'Hey Da ...Barnsey and me are heading out on the town, like. Want me to phone oul Maureen and see if you can stay out to ten?' Paul says, finishing his pint.
'Ten? ...Sure you'll be sleeping by ten, like a wee bairn. He always falls asleep, Mass Patterson,' Rory jokes back.
'Aye, you're right, like,' Big Paul laughs. 'Come on, Barnsey. Let's get out of this hole ...see if we can get you a woman, like.'

A shadow falls over the table as Paul blocks the light.

'Great to see you again, Pearl, love. You look after my oul mate,' he says, reaching for her hand. 'Right mate,' he nods, slapping my shoulder. Big Paul grabs Barnsey by the scruff of the neck and points him towards the door.

'See ya, Da,' he yells at the door. I laugh and watch Rory mumble to Pearl. He's probably explaining the *Da* tag. I smile.

'So what's the latest?' I ask.

'They can't match the gun found on Johnston.'

Pearl looks at me.

'Anything else, Rory?'

'No ...just the imminent departure from custody of that skitter Johnston. Keep digging. We don't want half a story. Get me the whole thing. The others can keep up with the Johnston stuff. Stay low, Simon. Remember ye are on holidays so to speak,' Rory finishes, giving his knowing look.

'We're staying in the Manningburg tonight,' I tell him, watching Pearl appear surprised.

'Nothing but the best,' Rory smiles.

'Looks like it, Rory. Bit of a surprise, you know,' she adds.

'Right, let's go,' I say, scratching back my stool. I hate busy bars. Rory stands and fusses over Pearl Patterson. He's still standing when we wave from the door.

We stroll onto Great Victoria Street. 'What will I do with this?' I ask.

'Give me it,' she says. I haul it from my pocket and watch her look at it again.

'Are you okay?'

'Fine,' she says quickly. Her hands grip the plastic bag and she removes it reverently from my palm. She sighs and throws it in the litter bin.

'That's the end of that,' she states, dusting her hands. 'Do you want to keep the tape of Mulholland?'

'No point, Pearl. It was only to spook him. Anyway, you were giving him the come on.'

'You can't catch a mouse with a tortoise, you know,' Pearl smiles, handing me the tape. I break it in two and toss it in the bin, also.

'I'm proud of you, Pearl.'

'I'm proud of you.'

We hug and I lift her high, swinging her around. Robinson's is bulging. Dark, dressed doormen scrutinise patrons approaching. We both stare at the Manningburg Hotel in all its splendour and cross the road. Formal dinner guests mingle around reception. The large foyer in fawn marble with soft easy chairs looks brilliant. I check in with reception and we take the lift to our room. Pearl snuggles close, watching us in the mirror.

'Damn ...the bags.'

'In the car,' she adds.

'And the car and RAV4 are in ...'

'*The Scribe* car park,' she finishes, laughing.

I open the door and stand back. The magnum of champagne is waiting by the bed and the chocolates are resting on the pillow.

'Oh Simon,' she says, hugging me. 'It's such a beautiful room.'

'See anything else?' I ask, raising my brows. She spins around and scans everything from the doorframe.

'A banana?' Pearl laughs.

'Yes ...a banana,' I reply confidently, smiling.

'A banana?' She gives that little groan again.

Chapter 19

It was a banana to end all bananas. It ends. My mobile rings.
'Shot… I'm shot… Mulholland …you next.'
'Paul. What's happened? Are you at home?'
'Yeah.' The line goes silent. I dial 999 and direct the paramedics to Robinson Park. Then I ring reception. Pearl leans on my shoulder, straining to hear.
'What's wrong, Simon?'
'Paul's been shot. He managed to dial here somehow to warn us. The paramedics are on the way. There's a taxi waiting downstairs. It'll take us. It was Mulholland,' I blast, grabbing my jeans and balancing myself into them.
'Shot?' Pearl yells, more for her own comprehension than mine.
    I scamper from the room. Pearl is lagging behind.
'Hurry up. Mulholland is coming after us as well. He told Paul.'
My mind focuses on Mulholland or anyone with swarthy features and short dark hair. The lift seems to take forever.
'Mr. Rogers …your taxi is right there,' a man says, pointing. He startles me and my fist is ready to land a punch. I grab Pearl by the hand and we bolt through the foyer. The receptionist is standing all tense on the steps and crying. 'I'm so sorry,' she mutters.
'Where does Paul live?' Pearl asks.
'Glengormley,' I snap out. 'Take us to *The Irish Scribe*,' I say to the driver.
    He doesn't bother to stop at the lights and hurtles around the one way system, past Castle Court and into Manford Street against the flow of traffic. The city's quiet. The drunks have gone, only the homeless saunter. I'm out and running before he pulls up. I fumble

for my keys and pass. The security man relaxes and returns to his hut. I ram the RAV4 into first and it squeals like a baby on the slick car park floor. Pearl is running towards me.

'Phone Rory, press button two.' Pearl looks impatient. 'It'll take him awhile to answer,' I blurt, narrowly missing the kerb.
'Don't get us killed,' she yells. I run the red light in High Street and bounce across the lanes towards the M2.
'Simon,' she yells. I grit my teeth and hold back the profanity.

'Rory, it's Pearl Patterson. Hold on,' she says handing me the phone. Rory is barely awake.
'Paul's been shot,' I say, in a soft tone. 'He's at the house. It was Mulholland. I'm putting you back to Pearl, I'm almost there,' I finish. Rory hadn't time to utter a word. I know what he thinks of Paul, and me, for that matter. He'd told many people we were his boys. Pearl talks calmly to him. I check any cars we meet. None is a blue Mercedes.

We arrive in chaos. Flashing lights of emergency vehicles cast circling shadows on the red-bricked houses of Robinson Park.
'Phone Mandy, her number's down there.'
The uniformed policeman puts up his hand to stop me. I run past his yells. Barnsey's at the door.
'What's happened? He phoned me.' My head is spinning and my lungs burn.
'He's in a bad way, Simon. You can't go in. The paramedics are with him.'
'Where's he shot?'
'Twice in the stomach and a couple on the arms and his left leg. Here ...sit down here.' The strong arm of Barnsey and the law helps me onto the stairs in Paul's hall. A paramedic goes outside.
'How is he?' He doesn't answer and runs quickly to the ambulance.
'Said he was coming after me, Barnsey.'
'Aye, I know. Thought as much. I've circulated his plate, units are looking for him,' Barnsey explains. The paramedic dashes back inside with a black bottle. It looks like oxygen or something. I push myself off the stairs and try to duck under Barnsey.
'Sit down. Let them do their job, for Christ's sake.'

His face comes and goes. The champagne is rolling around in my stomach, trying to find an outlet. There's a bustle behind the door and I stare at the handle. It turns slowly. A tall, thin paramedic with a bald head nods at Barnsey. They huddle and whisper. Blood is pumping in my ears. I try to listen. My stomach is heaving. Barnsey turns quickly. I barely make it to the door. My vomit lands in Paul's front garden. Barnsey and one of his colleagues grab me. One of them wipes my brow.

'You'll be all right in a minute. Come on and sit down,' Barnsey says.

He leans on his hunkers in front of me. I see his wrinkles and his awesome shoulders. 'Big Paul's dead. He was pronounced dead at two, forty-four hours,' he says calmly.

I wince and the stairs move. It's as if Barnsey is giving the result of a football match. He doesn't give a shit. He'd been out with him before Mulholland called.

Two, forty-four hours, echoes. It bangs around like a car tumbling along the racetrack, taking new flips with each obstacle it comes in contact with. I'm at the mercy of my memories. Flashes of Paul shouting *Heh Da*. Us, laughing over a pint. The way he reached over to shake Pearl's hand in Nugents and the way he always rocks on his heels.

The stale taste of vomit and shoals of shivers cause goose pimples on my arms. I look at them, clutching my forearms and huddling on the stairs. Footsteps are close, female footsteps. Barnsey nods to let Pearl through.

'Simon ...Oh Simon, I'm so sorry,' she shouts somewhere close. I watch the dado rail in the hall. It was only yesterday, we watched the orange Yugo swerve off with the Big Man inside it. His outstretched arm flicking a farewell.

Pearl wraps herself around me. I chance a glance at her. Her eyes are red and runny and her face and lips search for words. She gives up and puts her head on my shoulder and we rock. Where's all my beliefs now? The casual way I had said, *when your time's up, your time's up*. My dad always said that, too.

Pearl is sobbing and her tears wet my shoulder. I haven't reached that stage yet. My throat is thick. *Two, forty-four hours,* echoes, with the image of Barnsey's wrinkled face kneeling in front of me. 'You're dead Big Paul. Dead. What will I do?' I mutter. Everyone dies. I'm sick of people dying. A tear escapes and it itches my cheek. Pearl's warmth helps with the shivers. I shake violently and Pearl grabs me. It's no good. My cheeks are wet and I give in.

'I love you, Simon,' she says, rubbing my hair like her child. She had done this when I was a child, comforting me or putting my crap drawing up on her door.

Part of me wants to see Paul and the other part doesn't. I've seen too many dead bodies recently; my mum and dad. I find it hard to remember them alive, after looking at them dead. I feel safe in Pearl's arms. Blue lights flash in the darkness midst the silhouette of the neighbours, standing, swaying in whispers.

Rory appears at the door. Barnsey shakes his head and huddles him into his arm. Rory will look back. He does, around the collar of his green wax jacket. I see his shoulders twitch and his fingers bridge his nose.

'Mandy's on her way, Simon,' Pearl whispers. She holds my cheeks and kisses me. 'I love you, you know.' I sniff and nod my head. Pearl lights a cigarette and helps me outside. People stare, whisper, in dressing gowns. Part of me wants to yell at them, project my anger and pain onto them. It's not their fault.

Rory grabs my arm and hugs me tightly. 'Big Paul. Why?' Rory quivers in my arms.
'Get the presses stopped, Rory.' He stands back and looks at me. What's a press? I can see him ask himself. It shocks him back into the real world, the world that goes on. Death doesn't stop it. He dials and talks quickly. A black van arrives and separates the onlookers. They drive to the tape. Barnsey runs and talks to the huddling men. Probably Forensics. They wave their arms around and Barnsey grabs his waist. They look pissed off because so many people have trampled around the murder scene. I walk with Pearl to the Toyota. We hold hands.

'Are you okay?' I ask. She smiles and squeezes my fingers. *Two, forty-four hours* rattles around.
'Ask people what they heard or saw,' I say. 'You know how to work it?'
'How could I forget.'
The psychology of a disaster: keep people busy, involved, like passing bricks in a chain gang after a bomb or earthquake. It's usually nothing more than to relieve stress and give a feeling of usefulness. Shock makes people do many things, usually feel angry and useless.

I phone the report of Paul Morgan's murder in to the night desk. They will fix it up. The word *alleged* is everywhere, just to be

on the safe side. Rory arrives beside me and looks much better.
'Tam McGhee has it stopped for the new page,' Rory explains.
'Did you warn him what it was?' I ask.
'Aye ...I did that.' Rory nods his head and tries to fight back the emotion. 'They'd forty thousand run off. I ordered a complete re-run with this? Tam McGhee and the boys don't mind. Big Paul and them were very great. Tam McGhee says it'll be on the streets before you can say Jack Robinson. He was asking about ye,' Rory finishes.

I sigh and tap his shoulder. Pearl's busy taking quotes that won't be needed, although someone might have seen something. The press crew will be stripping plates off the metal monster. The comps rescheduling the front page. Not one of them will mind. It'll be an adrenaline rush. Shock, when people do things and push themselves beyond what is expected. Then the tiredness comes, the still moments, which saunter and stroll in the recollections of what has happened.

How bits seem to fall into place with the comradeship of helping. See I'm not a bad person after all. I did what was right. I can do it under pressure. All of it seems to help, to encourage reason to look at personal problems. Maybe she's not that bad. Or I will apologise. We all crave to be loved and show love. Yet, sometimes it takes a glimpse at the unfinished to hone our focus.

The bad dreams. The alimony left unpaid. The doctor uttering bad news and urging that we stop smoking. The unfinished: six months to the finished. The thing we try to avoid, yet we smoke, drive too quickly, take chances, thinking it won't be me. Sometimes the passing car, headlights flashing, too close for comfort, sets it off. That was close. The beginning of the things which vodka obliterates or the children playing lessen. We wise up, revert to the seen and leave the unfinished dangling until the next time.

'Barnsey thinks he'll take a pop at you too,' Rory says somewhere. I shake myself.
'Big Paul said he was going to have it out with Barnsey when they were out. Maybe it wasn't Mulholland. He's worth watching, Rory.'
'The smart money's on Mulholland, Simon. Oh, Barnsey's mixed up in it all right, but we'll sort him, don't you worry,' Rory says with certainty.
'You see, if Mulholland dies it's home free for Barnsey. They can blame old Tom and Nancy's murder on their deranged son, Trevor.

That's if they ever need to. And, if they get rid of me then it's happy days,' I add.

His hands rub his face and he puffs at the night sky. 'I have lost one of ye.' Rory stops abruptly. I grab his arm. His eyes fill again and the blue lights reflect off his forehead.

Some neighbours leave and go back to their homes, giving us an apologetic grimace en-route.

'It won't be long before the others are here, Rory.'

'They'll not make the morning, Simon,' he says, with some relish.

'Get you away home with Pearl and get some rest,' he adds.

Some rest. That's hard to imagine.

If he is coming after me he'll go to Tullydeen. It would be perfect. Call with me the way I called with him. Tinges of guilt mingle in my mind as I replay the events of our meeting, earlier. My recklessness maybe broke the camel's back.

'Penny for them.' Her voice is comforting, shaking me from the despair I want to plunge myself into. Barnsey runs towards us, his jacket flapping around and he's puffing hard.

'We can't get him. He hasn't went back home and there's no sightings of him.' He breathes through his nose. 'He's not tried the ports either.' I look at Rory and his gaze remains on Barnsey.

'I take it you found Big Paul's relatives all right, Barnsey. Ye didn't have to set up roadblocks or anything to locate them like?' Rory spits.

'They'll be here soon, Rory.'

'I'll wait until they arrive,' Rory adds. 'Away ye go Simon and get some rest.' Rory places his hand on my forearm and squeezes it tightly. It's a touch, maybe to give me his pain or to say what Paul meant to both of us. It's that type of touch. 'Bye-bye, Mass Patterson,' he smiles. We walk to the Toyota and he corners Barnsey again.

'He'll lay into him no doubt,' I say to Pearl.

'Don't like him,' Pearl says, decidedly.

I start the RAV4 and reverse carefully out of Robinson Park, taking one last look at Paul's house. I never want to see it again. *Two, forty-four hours* and Barnsey's wrinkles cloud the road. I find myself drifting from lane to lane.

'Do you want me to drive?'

'No ...I'm fine ...just thinking, sorry.' I feel a bit edgy crossing into East Belfast. 'I'll drop you off at the Manningburg.'

'No I don't think so, Simon.' Pearl takes off her seat belt and turns sideways, towards me.

'I'm going to Tullydeen with you,' she says. I can do nothing but smile. I shouldn't be smiling. Paul's dead.
'How'd you know?'
'I paid a penny, you know.'

A milk float pulls out of a street just past Ballyhackamore. I jump. I'm constantly watching the mirror for lights coming charging out at me: a blue Mercedes. I take the road for Comber and a circling red light stands on the road. My grip on the wheel tightens and my stomach feels the way it does when I eat too much corned beef. 'Police,' she says softly. Maybe she has visions of me charging through the roadblock, bullets ripping after us.

'Step out of the vehicle, sir.'
I can't believe my ears. What an asshole. He shines his torch on me, back to my pass. His burly colleague walks over to examine it. They look at me the way cops look.
'Step out of the vehicle, now, sir.' I comply with a huge sigh.
'Have you had a drink, sir?'
'Yes, a glass of wine this evening,' I reply, trying the nice route. 'I've just left Robinson Park, Constable. My colleague was murdered up there.' He glances from his peak and doesn't reply, like a teenager paying no attention.
'What's wrong?' Pearl asks peering over.
I shrug. 'It'll be all right.'

One of them mumbles into his radio and the crackle hisses through the early morning. I'm all shivery now. Part panic: part this is all I need. The bigger of the two policemen produces a breathalyser.
'Could you blow into this, sir?'
I sigh and comply, nervously. I'd a few drinks. The champagne back at our room. Drinking and driving was the last thing on my mind when I received the call. I blow. I hand it to him. Lights near the tube glow.
'I doubt you've had more than one glass, sir. You'll have to accompany us to the station.'
'What?' I scream. 'Have you nothing better to do than harass me? Why the hell aren't you out looking for a fruitcake that's trying to kill me?' It's out before I realise. I'm seething. I've had it now anyway.
'Youse probably waved him through, you stupid shites.'
'Simon,' Pearl yells.

'Shut up.'
'Simon, what's happening?'
'Ask these dickheads.' I yell, whipping my arm.
'Now sir ...I must warn you ...'
'Just piss off,' I rant with my finger pointing into his face.

One of them spins me around and marches me to the police car. 'Leave him alone,' Pearl shouts after us. I try to turn, but he's strong and my feet barely touch the ground.
'Are you arresting me? Are you? Are you deaf as well as stupid? You even have to dress the same ...can't even pick your own clothes.'
I land in the back seat and kick the seats in front.

He looks at me and I turn my head. 'Calm down, sir.' Already I'm regretting my outburst. He jumps in and I bite my lip. The air freshener is getting up my nose. I sneeze. What would Grace think now?

I'm a little calmer when he opens the door. I'm in Dundonald RUC Station. The Toyota RAV4 arrives behind me with Pearl and the other cop. He marches me in and up to the desk. Another cop takes my press pass.
'Are you Simon Rogers?' he asks. His doleful eyes wait for an answer. I want to say, *No! I'm Superman* or *Hugh McWhinney, the butcher in Comber Square.*
'Yes,' I concede.

He shuffles a sheet and writes. 'It'll be some time before the doctor arrives, sir. I'll have to put you in a cell until such a time, sir.'
'Where's my friend and my vehicle?' I already know Pearl's here. I just want to be awkward. 'They will be fine, sir.'

It's blue and green everywhere: all new and blue and bloody green. I sit on the bed fuming. A drunk next door sings *Danny Boy*. At least he's drunk. If I'd known I'd have given it the whole treatment. Might as well have been hung for a sheep as a lamb. I sigh into the wall. At least I'm alive. Paul's dead.

I walk to the little slit in the door and bang. 'Yoo,' I yell at the top of my voice. A grey haired policeman with piercing, blue eyes looks in.
'Can I have a cigarette, please?' He returns with a single cigarette and waits for my lighter. They've taken my belt and laces. Just on the off chance.

The other papers will be onto the story of Paul's murder. They won't make the morning, at least we did. I slump down on the bed and wait. The drunk next door is coughing and sort of being sick. It's better than his singing. I jump now and then. Sometimes I think Mulholland is behind me. My eyes are heavy and the sickly aftertaste of anger takes its toll.

    A wrinkled face smiles at me, nipping at my shoulder. I try to get my bearings. It's Barnsey.
'Say cheese for an old dyke, Rogers.'
The camera flash dazzles me. Mandy stands laughing, throwing her head back. 'We are even, Rogers.'
'We got him ...he's dead,' Barnsey says.
I think of Paul, but I know that he's talking about Mulholland.
'Where's Pearl?'

Chapter 20

IRISH SCRIBE REPORTER MURDERED

The sub editor had used as the headline above the story of Big Paul's murder. The rest were onto it. *Cool FM* led with Paul's murder and now their reporter is at my house with the rest. The police are holding them at the entrance. They shove tapes and cameras at the Toyota as we arrive.
'Come on Simon, give us something. What's the score, mate?' Tommy Dalaney shouts, running alongside.
I shrug. 'Jesus, this is all I need,' I say.
Pearl looks back at them and I flick at my hair. 'Bloody nuisance ...reporters, you know,' she smiles, trying to lift my mood.
'Ach ...I suppose you're right,' I manage, with a lot of effort.
  A shiver crosses my soul, seeing Mulholland's blue Mercedes parked in the yard. The police are doing their bit. Barnsey and Mandy are down at the scene. Sean Gribbin, freelance photographer, wearing a green boiler suit is sneaking across the barley field trying to get exclusive pictures. Sean's slipped the police, I muse. The fingerprint cop flicks his brushes over the panels on the door of my home. Pearl looks wearily at me. We haven't spoken much. A surge of emotion wets my eyes. There's no turning it or holding it back. I sniffle to the window of the Toyota.

'Simon,' Barnsey waves. I swipe at my face and walk towards him. His white shirt looks the way I feel. 'This's where he topped himself,' he says, pointing to the pool of blood. Will I ever be able to look around this yard again and not think of him or imagine him lying dead?

'Where's his body?'

'Our boys took it to the morgue. We'll have the match on the bullets in an hour or two.' Barnsey places his hands on his hips. 'We gave him every chance to surrender. He took a pop at our officers and then shot himself in the mouth.'

I have a visual picture of the scene. Something like the one I'd watched on videos.

'Lifting you last night was the safest thing to do,' he smirks. I cringe, recalling my performance.

'I made a real asshole of myself when they arrested me.' I say, swiping at my hair.

'Aye ...I know. We taped you,' Barnsey grins, wrinkles and all. I shake my head once more.

'Is it all right to go into the house?'

'Aye ...away you go,' Barnsey says.

My home is mayhem. Passive police stand around, looking bored while the Forensics pack up. They don't take long. I suppose they get plenty of practice working in this country. Pearl prepares toast and coffee. Rory arrives, looking drawn. Mandy is chuffed with her shot of me in the cell. God knows when that'll appear. We work on a press release and it helps to distract me a little. Several times I sigh deeply, as fingers of faith seem to want to poke at me.

After about half an hour we are agreed on the release. Rory takes it outside and distributes it to my waiting colleagues. It basically states the facts that Mulholland allegedly shot Paul Morgan and then travelled to Tullydeen to attempt the same fate with me. I took the angle that Mulholland was a mentally disturbed individual who turned the gun on himself rather than surrender to the police. We gave no indication that Mulholland was the possible mastermind behind the Andrews Corporation. That would've swayed massive, public opinion harshly against him. Despite the fact that he allegedly committed murder, many people would continue to give him the benefit of the doubt, remembering what had happened to his parents in the car bomb.

The door opens again and several of my colleagues peer in and pass on their condolences. I salute them with the can and they're gone. Too much to do and speculate about. Mandy shouts a farewell and runs to her car.

'Phone you later, Mandy.'
'Perhaps you will. Oh ...you appear rather pitiful first thing in the morning, Rogers,' she adds, ducking into the car. 'We are even for the moment.'
Rory pats my shoulder. 'I'll have to go, Simon. Take it easy. Bye-bye, Mass Patterson. Don't answer any more questions. I don't think they'll bother you now,' he says. Pearl waves and flashes a smile at him.
'How are you doing, Rory?'
'Ah ...good question. Good question.' He taps my shoulder again and goes. He probably coaxed Barnsey to arrest me. Mulholland's car is gone and only a tiny bloodstain remains. The door is grimy and black from the Forensics' brushes.

I place the laptop on the table. Pearl squeezes my shoulders and runs her fingers through my hair. 'I need beauty sleep, you know.'
'Give you a shout next month,' I reply quickly, turning.
'Huh. Best ride you'll ever have,' she grins, wrapping her leg around the door.
'Ever want.'
She goes and I flick up a clean page.

I write my piece and stick to the facts. I don't want anything to slip in that isn't congruent with my press statement. Or, to raise suspicion, link things and give the others ideas. It will be interesting to read their articles in the morning.

The legacy of becoming the recipient of crime makes me lock the door at Tullydeen. I refuse to call myself a victim. I hate that bloody word. My paranoia will leave soon. It's just normal behaviour after the events, and shows that I want to live, I remind myself. *Paul's dead*, I stop and say now and then. I read over the siege of Tullydeen where Mulholland turned a smoking gun on himself rather than surrender to police. I suppose he knew he would disappear anyway or something to that effect.

My article takes the angle of his personal loss and the emotional pain he must've been suffering, following the tragic murder of his family. I certainly don't mention he may have planned the bombing. It's a conservative piece. The others will dramatise the events leading up to Mulholland's suicide. I suppose, it's every journalist's dream to have this happen, right on their doorstep. For me it's not. The spell-check stops on Tullydeen – *word not found*, the package tells me.

'Tullydeen is more than a word, Doris,' I tell my laptop, smiling. Grace named it Doris, not me. I touch the keyboard and Doris runs on. I wonder how Grace and Pearl will get on …probably like a house on fire.

I close the file and take Doris upstairs to the printer. Pearl is blowing bubbles again. I run the printout and read the copy for errors and try to speed it up a bit. There comes a time when it has to do. I make the changes and email the file to Rory. Pearl is gone: in REM sleep. Amazingly, I had slept in the police station, Pearl didn't. She waited at the desk until Barnsey arrived. No wonder she's tired. Her back is bare. As usual she is cuddling the pillow, moving ever so slightly as she breathes. I watch her for a moment, then tiptoe out. Tomorrow the story will appear. Tomorrow always appears unless you are dead. I think of Paul and my eyes are filling up again.

I bounce awake and Pearl grabs me. 'It's okay, Simon.'

Shivers cascade down my legs. I'm in Tullydeen, not Mulholland's house with a gun firing at me.

'Here.' Pearl hands me a cigarette and I relax slightly.

'What time is it?'

'Almost four.'

'Morning or afternoon?'

'Afternoon. God …I was tired.'

The news is just beginning on *Cool FM*. The broadcaster talks quickly and flicks over to the reporter at Tullydeen. Pearl rubs my leg and smiles. They move to the farmers complaining about the drought and I tap it off.

'They're giving it the works,' I say. They were taking the angle of Mulholland being a desperate man, going on a rampage and being killed in a bloody shootout. I suppose that's how it was. It sounds worse coming over the airwaves – more dramatic or something. They did a good piece on Big Paul. Everybody liked Big Paul.

'Penny for them.' I don't answer and spin myself out of bed.

'I take it you are blaming yourself.' Pearl spins me around. 'You did not pull the trigger, Simon,' she says slowly. Her body heat blooms into me. 'You did not make him do anything. Some people are just evil,' she says. 'I know him …he's not normal. He loved to hurt people and the bastard got what he deserved. Look at all the people he wrecked and killed. He didn't care about their lives. Did he?' she finishes.

'I don't agree with people being evil. Sick maybe. I don't like the word evil. Ach ...I suppose you're right.' It will keep her off my case. She's concerned. My forced smile emerges as I push past Pearl.

'Simon.'

'Going for a walk,' I yell from the room.

My feet squeeze into the trainers. I'm in no mood to see someone else's version. Quickly, I sprint down the stairs. Pearl's on the landing and I'm gone before she can ask if I'm okay. Jesus I hate people asking if I'm okay when they know I'm not. The bloodstain in the yard takes my gaze. The little trickles have dried in the Tullydeen sun. Little arm-like things trying to run away or reaching out for help. I pull my eyes away and look at the sun. I wince and hurt. Need to punish myself. I suppose I will always have empathy with someone that takes their own life. He asked for my help. What would've happen if Liz McFarland hadn't bothered helping me? She didn't bang my head off a wall and gloat. I run into the garden and leap over the wall, landing in the clover and long grass, hiding close to the wall.

Quickly, I try to outrun the post-mortem in my mind. No one ever condemns me like I do – if they do they don't say. The black rocks, slack tide and seaweed appear uninterested as I stroll. The yachts far out in the Lough wait for more wind. Scrabo Tower marks Newtownards and the top of the Lough in the distance.

There's no one around, just me, and my ghosts. Ghosts of Paul and Mulholland. I stop on the rocks and sit, staring. The seaweed crackles like my thoughts racing around. Each one hitting harder than the last. One instant it's Paul's laughing face, the next it's Mulholland, spinning in the bathroom when I'd hit him. I lie flat out looking at the heavens. They're moving ever so slightly. As a kid I used to do this when things didn't go my way. It works better with clouds in the sky. Today there are no clouds – in the sky at least.

Liz McFarland's face pops into view. Her smiling face and the way she laughed when I asked about the shocks. I see myself sitting on the Strand in Portstewart passing on all this knowledge to Pearl. Mulholland's bucket was more than full. Everything pointed to it and then I had to kick it. Kick it right to Glengormley and cost Big Paul his life. *Every experience is a learning experience*, I can recall Liz McFarland saying. If you learn and don't put it into practice then look what happens. Mulholland put me onto all of this and all I could do was hit him. Ignore the full picture. I played the hero. Jung was right. The archetypal hero getting the hinge: hero to zero.

'I think it's time you wised up, Simon.' I jump and turn. Pearl is standing peering down at me. I sigh and return to looking at the sky. 'Get up and grow up,' she says, sternly, her words drifting off towards the other shore in the gentle breeze. She grabs my arm and I shrug it free.
'Where would I have been if someone hadn't helped me?' I ask.
'You would've died like Mulholland, Simon. But you didn't. Mulholland was a pig. An evil person who took pictures of me and blackmailed me over the death of my husband, for years. You see I said death, not murder. Peter died. At the moment I'm strong enough to say that. Mulholland murdered your best friend. And all you can think off is how sad it must be for him to go through what you went through. Did you ever stop to think that Mulholland knew you were a psychologist? He was playing you at your own game. He wanted you to feel sorry for him,' she pauses and her voice is shaky.
'Just take a look at me. That bastard used me as his whore. The world will be a better place without him. But, that's not good enough for good old Simon. No, he sits on the rocks and kicks himself because he couldn't draw his little bucket in the sand and save his soul. There, there, Trevor, you are just sick, not an evil scumbag. Don't worry about all the things that happened,' Pearl spits out, nodding with her words. 'Well, Simon, take at look at me. I had to have him slabber all over me. So just you lie there and cry for that scumbag. You're certainly not the man I thought you were.'

  She turns, staring into the fields. The fields ploughed and waiting for cabbages in the autumn. Pearl blows smoke high into the Tullydeen sky. Her arms are folded. She's put some reality back into me, a reality that I agreed with anyway. I struggle up and watch her. She doesn't move or acknowledge my presence. I want to say I'm sorry. But I don't. I just stand. Saying sorry is something that seems so shallow. I killed your dog, sorry. Sorry to hear about Uncle Harold. Too many people said they were sorry at my father and mother's funerals. I was sick of it. They meant well. The outstretched hand and sorry. But what would they say in place of sorry? They were all good people. They meant well. Many of those people help me no end. It was me that was touchy, not people being sorry. It's easy to blame outward I remind myself.

Pearl's shoulders move in little ripples. She's sobbing ever so gently with her arms folded across her chest. I place my hand on her shoulder and she freezes.

'Just don't say anything, Simon. Nothing.' I tap her shoulder and walk off to the edge of the field and duck under the wire. The ruts are dry and crumbly. I slip and slide trying to keep my footing. Its smell is something which I can never describe. I suppose it's just earthy. I walk between the drills to the top of the hill and survey Tullydeen. The sun is beating into my face. The house and barns glow, past the field of barley. I turn to look at the ruins of Pearl's cottage and the memories of our frenzy and my picture on her door. I was about five then. Now she's my lover. Susan's hyper and up to her neck in terrorism. Could we all start again? Use a big rubber and wipe out the wrong turns.

Pearl is tossing stones into the mud of the Lough. The gulls and waders all swoop about. Life in the Lough goes on without water. The birds feed in the mud midst the crackling seaweed. White rump rabbits sleep and the crabs and jellyfish wait for the tide. Will they survive or shrivel up in the sun?

The islands glow brown: Trashna, in the distance. I used to go there with my dad and have picnics while we fished. Life goes on. Trashna didn't mourn my parents. It didn't cry for them or Paul. Pearl's making her way up the hill towards me. I walk slowly down and she stops. Her eyes are red and little dried tear-tracks are exposed by the sun. Pearl shades her eyes and stands in her jeans and black top.

'Well?' she asks.

'Well,' I reply.

Chapter 21

The rain rains. Mark McCreery waves as he dodges the traffic on the road. Pearl grips my hand. 'Let's go in, Simon,' she says softly. The wreaths sit beside the church, men in black pinstripes shuffle around. They are used to this.

Hordes of press hide under the willows, perching on the stone wall all around the tiny church. They click in my direction as Pearl and I approach Ballymillan Presbyterian Church. I grimace and acknowledge the empathic gestures from my colleagues. Pearl squeezes my hand once more and the smell of old wood drifts over me. The way it did as a kid going to church, on my wedding day and at Grace's christening.

Rory and Maureen are already inside, sitting with their heads bowed, wilting with the soft organ music. People walk sideways, gesturing respectfully as they slip into the pews. Paul's coffin sits beside the altar at the front of the church. My father's coffin was the same colour. My hands start to shake and I land in the pew beside Rory. He's studying his toes and doesn't hold my eyes. Maureen looks over her tissue, stifles her sob, just for a moment.

'Did ye see the crew outside?' Rory asks, not looking up.

'Aye,' I answer. Pearl grips my hand firmly. To have her with me means everything. The church fills and the music grows louder. The shower has passed and once more the sun glistens in from the stained glass windows. Christ on the Cross shadows Paul's coffin. We stand and Pearl hands me the Order of Service.

Frank Morgan walks into the church, here to bury his son. The hopelessness of trying to work it all out glows from his ashen face. Paul's only sister, Elsie, is ushered in by two women on thin legs, clutching her arms. Paul's father cradles her under his arm and the man in robes utters sombre words. A baby murmurs and *The Lord's My Shepherd*, begins. I stare at the sheet and curse who ever chose this hymn. I can't see the words and my eyes smart. The strong voices sing with pride, the way they did at my father and mother's funerals. *Pastures Green*, ring in my ears and a tear falls, blotting the print. I shoot a glance at Pearl and the beautiful black coat and hat that she's wearing.

Why does everybody I love, die? Why? My mental memories see my mother alive in the kitchen in Tullydeen, putting the potatoes onto the big plate in the middle of the table. Her eyes rolling in contempt at my father leaving muddy prints on her polished floor. My father shrugging his shoulders and sticking his tongue out when her back was turned. Him pushing the boat out and jumping in. The first day he took me to Trashna, the big island I always wanted to explore. *Quick dad, I've caught one*. I'll never forget that. Grace said the same when she caught her first fish. How they loved Grace. After her visits they talked about everything she said, laughing at her imagination. Then ...they always said I was the same at her age, how we looked alike and had the same amount of stubbornness.

Pearl traces a tiny circle on the back of my left hand. I watch her finger move like my thoughts. She's buried her husband. I wonder does she really believe she didn't murder him? I chance a small glance at her and all of her soul is propping me up.

What was special to Paul and his father? I know they had a pint in the pub every week after watching Linfield play. After that I don't know. I have no right to know. Christ's shadow is hugging Big Paul to his bosom, blasted by the recovering sun. Yet it's just his body in the coffin, his spirit will walk with me forever.

A shudder sways me as I think of Barnsey's face saying *two, forty-four hours*. Rory comforts Maureen and we all sit once more. The man with the book speaks with conviction and Elsie Morgan is helped from the front row – a woman kept from folding in two by her human friends. Paul's father sits straight and proud with his brother shuffling across just to be near him. Just to be there is always enough, when words have no meaning.

My father tiptoes across my soul with his soft voice: *You'll not die before your time, son.* Even my mother agreed with him on that one. I place my arms around Pearl and she snuggles into my neck. She gives a tiny sniff and touches my leg. Rory reaches for my arm and gently squeezes it. His head bows to the floor once more.

Suddenly, we all stand. The music grows, muffling the sound of uncomfortable clothes. A man in black pinstripes whispers into my ear. People shuffle out to greet Frank Morgan. Elsie has recovered and hugs me tightly with her trembling bones. She lets me go to her father. Frank Morgan shakes my hand and we hold the moment and speak in the silence of grief. His eyes tell me how much he loved his son. His cheeks, rubbery, tired.

The undertakers bring out Paul's coffin. Mourners line the tiny ash path to the grave behind the church. Rory saunters over wringing his fingers. Pearl moves to be with Maureen and they comfort each other. Maureen and Rory never had kids – only Big Paul and me. She treated us like her children. I'll never hear *Heh Da* again.

The men in black place Paul on our shoulders. If I have to I will carry him forever. Two of Paul's cousins are at the front. Rory and I link our arms around the remains of our best friend. Frank Morgan clutches his daughter to his side and we begin the walk. A woman in a mauve dress looks at me and her eyes show no colour, only tears. We shuffle along an ash path. The cameras click like a salute, paying respect to their journalistic friend. Mandy snaps with the others and each of them seem to talk to their God as the shutter closes. The coldness of the oak rests on my cheek and digs into my collarbone.

The journey's over. The men in black pinstripes step forward to remove Big Paul from our shoulders. I don't want to hand him over. The robes on the man with the book sway in the August breeze. He reads from the pages that he had marked, before closing the book and reverently uttering, *amen*. It murmurs into the willows and perhaps heaven.

People move away and talk silently about things people talk about after funerals. Frank Morgan is sheltered by his brother and helped away. I stand and stare into the grave. People pat my shoulder in the remoteness of the moment.

It's just Big Paul and me. My thoughts spin like a carousel. He helped me come to terms with many things. The serious look he held when he handed the rings to the Minister on my wedding day. How he hugged me when he flew from London when my father died. Then a few months later he did the same when my mother slipped away. The shrinking, lonely woman who found the November days too long with no one to scold. How Grace loved him. He carried my mother and father's coffins, took care of me and now he's dead. I choke the tears and fire my head to the heavens.

A little flurry of rain spins across us. I know Pearl's behind me. I can feel her, yet I don't turn around. Mulholland's dead, I almost mutter, but it's not important now. I want to throw something into the grave, just something, something to say farewell. The taste of tears in my mouth drowns any control I have. Little pieces of earth speckle the dark oak. I look down, all the way down. Slowly I pull off my watch and readjust its hands, I promise never to wear one again. I grip it firmly until it snaps and breaks in my fist. Little bits of glass have pierced my skin. They glisten. I let it fall gently onto the wood.

'Goodbye, big man,' I whisper. '*Two, forty-four hours* was just your time ...just your time.'

Chapter 22

We'd spent a couple of days thinking about life, which is always harder than living. The reports on the bullets from Mulholland's gun had returned a match from the ones that killed Paul. I still thought it was Paul when the phone rang. His number was stored on my mobile and it was hard to think that he would never answer it again, if I pressed the green button. The reality of his death was looming, swirling in my mind.

Mulholland's funeral was not for a few days yet and my colleagues rang constantly, hoping for an angle or a slip. I slipped the phone off the hook. Various papers and television networks grappled with the idea of Mulholland's mental health and they wheeled in experts to give opinions. There's nothing like a good scandal to focus people's attention, Rory always said. He was being proved right once again.

Mario's pizza is a welcome taste. 'I've had enough,' Pearl says, pointing to the last slice.
'Thanks. Just love sitting here and watching the world pass. I think the City Hall is such a beautiful building,' I say, swivelling around.
'If they don't start bombing again. I get a bad feeling this Ceasefire won't hold, you know.' Pearl's statement sort of takes me by surprise.
'What do you mean?'
'Oh, it's all too good to be true, Simon. All this happening as well,' she exclaims, flapping her arms around.
'All this with Mulholland, you mean?'
'Yes.'
'Is there something you're not telling me, Pearl?'

She looks seriously at me, then turns to watch a plane drift across the rooftops of the city.

'No. I just have a bad feeling that's all.'

I stuff the last bite of pizza into my mouth. 'Are you worried about Johnston being out?'

'Worried ...course I'm worried, Simon. We think my daughter is engaged to him and we think he's here to kill you,' Pearl says, getting rattled.

'We think,' I smile, raising my brows. She slaps my arm and the both of us concede a small laugh.

'Let's go for a walk, Simon.'

We stroll along Royal Avenue and gaze at the windows. Pearl matches garments and discards others for reasons of style or colour. 'Let me help you across the road, darling. There's one of those big, red buses coming,' she says, wryly.

'Why thank you, dear.'

'Wait by the kerb and mumsy-wumsy will tell you when it's safe to walk.' She makes a big thing out of checking both ways for traffic. We both see the blue car driving slowly.

'It's him,' I yell. Pearl looks at me, bewildered. The car stops by the kerb and something drops from the window, thrown by the driver. I was braced for a bullet, yet the car cruises on as if nothing had happened.

'What's that? It was Johnston,' Pearl mutters, quickly. I stoop down and pick up the picture. Pearl is focusing on it beside my shoulder. 'Oh my God. Oh my God. How did he get this?'

I can't speak, only stare at the photograph of Grace and me with two bullets forced through our foreheads. It was sitting on my desk when we left Tullydeen. Pearl goes to point out this fact and my nod makes her stop. She clutches my arm. 'Oh my God, Simon,' she whispers over and over. The blue car parks across the road and Johnston waves over with a large smile.

If there are buses it's too bad. I run straight for him and his throat. He slips the car into gear and drives off as I manage to kick the driver's door. 'You're going down, Johnston,' I yell to the evening street. But he's gone. Pearl hurtles over and almost knocks me down with a crying hug. 'Let's get out of here,' she whimpers. The whole street is spinning. I check around. There's no one. All the shops have closed for the day. It's after 9pm. Only the buildings witnessed the happening.

I grab Pearl and we run toward Manford Street and *The Irish Scribe* office. The newsroom is ghostly silent. Paul's desk is sitting as he left it. The little tiger on top of his computer and the slogan-signs stuck to his desk, telling the world how he was used and abused by his employers. He had been the life, but now he was the soul of this place. Yeah, he'd have liked that. The night desk crew twiddle their thumbs and drink coffee. Rory's in his greenhouse midst the everpresent drone of the presses below us.

One of the night desk guys reaches for the incoming text. Rory has spotted us. I call him with a wave. It's hard to breathe. 'Johnston's been released,' I say, to the night desk guy. He looks at the text and then me, 'yeah.'

Rory slammed the desk when he heard the news.
'Here, take a gawk at this,' I say, somewhat casually as if it was a holiday snap.
'A ...Jesus.' Rory says, straightening his lips.
'That picture was sitting on my desk this evening. We only left Tullydeen around five.'
'It was five exactly,' Pearl confirms, nodding.

A cold reality runs down my spine. I picture Johnston stepping out of my lane with a smile on his face waiting to pull the trigger. I walk to Rory's greenhouse and use the filing cabinets as my support. My legs feel unsteady, yet my mind is alert.
'That boy Barnsey is worth a watching. He couldn't find Mulholland the night Big Paul was murdered,' Rory says, angrily.
'He had to lift ye, Simon, because I asked him to. If he hadn't it would have given the game away. He wanted Mulholland to get ye,' Rory finishes.
'Looks like it, Rory,' I agree. 'It's all starting to add up.' I pause and stare at the ceiling. 'So what. I've opened a can of worms with the Andrews Corporation and Barnsey's crawling about in there somewhere. What's new about Barnsey crawling.'
'Never trust people that take a bribe, Simon. It's all right to offer a bribe, yet taking it is a different thing,' Rory says, shaking his head.
'Well now, keeping ye alive is the main concern ...isn't it, Mass Patterson.'
'Sometimes I wonder, Rory. Sometimes I wonder if it's all worth it. I don't know,' Pearl dismisses, with a swipe at the air.
'He'll go to Jersey after he finishes me off,' I say. 'So in that case

we go to Jersey now, well in the morning. That means he has to follow and it messes with his plans.'

'Aye,' Rory nods, looking to Pearl.

'It means we can get to Susan before him. And, he'll know we've been there before. Susan probably told him. He has to marry her to get all the money.'

'What money?' they ask.

'Mulholland's money,' I say. 'I bet he left Susan everything. He was besotted with her.'

'It was suicide. They won't pay out Simon,' Rory adds.

'Doesn't matter about that. Mulholland would have the money all signed away to Susan years ago. She probably got access to the money last year or before that. Mulholland probably had it witnessed, say ten years ago. Can't prove and predict someone will commit suicide for that length of time,' I explain. 'There's a double bind because Johnston had also blackmailed Mulholland about the car bomb. However, Mulholland was a genius and it *only* seemed he was getting done over. Johnston will get a nasty shock someday soon when he goes to collect his nest egg. Mulholland will get his money back, despite being dead. He hated Johnston.'

Pearl's catches my drift and Rory takes a minute to catch on.

I grab the phone and call the airport. At least there are no more flights tonight. We are on the first flight out tomorrow morning.

'So Johnston goes to Jersey to get married. Susan said she was getting married, right, Pearl?'

'Right.'

'Till death do us part,' Pearl adds, softly and resolutely. Rory looks at me and rubs his scalp. Pearl has gone remote, even the colour is leaving her tan.

The phone rings and all of us look at it, as if it's a bomb. Rory swallows hard and looks somewhat apprehensive as he prepares to pick it up.

'Guess what?' Rory says, holding his arms out. 'That was Barnsey. Johnston has been released. As if we didn't know.'

Pearl lights up and paces around Rory's greenhouse, clutching her right elbow the way she did when I told her Susan had a clone in Belfast.

'Can Johnston get to Jersey before us?' Pearl asks. I knew she would ask that one.

'I don't think so,' I reply, looking at Rory. She draws hard on her cigarette and blows the smoke at the ceiling.

'He'll not be flying with us in the morning, you know. He'll get there some other way.'

My gut churns as I think of Grace. I can't go to the police. If I do, Barnsey will know. I phone Pauline and make up a bit of a story. I mention Big Paul's murder and she agrees to take Grace to the caravan. It was easier than I had thought it would be. She informs me Barnsey had called. I can hardly swallow. He played with Grace. Barnsey never called like that. There's evidence for my paranoia.

This way Grace will think it's just a holiday. She isn't stupid. It was only a few weeks ago when Grace said her mummy was spelling words, so it must've been important. All I could do was laugh. I remember my folks doing the same like *we'll get him that from S-a-n-t-a*. It's back to time. If it's Grace's time I don't want her knowing it. My teeth lock and I'm as sure about this as anything. No one knows where we have the caravan. At least I don't think they do.

Rory waits for the answer to his question and I haven't a clue what he had asked me.

'Sorry, I was miles away.'

'Where are ye staying tonight?' he repeats.

'Tullydeen,' Pearl snaps in before I have time to answer. 'If he's coming to kill us then we'll be there.'

A smile shoots across her face, accompanied by a positive nod. Rory doesn't look too keen on the idea, yet he doesn't say. He collapses into his chair and clutches his hands.

'Keep in touch if anything happens ...'

'What ...call the police, Rory,' I interrupt. He shakes his head.

'So far so good,' Pearl says, as we enter the lane. On the way she decided against phoning Susan. I thought she might have wanted to. Perhaps she did, maybe it's better not to know when you're going to die. The floating moon swings over Tullydeen like a piece of paper in the tide. Tiny clouds pass like smoke, now and then. I check everywhere. There are no bodies lurking around or cars parked in the fields.

'Look,' Pearl points.

I zoom in on the circle resting against the door.

'Oh my God, what a sicko,' Pearl says.

'Yeah ...sick and deadly.'

I pick up the black wreath, making sure there are no wires attached to it. All of the flowers and greenery have been sprayed black. The typed message rests at twelve o'clock.
Bye-bye, now. Will both of you be buried in the same grave? That would be nice.

Pearl mutters and walks over to the barn wall. I set the wreath down and puff out my cheeks. I'm bound to waken up and find out this is just a bad dream. I fumble for a Marlboro and feel remarkably calm. It's like a form of resignation to fate. Pearl has walked off towards the garden, clutching her elbow again. I turn the key in the lock and wait for the bang. There's none.

I scan the kitchen. Nothing's been touched. I run upstairs and the empty picture frame sits in its usual position. Nothing: no flashing guns or masked men. I run back downstairs and into the approaching night. Pearl's sitting on the wall, looking over the Lough. Little gangs of midges breakdance close to her.

'There's nothing amiss except the photo. He put the frame back together and it's in the same position.' I explain.
'How long would it take to get to Jersey by boat?' Pearl asks.
'Hours ...from Ireland ...he wouldn't be there before us, Pearl,' I say, putting my arms around her.
'What if he flew? There's an airport over there. He could hire a private plane and be there in no time.'
'Those planes wouldn't fly that far,' I reply quickly, not knowing if they would. I don't want to even think about that.
'We'd better grab a few things for tomorrow.'
'I'm grabbing nothing except the flight. If I need anything I will buy it over there, you know. Simon, let's get drunk. This could be our last night.'
'Ach ...Pearl come on, this's not getting us anywhere.'
'We've nowhere to go, Simon. Nowhere, just like Billy Thompson and Fast Frank. We're sitting ducks.'
'Sitting, but not dead ducks,' I interrupt. 'I could murder a beer.'
Pearl spins around and gives a loud laugh. 'Stuff it, let's drink to murder,' she sighs.

Nobody meets us in Jersey. We hire a car and drive to St. Tanons. The sun sneaks through the trees and across the large lawns in front of the hospital.
'You wait here.'

A man in a brown sports jacket with stringy fair hair smokes aggressively at the door.

'Is Susan Patterson on duty?' I ask at reception.

'Yes, she's here.'

'What ward?' I'm already running, looking back for directions.

'Number Seven, third on the right.'

The long depressing corridor, with heating pipes and rounded door frames slides under my shoes. I skid to a halt and look in. Number Seven is written on the door – lucky seven. I hate the smell of hospitals, which hasn't been helped by the recent food odour. It's a female ward. Everyone studies the stranger – me. The woman that sat beside me on the bench smiles. A male nurse, turning off the ward corridor up ahead, fails to notice my wave.

Doors intermittently break up the dour paint job. I search madly for directions. The television is blaring with no one watching it. The woman I had met on my last visit here is telling everyone I'm called Simon. I'm also her husband, she relays.

'Susan,' I yell. She appears at a doorway and stops abruptly. I run towards her. 'Susan, we've got to get out of here.'

'What?'

'Tommy Johnston's on his way here and I think you don't want to see him,' I add.

'Course he's coming. We're getting married. After what mummy did I just brought it all forward. I won't let her talk to me like that. I heard about your friend. How ...'

'Shut up, Susan. He's not going to marry you ...well, he might but.' I grab her arm and force-walk her along the corridor past the women and their eyes.

'You're hurting me,' she yells, trying to break free. If she doesn't shut up I'll hurt her a lot more.

'We've to get out of here. Your lover boy, alias Mervyn, a la Tommy Johnston, is coming looking you and me. He sent me a nice little picture of my daughter and myself with bullets stuck into our foreheads. Shut up, Susan,' I blast out as she tries to interrupt. Her eyes startle with shock. 'Did Mulholland leave you money before he died?'

'Yes. He gave me some. He said he loved me. I played along. He always gave me money. He said...'

'How much did he give you?'

'Simon, wise up. Mind your own business,' she snaps back.

'When were you speaking to Tommy Johnston last?' I ask. She tries to stop walking but I keep the movement going with the gentle persuasion of a push.

'This morning. He loves me. I told you to stay out of this. No. You couldn't ...'

'Look Susan ...Tommy Johnston might marry you all right. It's the line, *till death do us part*, that bothers me. And, he becomes *richer, not poorer*.'

Susan tries to stop once more.

'Nonsense. It's your fault. Mulholland got his folks killed. He deserved anything he got. He's evil.'

'So is blackmail Susan, and crying rape on Billy Thompson,' I bounce back. She tries to laugh it off, yet I feel it register beneath my grip.

I check the windows. Pearl is fixing her make-up in the car. A doctor approaches us with his head down.

'Tommy,' Susan says, looking at the pistol and becoming the recipient of a sudden revelation.

'Did you get your nice wee wreath, Simon boy? Was it the right colour?' Tommy Johnston asks from his chiselled face. The pistol pushes into my neck, crushing my Adams Apple. My ears go numb and Susan Patterson squeezes tightly on my hand. She's muttering uncontrollably.

'Let's go for a wee walk,' Johnston says, calmly. I look into his recessed features and his pupils never stay still. We turn around. The pistol is stuck fast to my lungs. I don't want to die. Pearl's still sitting in the car, dangling her arm out of the window. Will I ever see her again? Grace? Has he killed her? Susan cries uncontrollably. Any time we try to stop, the pistol or his arm pushes us on.

Johnston grabs Susan's hair and pulls her head backwards. 'I'll have to put off the wedding,' he laughs, in a thick Antrim accent. Susan looks at me, terror and the reality of doom, engulfing her. We had our first years together and what could be our last few minutes. The façade and complications of life have melted. We were the souls of Tullydeen. We were the parents of Peggy-Sue and Barney. The explorers of the black rocks and not even our imagination could have foreseen this happening. Yet we'd walked on the moon, played houses and wondered about being eighteen. Susan squeezes my hand and everything melts. We've both returned to Tullydeen. The little girl appears in her eyes – the real Susan

Patterson. The one I knew: not the clone. She could never be. The real Susan Patterson has just returned in the last few minutes.
'I'm sorry, Simon,' she muffles out.
'It doesn't matter,' I sniff back, feeling the tears trickling down my cheek.

Johnston pushes us into the ward we had just left. The women talk on. I stare over at Gladys and she smiles. I look for a way out. The windows are too narrow. I couldn't dive through them. Even if I did, he'd kill Susan. Johnston makes her open a door on the right, off the corridor. He shoves me into a soft chair. A huge grin lights up his face. I curse white coats. White coats in a hospital go unnoticed.

We're in the nurses' rest room with a kettle and cups and an old battered coffee table. I look at the tea trolley beside Johnston. It would make a noise, but I can't reach it. He tugs on Susan's hair.
'Maybe you'll meet someone in the next world, wee Susan,' Johnston says, smiling.

He pushes her across the small room and she slides down onto the floor, trembling and sobbing.
'Nice weather,' Johnston remarks casually. 'I'm off to Malaga.' His nods reinforce his words. Malaga bounces off my scull. The Andrews Corporation. I hadn't been paranoid. They'd hired him; well, the front men had on Mulholland's orders. The big façade that Mulholland had used to fool everyone. My hands begin shaking. Johnston stands with his back to the door. *Staff Only* is stuck to it. His body hides most of the letters on the glass.

I'm going to die in a mental institution. Many people have died here, although not like this. People turn a blind eye to mental illness. I glance around the room. The blue walls signal a cold death. Johnston fixes a silencer to his pistol and grins, showing me the way it fits. I can feel his breath hit my face, then he steps back. The old beige armchair I'm sitting in is the last thing I will see, the cupboards on the walls. I want to ask about Grace but I won't give him the pleasure. Susan has been reduced to a blubbering ball against the cupboard.

'Nice villas out in Spain, wee Susan,' Johnston says, putting the gun under her chin and lifting her head. 'Remember we stayed there.' I'm tempted to lash out with a kick. It'd be stupid. He wants me to do that.

The door opens and Johnston spins around with the gun at waist height.

'Are you hurting my husband? Simon is my husband,' the old lady with grey hair scolds. I land a kick into his back and he falls against the door. 'Scream, Susan,' I yell.

'Leave my husband alone,' Gladys keeps saying. Johnston still has the gun. I leap onto his back. He has to shoot himself to get me. I hear shuffling behind me.

'You said you loved me,' Susan screams, pouring the contents of kettle over him. A little of the warm water sprinkles around my arms, yet Johnston took most of it over his head and face. His squeal rips across the room.

People are running in response. The gun drops onto the floor. I punch Johnston hard on his kidneys. He's reeling around clutching his head and only slightly concerned about the hardest punch I have ever landed.

'Give me the gun,' Susan says. 'Gladys ...give me the gun.' Susan's hair is sticking all over her face. Gladys looks at me.

'Will I give it to her, Simon? I don't know if I should. Were you and her having an affair? I want a divorce,' she says, gazing at the gun.

'Don't move,' I say to Susan. 'Don't move. Gladys, give me the gun. It's me, Simon.'

'Yes I know it's you, Simon ...but her,' Gladys replies, pointing the pistol at Susan. A male nurse tries to come in and Johnston rolls on the bluish tiles.

'I want a divorce, Simon. You and her, well.' Gladys looks angrily at Susan Patterson through her tatty grey hair. I can't get to Gladys yet. Johnston's body is in the way.

'I used to love guns,' Gladys says, pointing it at Susan. 'We used to shoot, Simon.'

'Yes Gladys, we did.' I can't believe this.

'I want a divorce, Simon. I have caught you red handed,' Gladys scolds once more.

'Gladys, it's me ...Susan, the nurse.'

'Hummh, you are not a nurse. You only put me in here to get close to her, didn't you, Simon. I know what you did.' Gladys' face grimaces. 'You thought I didn't know what was going on, hummh. Well, Gladys is not so stupid. Not so doting.'

The bullet spits out from the silencer. Susan hits the tiles with a thud as I dive onto Gladys. I have the gun. Her hand is still around the trigger. She squeezes more rounds off into the ceiling.

Two male nurses push from the door, grabbing Gladys. The gun works free.

Blood trickles across the floor from Susan's ear and mouth. Johnston's red and blistering face is just waiting for the remainder of the rounds. I want to pump them into him and just for a moment I think about keeping one for myself.

Susan is stone cold dead. I stand with the pistol in my hand. The doctor finishes examining Susan and turns to Johnston. Police scurry in. Pearl's face looks to me for conformation. Two policemen push me against the wall. 'Simon Rogers,' I yell. They take the gun and let me go. The male nurse who grabbed Gladys rushes past with medical supplies. 'I hope you die, Johnston,' I mutter. Gladys is surrounded by police who take her to another part of the ward.

'Susan's been shot,' I offer as gently as possible. 'Shot dead, Pearl.' She slides down the wall, crying. I don't intrude. What it means to a mother to lose a child is beyond me. I don't pretend to know. I sit opposite her on the floor and light a cigarette.

Paramedics rush past with Johnston strapped to the trolley. 'Johnston, I hope you die,' I scream after them. People look. A second trolley appears with a black sheet strapped over it. Pearl's alert, scampering to her feet. Her face doesn't want it to be true. The two burly paramedics nod respectfully and drop their heads. Pearl looks at her daughter. In the brief silence it appears to register with her. She slaps the wall. A nurse wants to comfort her. Pearl shakes her off. There's always some asshole that can't stand people expressing their grief. They can't deal with their own pain, but they feel the need to touch yours. It's so patronising.

Nurses arrive and usher the ogling patients from the ward. A male nurse wants to look at a cut on my neck. I didn't even know I had it. He dabs alcohol on my neck and mumbles something about it being fine.

Pearl strides off. 'Wait,' I yell, gathering speed. Two police officers turn and watch. Pearl keeps running. I catch up with her at the car, slumped over the bonnet.

'Where are they taking Susan?' she mutters. Her face has gone into a world I never want to visit. Pearl runs over and clutches me, crying. Every cry rebounds off my body. I hold her like I never held her before. A tall detective waits until an opportune time to explain where Susan will be taken. He shows us to the car and we slump, entwined into the back seat.

'It's all over now, Simon,' Pearl manages, watching the granite houses pass. 'It's all over,' she repeats reaching for my chest. Her hands grip my shoulders. Her head rests against my chest. Pearl whimpers softly. Tears and tiredness grab my face. For what? ...For newspapers ...for circulation ...for truth ...for God and Ulster ...for a United Ireland ...for the law-abiding people ...for my memory of the little girl from Tullydeen.

Chapter 23

We arrive at the General Hospital in St. Helier. Susan's body has to go through the formalities of the Accident and Emergency Department. Johnston's here too. Pearl is taken by doctors to a tiny room and I slump into a red chair with a can of Fanta and wait. When she returns we saunter outside for a smoke.

Her face is distant, tired and resigned to a fate. 'Don't wait for me,' she says, catching me off guard.
'Of course I'll wait for you.'
'No, Simon. You get out of here when you feel the need. We're dead ducks if we stay together.' She turns, holds my hand and rubs her finger along the back of it. Her gentle touch sends tingles all over me. All she has to do is touch me and I'm relaxed. I watch her face, her eyes, her mouth, her nose, her eyebrows, her hair, her.
'I love you, Pearl,' I say pulling her close.
'I know you do, Simon. I wanted to get married to you, in the little church in Drumfiddy. Would you have?' she asks.
'Yes.'
'If I don't make it will you put flowers on my grave?'
'Pearl …stop it.'
'Will you?'
'Ach …Pearl …'
'Will you, Simon?'
'No. Yes. Look Pearl, we'll be fine. They can't touch you,' I say, not really believing it. But what else can I say? She grips firmly to my body and holds me. Her embrace is strong yet gentle. It's more than a passing notion. We unlock and we hold hands and look at each

other the way we did at her old cottage. 'Penny for them,' she says. I say nothing except my look hopefully tells her that I love her.

A doctor waits and doesn't want to intrude, but he obviously needs to speak to Pearl. We return to the Accident and Emergency Department where Pearl goes to a small room at the far end. More policemen arrive. Barnsey is with them. I knew there was something up, by the way they had treated me. Barnsey had obviously been in touch and wanted me to be kept safe until he could kill me. My level of sarcasm has risen like an autumnal tide. But sarcasm is never far removed from the truth, as it tends to navigate from a map of previous experience. A nurse dashes from Johnston's cubicle and I catch a glimpse of the faces labouring over him. Machines are beeping and focused minds talk rapidly over the self-employed terrorist. I still hope he dies.

So Johnston was off to Malaga. Pride before a fall, my mother always said. Johnston had boasted about it, not figuring on Gladys. Barnsey's talking to his counterparts and taking the odd look in my direction. I saunter through the sliding doors, into a busy St. Helier. Traffic, three lanes deep, cruises along in the heat, music of varying tastes drifts in my direction. I lean against the wall and savour my cigarette. I can't work out if it's better if Johnston lives or dies. In some shady bar they struck a deal to get even with me. Barnsey's in on it, too.

I return inside once more, to the fresh flurry of activity. Police huddle around the doctors and nursing staff.

'He's dead,' Barnsey says, shrugging.

'Good,' I snap back. 'Just throw him off the pier. What are you doing here?'

'We thought he'd come here,' Barnsey says, resting his arm against the wall.

'Susan Patterson is dead. Pearl's in with the docs now,' I say.

It's easy to see that Barnsey is itching to talk about something. He has that look on his face, his eyes and wrinkles darting about not really listening to me, more in the act of rehearsing what he wants to ask.

'Listen Simon. Word has it the Andrews Corporation employed Johnston,' he begins. I want to laugh at this great revelation, yet Barnsey holds the key to my freedom at this moment.

'Surprise, surprise,' I reply, watching him straighten off the wall.

'He told me about Malaga. He was counting the money in the

hospital ...whatever they had paid him to get me. He sort of jumped the gun, Barnsey, if you'll pardon the pun.'
'He told you?'
'Yeah.'

Barnsey sighs and wipes the sweat from his brow. 'Do these assholes know that?' I give him a look, which makes him feel stupid for asking the question.
'I must've hit close to the truth with the story, Barnsey.' I notice his stare drift off around the cubicles. Barnsey only does this when he wants to hide something.
'Spill the beans, Barnsey,' I whisper. I'm playing with his anxiety. It's dangerous, yet after what's happened I don't care. He fidgets a bit and I let him run.

'I sent the fraud squad into Mulholland's HQ this morning. Complete media blackout. Big mate of mine says there's already much amiss.'
'What like? Did you go to his house as well?' I ask.
'Yeah went to the house too. You know how those boys work but it takes ages. Anyway he's rubbing his hands, saying this's big, but it'll take months to decipher.'
'Give me something, Barnsey.' He looks around very suspiciously, drawing attention to himself. I want to laugh, however, I don't.
'The Andrews Corporation. There was stuff belonging to them in the safe at Mulholland's office. Some of the businesses on the computers were well known as paramilitary money laundering rackets. Could never prove it before, but this might all add up. I'm telling you, Simon, if it's as good as the boys first think, then there'll be some shit hitting the fan,' Barnsey finishes, looking pleased with himself. I don't believe a word of it, yet I'll play along.
'This's always threatening to break, Barnsey, but it never does,' I say. He's bursting to win me over.
'But this's different, Simon. Say this money they take from Joe Bloggs, for protection is put into their false firms. Do you follow?' I nod. His wrinkles smooth out. 'It doesn't. It was put into or at least they think it was put into every business Mulholland had and most of it into the Andrews Corporation. Mulholland was a nutcase, a loon ...but a wizard with figures. My big mate's saying it's all over the place. Every citizen in the country's handling it,' Barnsey pauses and taps the wall, 'Mulholland handled the police pensions. It's going to look bad,' he explains.

I laugh and shake my head. Barnsey watches me and doesn't appear amused.

'So what's this got to do with me and the contract on me?' I say, putting the connections together. Billy Thompson was right, *money and patches*, he had said. 'It would take years in the courts to prove and loads upon loads of paperwork to convict them. So what's it all about? I was only wanting to warn people about being swindled.'

'Aye, that's what you did do, Simon. But the shit doesn't stop there. That's why Johnston's lying dead in there. Do you honestly think they gave a shit about you and your story?' Barnsey pauses. He almost told me what he wasn't going to tell me. He rubs his hands and walks around, looking at the posters on how to look after your health.

'Come on, Barnsey, what's the rest?'

'They sent Johnston after you and killed Mulholland's parents because old Tom Mulholland got too close. The same will happen to you. It's big business. None of us could afford peace. The paramilitaries are in business together,' he says.

'Don't forget about your crowd ...the police. Youse need the Troubles more than anyone, look at the money a cop earns in Northern Ireland. Anyway it's common knowledge, Barnsey. People know that the paramilitaries from all sides buy guns together and split them. Sure the police had known that for years,' I say. I'm not going to let him off the hook. He knows that he's cornered.

'Look Simon, if you don't stop this story, they'll kill you.'

'They'll kill me? Is that the Loyalists or the Nationalists?'

He glances away again and talks for time. He tells me about the country going bankrupt and the consequences of the complete picture coming to the surface.

'Just stop, Barnsey,' I say.

'No I won't. If you don't stop this Simon, you'll cause a civil war. The Prods will think the Catholics took the money and vice versa. The police will be caught in the middle and all hell will break loose.'

'Is there something new about that?'

'There'll be ways and means. Mulholland's dead, now. He'll take the blame and the crooked dealing. They'll pawn it off onto him, because of his state of mind. All that shite you study.'

A piece of Barnsey's personality comes to the surface. I knew it was there, yet I sort of hoped it wasn't. What's he in all of this? He's giving me the hard sell to drop the story. Mulholland will be blamed for the Andrews Corporation and Big Paul's murder. In other words I've to put the lid back on the can of worms. I feel as if I'm going mad. I'm damned if I do and I'm damned if I don't. If Barnsey is telling me all this, I'm under no illusion that I will be allowed to live. Have all the divisions been together in one huge conglomerate, working for a mutual richness while killing each other and talking about peace?

'I'll let it drop, Barnsey. Look, I'm worried about Grace. It's not my scene anyway. I investigate other sorts of things,' I explain, watching his face. 'I heard you called.'

He nods.

'Were you there when Big Paul was murdered?'

'Simon,' he pleads.

'Were you? Yes or no?'

'No. I had left about two hours before that. Do you not think I feel stupid and useless, eh Simon?'

I nod.

'I had to ask you, Barnsey. I'm going for a piss, be back in a minute,' I say, as Barnsey nods and takes his seat. He was telling the truth about Paul's murder. I'll stake my career on it. But his other story was rubbish or most of it was. His speech is over. He can sit contented and reflect upon his performance. I have my Barclaycard and about fifty quid in cash. I run my fingers across the edges of the notes in my pocket.

I look in the mirror above the wash hand basin and decide. Pearl will have to fend for herself. There's no way both of us would make it. She was right. Anyway, she'll want to be with Susan. Shit, what a mess. My face is haggard, tired with black bags under my eyes. I scramble onto the window ledge and force my head through the opening in the frosted glass. I look down into the car park and jump the ten feet or so, landing between two BMW's.

The hospital is a tall, red bricked building, luckily I had been on the ground floor. I squint around in the sunshine and a couple of people are walking towards their cars. They appear to be discussing their latest diagnosis. A large wall separates me from the busy traffic. I take a deep breath and walk confidently towards it. Trust me to be on an island. *No man is an island*, yet getting off one is awkward. I make for the harbour. There's no activity or police running behind me. Holidaymakers strolling around give me some cover. It would be crazy to try the ferries or airport. A bus to Gorey stops to allow people off. I jump on and look over my shoulder once more. Sweat is pouring into my eyebrows. I'm certain that I'll never see Pearl or Grace again. I push the thoughts to the back of my mind and it helps to stop the sea whistling in my ears and that pumping sensation.

It's everyone for themselves now. Barnsey could dream up a charge and I am under no illusion what the consequences would be. He wants it dropped all right. Even if I did, they couldn't take the chance on my silence. A bullet would ensure silence. Johnston had failed in his mission to kill me. Barnsey could've mourned me, all cut up in the knowledge their little scheme was secure. Mulholland got Big Paul but missed me. That didn't matter because Johnston was there to sweep up. If it hadn't been for Rory I was already dead meat with his scheme to have me arrested and thrown into the cells.

As usual the talk about peace in Northern Ireland was down to money: same old song. What would all the policemen do if peace arrived? Where else could they earn that sort of money? Nowhere.

I was right about Tom Mulholland. He had stumbled onto the same thing as me. So it's, bang, you're dead. Any price for a cause. If they can't get me they'll use Grace and Pearl to draw me out. Everyone is leaving the bus. It's the end of the road. Gorey has arrived.

Chapter 24

An influx of French tourists gives me some cover. I try not to think of the future. How things will work out is beyond me. It's boiling. Jersey's well in the eighties and my throat is taking the toll. I sip a Coke and sit on the wall looking at Gorey harbour.

The only person in the world I can trust is Rory. Big Paul's dead. Well, Mandy and Matt Brown, too. It's sort of ironic that I'm living on borrowed time, marooned on an island or at least it feels that way. There will be sleepless nights ahead when Pearl's spirit questions my desertion: the sound of Susan, hitting the floor and the sight of her staring, dead eyes. Why me? I bounce from the wall and lift the receiver, Grace was coming next and I can't afford to think about her at the moment.

Rory answers quickly and I put him in the picture. He wants to print something, draw attention to my situation and perhaps make my killers think twice. I tell him about Barnsey and the story of the fraud squad going to Mulholland's office. Rory's reaction is the same as my own — *load of old rubbish*. Nothing about Johnston and Susan Patterson's deaths had reached the news networks. We figure it's a blackout, *free press my arse*, he drawls as usual. His voice is anxious and firing thoughts down the line and eventually he agrees not to print anything. Someone else knows what has happened. If I die it won't be an accident, with a grieving Barnsey sniggering up his sleeve. I recite all I know over the phone and it will hit the streets if a bullet hits me.

France looks like my best option. The boats drift to and fro in the harbour on the high tide, making the most of it before the sand returns. They'll track me to Gorey. I'll draw some money ...leave a trail. They'll be watching for transactions. The goldfish bowl of computerisation might give me a bit of time and a break for once.

The air-conditioning inside the bank is pleasant. This time I will volunteer my identity to the cashier. My driving licence does, along with my cheque card. I could have used the cash machine but I wanted to make sure I was recorded on CCTV.

'Love the badge. Everybody wears a badge ...don't they?' I say, making her smile. 'How do you feel about being a badge ...Maggie Dawson?' She flicks at her shoulder length, brown hair and gives me a smile of fluorescent teeth.

'It's okay,' she replies in what appears to be a Dorset tone with the edges knocked off.

'You're from Ireland?'

'Yes ...I'm over to blow up Jersey,' I whisper, as she smiles and taps the keys on her computer. She's putting me on the map and throwing a trail, which will be handed to Barnsey or his cronies soon. Maggie Dawson counts the money twice. I don't care if it's right and I almost grab the £500 before she has finished.

I filter through the strolling tourists towards the advertisement offering trips to France. I buy a ticket for the catamaran leaving in an hour and once more a record is kept. I start walking toward the large hill leading away from the village. It was the route I'd taken in the hired car going to meet Susan Patterson and Gladys at the hospital. What is in store for Gladys, I wonder?

This heat doesn't help and makes the hill appear larger. Every vehicle that passes dislodges my tiredness to a high state of alert. I must look suspicious because each motorist gives me an extra stare. Maybe they're just wondering what sort of an idiot would climb the hill in such heat. Three teenagers whiz past on bicycles; they must have no fear. I'm full of it, yet I know fear has great motivation. I rest close to the high verges and look down on the tiny village of Gorey. A large blue van labours up the hill, stuttering as the driver selects a lower gear.

The large van moves towards me. It's one of those refrigerated wagons which no doubt carries fish. The driver pulls up beside me and I open the door, apprehensively. The stocky man signals for me to get in. My immediate perception tells me he is French.

'Granville?' he utters in a nasal tone.

'Thanks, yeah.' I'm trying to work out where Granville is.
'Vacance? Holiday?' he asks, coaxing the van back to the remainder of the hill.
'Yeah ...something like that.' He casts a wicked grin across his weatherworn cheeks. I want to ask, why, but I sit in silence. He flicks at the radio button and the news blares out. Even the Andrews Corporation is getting a mention in Jersey and the imminent funeral of Trevor Mulholland in Belfast.

'Simon Rogers,' he says, almost knocking me off the seat with his words. I look at him. He grins, blowing a half whistle through his lips.
'Yes ...how did you ...?'
'Police ...down at the harbour. I was in the bank when you were in. Then I put one fish on top of the other and netted both of them,' he explains, quite pleased with himself. 'I saw your picture on TV. Where the crazy man killed himself at your house. The accountant. One coastal man to another,' he smirks. 'Pierre Gireau,' he adds, reaching out his hand.
'Well, I'll be damned,' I half laugh, meeting his gesture. 'What did the police want?'
'Sad, they missed the ferry ...they're waiting for you at Catheret. Asking about ...you know. Nobody saw anything because you were not there,' Pierre smiles, making his hand swim to accompany the shrug.
  We pass the little village of Granville and take a left toward the hospital. Pierre taps the wheel to the Cranberries, it's almost comical him even liking the Cranberries. He grunts at the wheel and we take an old dusty lane. 'My place,' he says briefly. We end up at an old Granite house with a large green shed and pallets sitting against one wall.
'Tomorrow I go to England ...I'll give you a lift.' He jumps from the cab and I can't believe my ears. He walks towards the shed and an old collie walks stiffly towards him. I follow him to the darkness of the shed and a few birds flap around high in the rafters.

'How will you get me to England?' I ask. He stops and stuffs his hand into his pocket. 'Mollie,' he says, motioning at the old collie dog. Mollie sniffs my hand and I pass the friendly test. Mollie returns to her master's side.
'In the van,' he says casually. Ask a stupid question, Simon, I think.

'In the van? ...If they're looking for me that would be too easy.'
'Old Pierre will take care of that. Reach me that pallet,' he says, pointing to the entrance. I give in and feel relaxed by his presence and confidence. I grab the pallet and drag it into the shed.

Pierre fixes bags of meal to his liking, then takes me to the house. It appears to be deserted. I reckon he's mid-fifties, hardy, with the build of a Marine. He must be an old soldier, it oozes from him.
'No one will bother you here tonight. I live alone now. This is my family home. My mother died four years ago,' he explains, showing me the photo on the kitchen wall. 'Never been to Ireland. Was that the Irish Sea ...beside your house?'
'No, Strangford Lough. It sits like a lagoon between the sea and the coast of Co. Down. It's about half an hour from Belfast,' I tell him.
'No bombs?'
'No bombs, Pierre.' He reaches me a can of beer and we toast.
'To Ireland,' he says.
'Pierre, I'm in big shit ...I just want ...'
'I don't need to know,' he interrupts. 'I knew you were on the run ...the way you acted in the bank. It's the eyes. I was on the run once in Algiers. Someone helped me ...so now I help you,' Pierre explains. 'That's me,' he says proudly, throwing the photograph of a young uniformed man at me.
'The Foreign Legion?'
'Corporal-Chief Gireau. Old Legionnaires don't die, they sell fish,' he chuckles. 'So I don't need to know ...any more than I already know. See ...I'm repaying God and the people who helped me. Let's eat.'

I study the young man standing proud in the photograph, wearing his *kepi blanc*. I visualise Pierre storming across the desert, gun at the ready, striking fear into his foe. I give a silent chuckle and feel as if I've won the *Lotto*. It's amazing what turns up when you least expect it. An old line from a book Liz MacFarland gave me following my attempted suicide comes to my mind. I always loved it. I don't even remember the name of the book, yet the impact of its words always helped me.
'In your darkest hour you will be looked after,' I say aloud. Pierre looks at me and I will my words to Grace, Pearl and to whatever makes my spine tingle when I rest my faith in my favourite verse.

Sleep was hard to come by and bumps in the night made me stare rapidly around the room. I could relax once my senses pinpointed the location as Pierre's living room. I picked up a lovely feeling about the room and the entire house as soon as I arrived. It wasn't hard to imagine his mother and a young Pierre chatting in the mixture of French and English, which he can slip in and out of without batting an eyelid.

The dawn arose around five and the drone of the refrigerated unit on his van competed with the birds. The ducks from the reservoir beside the hospital squealed and yelled occasionally, as if a row was developing. Maybe some other duck had eaten their porridge.

I saunter through the apple trees behind the house, soaking in the tranquillity. The powers that be will already know I did not arrive in France on the ferry. Surely they will have had a look at the cash transactions on my bank accounts by now. I want to phone Mandy or Rory but it would probably be traced. Rory knows what has happened and he knows I will not make contact with anyone directly. Plans came and went in the small hours of how I could keep tabs on the progress of my pursuers. Pursuers, I smile …I sound like Mandy. Killers, let's be honest about this. Keep the word killers foremost, Simon. Another phone call could cost me my life. I take my mobile out and remove the SIM card and break it in two.

'Bonjour,' Pierre shouts from the door.
'Morning, looks like another scorcher.'
'*Oui* ...you'll keep cool today,' Pierre states, nodding in the direction of the van. I smile and return to the house. Pierre has a pile of blankets on the table waiting for the off.
'Don't worry, Simon ...no one will find you.' Pierre made the traditional French breakfast: a bowl of hot chocolate with bread to dip into it. I devour one bowl full and several chunks of bread. Pierre rises sharply from the table and we are ready to depart.

Mollie greets us at the shed. The old collie waits for her breakfast and a fresh supply of water. I wait, watching the routine and his mutterings in French. Pierre seems lonely. ...I don't know what happened to him. A kind of sadness seeps out now and then. When he realises it has happened he cracks a joke and smiles. Maybe he had a young love and she jilted him or she was killed and he ran away to the Foreign Legion ...who knows?

He pats Mollie for the last time and opens the back doors of the boxvan. 'Up here, Simon,' he shouts, wanting me to follow. The whiff of fish is sickening at this early hour. I huddle the blankets close to me and already my teeth are starting to chatter with the cold. Pierre is removing a piece from the floor, a bit like a trap door. 'You will be in here for around an hour, at the most, two. Keep moving your arms and legs. Keep the blood moving. When you hear the vehicle stop, stay silent ...still. Do you need a pee?' he finishes.

'No.'

'You will when you get out.'

I crawl into the coffin-like hole. The blankets are a must in the chilly air. 'Can I breathe all right in here?'

'*Oui* ...the air will come in from the road. It may be a bit fumy from the exhaust. It should be okay.'

Pierre smiles as he replaces the cover of my coffin. Initially, I gasp for air more due to the suddenness of my claustrophobic introduction. I am good in confined spaces. The tartan blankets around my body are comforting in the darkness. It's like getting into a cold bed and already my chatters are starting to leave. We rock down the lane, then turn right towards Five Oaks, beginning the descent towards St. Helier. The vibration of the lorry is the worst part. It bangs my head up and down. I think of Pearl at the hospital. Is she lying dead somewhere? Or being held until her daughter is buried? I wish I could talk to Grace she would fix me up ...give me a telling off and coax me to be brave. We don't own our children, yet I suppose we think we do at times. Could I live without Grace? Often people say how could they survive without me? It's merely projection. If they kill Grace I'll go all the way. I won't care. I'd get them, even if I had to spend the rest of my life in jail. I'm hard to get going, but when pushed I really go mad and nothing stops me.

The early morning traffic thickens as we approach St. Helier. The hollow sound from the road tells me we are going under Fort Regent, the big tunnel dug through the rocks close to the harbour. I keep my toes and muscles flexing to avoid cramp, and clutch the blankets around me tightly. God, don't let the boat be delayed. Voices question Pierre as to his journey. I'm like a statue.

Suddenly, Pierre revs the engine and I imagine we are being guided onto the ship. The cold is taking effect and my bladder is pushing at my jeans. My toes are sore with cold and the hideaway does not allow me to move enough to get the blood going. We are turning. Voices shout directions and the murmur of the ship is a welcome sound. We've made it this far.

The back doors open. I just hope they are Pierre's footsteps. They stop beside my left ear and the lid lifts off.

'Follow me, there's a cabin,' his swarthy features beam.

I pull myself free from the hole and waste no time getting into the warmth. The car deck isn't completely full. Other passengers make their way to the stairs. Pierre exchanges hellos with some of the crew and I try to rub some warmth into my arms. 137 is stuck to the flimsy cabin door.

'I'll be up on deck,' Pierre says, letting me in. I am already warming up.

'I need a piss,' I smile. His eyes point to the sink. It'll do. 'Oh, have you a pen?' He fumbles inside his blue jacket and hands me a chewed *Biro*.

'Do not leave this cabin. I will check with you from time to time.'

  It is a beautiful Jersey morning. People are walking past the porthole, on deck, taking a look at the end of their holiday. Gulls screech and wait to be fed. The dock is a hive of activity. I hate berths on ships. As a kid I used to travel all night on the Belfast to Liverpool ferry. It was a terrible experience, setting a pattern for the remainder of my life. People next door are rumbling about and the passageway outside seems to be busy with passengers getting their bearings. I kick off my trainers and grab a handful of paper towels. There are four bunks to choose from. I pick the top one on the left-hand side. Never in my wildest dreams could I have imagined being so excited about being on board a ferry. Dry land is easy to cross. However, water poses a big problem with Customs and their suspicious stares. I still have another piece of water to cross the Irish Sea or *The Shuck* as it is affectionately known in Tullydeen.

  It would look bad if they told the truth of Johnston's murder in Jersey. It would be bad for tourism. No doubt the powers that be will be whispering rapidly about a plan. The way the doctors talked quickly over Johnston's peeling face. Gladys won't be much help to them. They'll push and push at Pearl, but she won't budge. What's she got to lose now? Susan's dead. She will know something was up when I left. It was her stupid idea. Sometimes sense is stupid. She's shrewd. We talked about trust. They might tell her I'm dead or being charged with the murders. I just hope she saw Barnsey. She knows what I think of him. Pearl knows he can't be trusted.

  The island of Jersey drifts off. We are moving. The door rattles and I tense. I jump off the bunk and push on my trainers. If I have to make a run for it at least I will have shoes. It's hard to run on a ship. Overboard is the only option. Overboard means into the propeller, sucked in by the motion of the ship.

'Who's there?'

'Pierre, some food.' I sigh and slowly open the door. Steam rises from the coffee and full breakfast. It smells beautiful. He reaches me the tray.

'Be back later. We arrive in Weymouth at 4.30pm. I'll come get you half an hour before we dock and put you back in the van,' he spits out quickly. I grab a tenner from my pocket and at first he refuses. 'Take it,' I say. His childish shy face goes even rosier and he eventually stuffs it into his pocket.

The eggs, bacon and sausages do the trick, giving me strength to think about the whole mess. I draw matchstick men on the paper towels. One for Mulholland, one for Johnston, one for me, one for Barnsey, one for the paramilitaries and one for the Andrews Corporation. I sit cross-legged on the bunk, looking at them. There is plenty of time to make them connect. Next, I draw a line from Johnston and the Andrews Corporation followed by a dashed line to me. They hired Johnston to shoot me. The Provos were supposed to hate the Loyalists and vice versa. What Billy Thompson said bounces back: *money and patches* it's all a racket, religion or causes no longer mattered. I have collectively put all the terrorist groups under the one heading: *paramilitaries*.

Corbière Lighthouse drifts past the porthole. I talk aloud to myself the way I used to read textbooks studying for my exams. So Mulholland shoots Paul, I had forgotten to draw Paul. I throw down the pen and look at the sketch. Nothing adds up. Nothing, that seems to make sense. Going on what Barnsey said, Mulholland was the key man behind all the money, moving it and hiding it in various systems. I'm not a financial wizard, yet I have a fair understanding of how it works. I make a few notes and something, which I try to ignore, keeps bouncing in and out of my vision. It's Mandy's father. Yes. He would know. He's a financier. Someone like him could sort this out or explain what I already know. He would know if it's possible. You don't ask a butcher what's wrong with your car ...you go to a mechanic.

Mandy's folks live in Surrey – Richmond upon Thames. I recall a mental picture of Philip Drummond from a few years back when I stayed overnight. I have talked to him many times on the phone and he always struck me as a good man with a good sense of humour. I suppose he'd have to, having to listen to Mandy.

We dock at Guernsey and wait for different passengers. Powerboats and yachts move in and around the harbour. I'd like to be able to go out on deck, but I can't have everything. Pierre brings coffee now and then although he does not stay.

I'm fed up looking at the drawings on the paper towels. An expert could spot the connection in a split second. Philip Drummond is such an expert. One thing's for sure: they cannot take the chance of letting me live. If they can't find me they'll use some method to lure me out. I sink my head into the pile of paper towels and think about Grace. What I'd give to pretend I'm enjoying one of her ham and mustard sandwiches. I hate mustard.

Chapter 25

'Bonne chance,' Pierre shouts over the drone of the diesel engine. Suddenly, I feel alone. He pulls into the traffic as a jumbo glides overhead towards Heathrow. This is the England of cricket, rugby, money and wine bars. Public school accents float around me as I try to find some meaning to my predicament. It's Mandy's homeland, her collective identity. Philip Drummond, Mandy's father, had always struck me as a genuine man. I have a mental picture of him retiring in his drawing room, midst the antique furniture. Mrs Drummond had been in York on my only visit to their home in Richmond.

Large wisteria mourns around the door. Borders of plants blast scent and colour from the pathway. A smiling although somewhat inquisitive woman attends to my summons. It's Mandy, only twenty years down the line. Mrs Drummond owns the same colouring and physique as her daughter; both have blond ponytails, athletic and a tad Swedish looking in appearance.
'Hello Mrs Drummond,' I say. 'I'm Simon Rogers, I work with Mandy at *The Irish Scribe* in Belfast.' Her face displays revelation. Perhaps she had seen pictures of me. Hopefully not the ones taken in the police cell. She stands aside, 'come in, Simon.' It's like listening to Mandy, same voice, grand and Surrey.
'I am delighted to meet you, Simon. Mandy talks about you constantly ...and eventually we meet,' she enthuses, showing me into a large, beamed room with classical music coming from somewhere. 'Philip is out at present. Out for his evening stroll.' She chuckles, pushing her hands into her denims. She appears to have been gardening before my interruption.

'He will be in Sadie's bar. He thinks I don't know, you see.' I mirror her smile and take an instant liking for Mrs Drummond. For the life of me I can't remember her first name. 'Are you over on business?'
'Sort of. It's a long story ...following a story. I have just come from Jersey,' I explain.
'I adore Jersey. I shall treat myself to a long weekend once the rugby season begins. Tea? Perhaps something stronger, Simon?'
'Anything's fine, Mrs Drummond,' I say, following her cue to take a seat.

She fixes me a large Scotch and flicks on two table lamps at either side of the bookcases. Volumes backed in leather, run in uniform along the bookshelves, enclosing me in a world of knowledge. Mostly money matters, I reckon. The soft leather chair mothers my body with its relaxing aroma.
'It gets dark earlier in Surrey,' I acknowledge, taking my glass. It has just gone 10.00pm, yet the dusk had pulled the night in upon Richmond. 'It'll still be light in Tullydeen,' I add, with a tenebrous melancholy zooming over me.
'To Ireland and its people and may they have peace,' Mrs Drummond salutes.
I shake myself and manage to utter *cheers*. Our glasses meet and I am touched by her finesse. The Scotch burns my tongue and induces tiredness and a feeling of wellbeing. It's a mental tiredness, one that hangs heavy with uncertainty. The weather and gardening keep us chatting and I compliment her on the blooms around the door.

Mrs Drummond exudes a tremendous presence. It's that thing which you can never quite put your finger on, like an itch, yet you can feel it. Her social skills are excellent, probably honed from years mingling with business colleagues of Philip's. Mrs Drummond fills my glass once more. My heart misses a beat when the phone disturbs the classical music and the squeakiness of the leather. Instinctively, I know it will be Mandy. She always phones around this time.
'Please don't tell her I'm here.' It's out before I realise. 'I'm in trouble. They could trace me.' The phone continues. Mrs Drummond searches for a meaning.
'What kind of trouble?'
'I'm on a story. If you tell her I'm here we're all in danger.' Mrs Drummond stands. The phone gives up. She sips her Scotch and seems to stifle her words. I spin sharply, following the sudden noise from outside.

'It's the gate. It will be Philip,' she assures me. I must appear nervous.

A cough accompanies the turning of the key. Philip Drummond is shuffling around in the small hall.

'In here, darling,' Mrs Drummond shouts, angling her head towards the door. I take another large swig of Scotch and watch the polished wood open.

'Good gracious, Simon Rogers,' Philip announces. He's wearing his slippers, blue cardigan and beige slacks. 'What a pleasant surprise.'

'Hello, Philip,' I reply, rising to meet his outstretched hand. 'It might not be so pleasant when you hear the full story.'

'What appears to be the trouble, Simon ...miss your flight?'

'No.'

'Scotch, darling?'

'Why not, Violet. Haven't had one for almost ten minutes,' Philip divulges with a wry grin and an acknowledgement that he had popped into his favourite watering hole. Philip sighs and slumps into his chair and begins to fiddle with his pipe.

'I need your help. I have been set up and it involves some sort of financial racket,' I explain.

'What's new about that,' he chuckles. Violet moves to the settee, clutching her glass.

'I was most upset to hear about your colleague,' he offers, slanting his glass.

'Paul, thank you. ...Yeah and this is part of it,' I add.

I launch headlong into the story as it has unfolded. Both of the Drummonds listen intently to my narrative. I pass Philip the paper towels from my pocket and apologise for putting him in this position. He quickly rebuffs my apology. I will never complain about human beings again. People have gone out of their way to help me. Right now, I'm sure there are more good people in the world. He studies my crude diagrams. Now and then, he scribbles something on his notepad.

'We need to phone Mandy ...let her know you are safe. I can relay messages from you. As a matter of fact,' Philip pauses. 'As a matter of fact, I will ask her to come over, make up something,' he dismisses. 'Don't worry, Simon, I will not say much on the phone. You'll stay here for as long as it takes.' Philip Drummond picks up his mobile from the table and smiles at me, 'makes me look young and trendy,' he chuckles.

'Hello, my daughter, and how are you?' he smiles. Violet Drummond places another Scotch in my hand. I would love to talk to Mandy. What I'd give just to be told off by her in her forthright manner. It is easy to see why Philip Drummond had been a top financier in the City. His manner and positive attitude would be hard to say *no* to.

He ends the call and smiles at me. 'Mandy gets into Heathrow at seven. I shall pick her up,' he says, decisively. He has the phone to his ear once more, making a reservation for his daughter on the 6 o'clock from Belfast. There is no question of a full flight. I don't think anyone would dare to tell Philip Drummond the flight was full. If he wanted on, nothing would stop him. In a light moment, induced by Scotch, I have a vision of him sitting proudly on the wing to spite all and sundry.

'Mandy is well. Have you eaten, Simon?' Philip's perfectly shaded grey hair moves slightly as he pushes out his words. He reminds me of Edward Woodward, the actor. The resemblance is uncanny.
'I had some food on the boat.'
'Would you like a sandwich?'
'I'd love one.'

Violet disappears into the kitchen. Perhaps it was her cue. The socialising is over. Philip Drummond reads virtually every national, daily newspaper he explains. He is adamant nothing had been mentioned regarding Susan Patterson or Johnston's deaths in Jersey. He was more than confident, he assured me, because of his love for Jersey. The mere mention of the word, Jersey would have drawn his attention to it, he stresses again.

His piercing blue eyes and healthy face gaze at me. 'This appears rather nasty, Simon. As you describe it, one big business, the one living off the other. Politics,' he chuckles. 'All money,' he adds, sternly. 'They have a go at us in the City ...at least we are honest. Of course, we are greedy. A million makes two million and so on. However, Mulholland appears to have been a wizard. I wish I had discovered him. And, you doubt if the fraud squad were involved? I doubt it, too. Mulholland would leave nothing unless he wanted it to be found. It would have been planned that way. That's the bad news. Or perhaps the good. Mulholland is no longer alive to argue or point the finger. It will look perfect. The unstable element concerning his character, his suicide and justice appearing to be done.' Philip pushes tobacco into his pipe and then he presses it with his finger. Smoking a pipe seems to be more of a hobby than an addiction.

'It would have simmered down for the fact you know about it,' he begins again, midst a cloud of grey smoke. 'I must warn you Simon, from my experience of greed and businesses hitting the wall ...anything goes. Anything, and to top that you are being chased by terrorists and the police. I'm confident you have had better weeks.' A wry grin slips from his lips. I see the funny side momentarily.

'In for a penny in for a pound,' I joke back.

'You cannot walk away from this, Simon,' he states in a serious tone. 'Perhaps this is your calling on earth. It has gone too far, I am afraid. First, staying alive and disappearing is paramount for you.' He's voicing all my thoughts. However, that old saying about the world being a small place has taken on a special meaning.

'I would love to see you pull this off. Forget all about going back to Ireland. I can take care of all that. I can raise you capital by selling your property,' he drops in.

I want to express my disapproval, yet I know it makes sense.

'You have a daughter, don't you?' He looks at me with genuineness and empathy.

'Yes. One daughter, Grace,' I reply, not sure what he's getting at. I feel a well of emotion surging inside me. I bury my face into the glass of Scotch and push it down with the burning sensation of its malt.

'We need to make plans Simon, move your daughter and wife.'

'Ex-wife,' I snap.

'Oh yes,' he says, unruffled by anything.

That's what I like about him, he takes everything straight on, no pretence, no flirting around the subject. I want to speak, yet I know his mind is in full gear. I've put my trust in him. I'm starting to feel I might actually live. Death and the prospect of death had in some way forced an acceptance upon me. *Where's Pearl?* X-rays my stomach, leaving an anxious feeling inside me. The way my stomach goes when I reach for my wallet and it's missing. The moments of frantic panic when hundreds of fears and scenarios, rush to my thoughts. I shrug it off and think what will be will be. Maybe it's just the Scotch. Maybe in the morning the depressive thoughts will be back. Maybe I will hate myself for leaving Pearl in the hospital. I had no option.

'Tomorrow I will send one of my best men to your ex-wife's home. Jot down the address, Simon. I will tempt her with a policy and say it is for Grace.'

'They're not at home. I told them to move for Grace's safety. They're at a caravan of a friend of mine on the Downpatrick Road just outside Killyleagh,' I explain. Quickly, I jot down the address and explain my concern for Grace's safety. Pauline could always be relied upon to protect Grace, despite our differences and the upheaval to her own life. But she knew what had happened to Big Paul. Even when he died he was easing life for me.

'Your daughter and ex-wife will be on English soil tomorrow evening, I promise you that. No one will suspect a thing.' Philip sits back, contentedly puffing upon his pipe. I drain my glass with an internal promise to kill if they harm Grace.

The Scotch accompanied me to bed. My mind went like a carousel and around 3.00am it ran out of steam. The noises of a strange house made me jump from time to time. It had been Philip up ready to go to Heathrow.

The water on my face eases the sleep and tiredness from my eyes. I make my way downstairs ready for Mandy's arrival. The smell of breakfast cooking greets my hungry stomach.

'Go into the drawing room Mandy,' Philip says, persuasively. 'Mum will bring breakfast through. She stops in the doorframe.

'Did the old dyke have a pleasant flight?' I inquire casually. Philip chuckles behind her. It's great to see Mandy Drummond lost for words. She turns and looks at her father. The realisation of the personal problem is making sense to Mandy.

'You rotters,' she smiles. 'What on earth are you doing here, Rogers?'

'Ach ...Mandy, just thought I'd drop in.' I rise from the chair and fling my arms around her. She's delighted to see me and has suddenly realised that I might have noticed that.

'You didn't call, Rogers,' she scolds, pushing me away. Good old Mandy.

'I'll leave you two to chat and fetch the breakfast,' Philip smiles, closing the door.

Mandy slumps down in her father's chair gob-smacked. I relay all the details of the Jersey saga. She knew as much as I did about the Andrews Corporation and their dealings. Mandy fills me in on the return of Barnsey and how he had visited Rory. 'Rory has been troubled,' Mandy says. I explain about the phone call from

Jersey, following my escape from the hospital. It fits Mandy's jigsaw together. She is confident nothing had come through on the Jersey incident. Mandy cuts her sausage as if it's Barnsey's throat. She always hated him. I think the feeling was mutual.

Philip pops his head around the drawing room door to assure me Grace and my ex-wife are being prepared for a quick trip to London. One of his men is in the air for Belfast at this very moment. Mandy looks at both of us.

'Grace and Pauline are being moved out, over here...your dad,' I say gently, waiting for the onslaught.

'How nice for you, Rogers. Perhaps you will rekindle the flame.'

'Ach ...Mandy.'

'Mandy nothing, Rogers. It will be nice to see Grace, forgetting the fact that I do not like children, of course.'

It's one of those days like Christmas Eve as a child. Just a matter of killing time until the time comes. I can't wait to see Grace. Even seeing Pauline appears worth it. All of us contemplate the risk of me surfacing in Richmond and the general consensus leads to an *okay*. I need clothes.

'I am glad to see you, Rogers. I am glad you came here. You knew my father would help. Let's shop.' Mandy's gentle touch on my cheek almost floors me. 'Come on, Rogers ...let's shop.' She looks stunning in her violet vest and white shorts. 'You'll find it much warmer here, Rogers ...better class of people, too,' she jests, knowing I'm shocked. If I didn't know her better, know she was a lesbian, I'd take it as flirting. She either twists her cheeks or frowns, as I try on many trousers, jeans and shorts. She picks my shirts, all bright colours, some with coloured hoops. Shirts I would have shied away from. She is boss.

'You are a big boy, Rogers,' she shouts across the Gents department, holding up underpants. She has a dozen pairs in her hand before I can protest. Mandy curses a sports bag free from the others on display. I dread to think of the bill. She reminds me of a bull in a china shop.

'Daddy's,' she explains, reaching the credit card to the cashier. 'Right Rogers, let's get drunk. If I've to meet your wife I will need to be drunk ...and so will you, come to think of it.'

I grab the grip and avoid the stare from the cashier. Mandy is already at the door, men glancing at her buttocks. The street is busy. The sunshine seems to have brought many people out to amble and shop.

'Down by the Thames will be fine. Oh ...Rogers, I'll get some drink.' Mandy disappears and I'm exhausted by her hyper mood.

    She slugs down a few beers in quick succession. It's going to be one of those times. She rarely drinks, yet when she does all hell breaks loose. The boats pass, people relax in the soothing heat. And, at this moment I feel as if normality has returned to my life. Had it all been a dream?

'Why, Rogers, you will be able to get remarried,' Mandy says sarcastically, already rouging up with the beer. I ignore the comment and toss a pebble into the water.

    Mandy refuses to walk and I carry her towards the house. 'Oh Rogers,' is the limit of her spoken word. The strange flirting behaviour is so out of character for her. 'One daughter,' I announce, rolling my eyes. Violet smiles.

'Hello mother. We are home. Rogers, let go of me.'

I drop the new grip full of clothes and reshuffle my hold on Mandy. I take her upstairs much to her disapproval.

'Get some sleep,' I say, dropping her gently onto the bed. She's entering her *piss off* stage and I know it's time to leave.

    Philip is in full flight when I return, charting things out from my basic diagram on the paper towel. He looks up from his half moons.

'Starting to make sense. Sit down. I heard Mandy arrive,' he adds, heartily. 'I have contacted some colleagues. My contacts need passport photos of you and whoever is travelling. You are going to my villa in Portugal. Pick a name ...one that is familiar to you. I want you to start using that name from now on. Call yourself it all day,' he finishes.

    I watch him and listen as Philip reels off the wisdom of his financial brain and I have the chance to become Mark Robbins.

'I am Mulholland's biggest fan, Simon. His work is sheer brilliance. Simple and brilliant. The Andrews Corporation I believe was set up to attract interest, divert attention away from Mulholland and the major money. Let me explain,' Philip says excitedly. 'Most of the policies were long term. A minimum of ten years. That gave the Corporation time to build up funds. Meanwhile, Mulholland and his cronies in Spain were grossing huge amounts of capital. They could invest this anywhere, make a quick profit and no one knew. The policyholders would not have known. They received a balance sheet each year that added up. All appeared normal. Mulholland would have been most particular to do so. Any discrepancy at this stage could have been the end of the master plan.'

'So everything happened except for the money being invested. The figures added up, yet in reality the money was in Mulholland's bank account?' I check.

'Basically, Simon. I expect you have policies or investments of your own. Well, the statement that arrives each year does not mean much. There are figures on it and expected sums. In reality most policyholders wouldn't have a clue how much they have accumulated or lost from this statement. It is so simple it's perfect. And, believe me, policyholders are too proud to have the figures interpreted. We all want to appear astute, Simon.' Philip smiles, satisfied with his explanation.

He's right. I get a letter each year about my own savings plan. It's all a load of crap to me. I just remember the guy that sold it to me, saying it would be worth £50,000 in twenty years or whatever 50 grand would be equal to then.

'So I was right?'

'Spot on, Simon. Let us say, for example, you have an account at the building society. Each week you invest £100. The cashier totals each credit and debit made and you have the balance. You know exactly how much you have. However, with the Andrews Corporation and Mulholland's kind of investment all you have is a letter and figures usually in units.'

'So the Andrews Corporation was a confidence trick? It was selling dodgy savings plans, like the way we exposed it in the first story?'

'Yes, Simon. You were spot on. Mulholland knew that part would come to light. In fact he was delighted, I believe, you exposed the case. I also believe he knew you would not rest with the simple fact of exposure. He kept throwing lures in your direction,' Philip adds, pushing his pen firmly into the notepad in front of him.

'In some befuddled sense I believe Mulholland was planning the downfall of the police and Loyalist factions in Ireland. You could call him a financial terrorist,' Philip chuckles.

I sit back and ferment over the logic of this statement. It seemed far-fetched, however, I had tugged at the idea of this several times. I light a Marlboro and little pieces come and go.

'Let me get this straight,' I say. 'You think Mulholland suckered the police and loyalists into handing over large sums of money and for argument's sake just threw it away?'

'Yes.'

'Jesus. What about the bomb? His parents?' I say, catching on to the logic of my own words. I feel as if the world has been lifted off my shoulders. 'Yes the bomb,' I say excitedly. Philip sits back and smirks. 'The police and Loyalists knew about the bomb. Meanwhile, Mulholland gains more respect and the police and Loyalists pour more money into his hair-brained scheme. They blackmail Mulholland while he promises to make them very rich. It's brilliant.'

'Exactly. Mulholland's father must have become suspicious or noticed some irregularities in the figures ...'

'So he was murdered, just as we had suspected?'

'Ahhh ...everyone misread Mulholland. The IRA would also become suspicious. He was fanatical about a cause and perhaps love ...the girl Patterson,' Philip adds, excitedly. 'They all took it for granted he was on their side.'

'So Mulholland was a Republican?' I laugh at the brilliance of his simple plan. It is as clear as day.

  I have a mental picture of the Loyalists and police coming to Mulholland with sacks of money, shaking hands while he sells them a get rich plan. Everyone was happy. They thought their money was making more money when in fact Mulholland probably burned the stuff or gave it away. 'Bloody perfect.'

'It was perfect, Simon.'

'Bloody right it was. What sort of a person would throw away money or cross these people?'

'You would if you were a tad crazy or a genius,' Philip says, smiling at the sheer simplicity of Mulholland's plan.

'Yeah, mad. Mad at having your parents killed and mad at having your girl stolen a la Tommy Johnston. Jesus.'

'I told you Mulholland was a genius and a dedicated genius. I had some inquiries made concerning Mulholland's financial status. Are you ready for this? He is entirely penniless. Broke. A gentleman of straw.'

'Broke? ...He's a millionaire,' I gasp.

'No ...penniless.'

'That's impossible. He's one of the richest men in Ireland.'

'He used to be or his family were. I surmise he used his personal fortune to mastermind the downfall of the police and loyalists in Ulster. Let me explain. Say a policyholder became suspicious, well, Mulholland refunded their money with a large bonus I suspect. All went well until he wanted it to be exposed. He most likely did the same with the Loyalists and the police ...perhaps inventing a policy that would give them a quick dividend. Perhaps he trebled their money in six months for example. It was simply a lure to gain confidence. Good God, if the returns were so good only a fool would not invest as much as possible,' Philip chuckles. 'I also believe he will have informed the IRA and the other Nationalist outfits of his scheme. You cannot fight a war without money, Simon. In fact they may have been involved, too. However, I think it would only be as another lure. Mulholland's financial mind foresaw no real peace in Ireland until the money was removed from the present power holders. That was his real genius. In short, until all the politicians and other leaders were penniless and forced to talk, they would resist change. They controlled the jobs and their voters had jobs ...most of them. Simple economics.'

'But sure the British Government would have bailed out the police and poured money in?'

'No. Not if all this came to the surface. The police are already under considerable suspicion of collusion with the Loyalists. This would be the icing on the cake. Besides that, Northern Ireland is such a drain on resources many MP's would gladly see it slip off. There are too many hot political issues where money needs to be used ...take the hospitals issue. What would the Americans have said finding out the truth about this? Old Bill Clinton and the others would have laughed their legs off. After all, we are trying to gain our respect following the Barings Banks swindle. We would look like fools. It short, Simon, I believe a political settlement will be reached to cover up the whole question. Perhaps the RUC will be put to sleep and a new police force formed. There will be many sweets used to hide the truth. Mulholland is a bloody genius,' Philip laughs.

'Yeah ...but I know the truth. I know what really happened and I know I will not have a hope in hell of living free,' I add, feeling the truth hit home.

'Yes ...there is that of course. But you do like a challenge,' Philip smirks.

'If Mulholland swindled everyone, people will want answers,' I say.

'Yes ...they'll want answers. However, they also want peace. Peace will be thrown to them as a carrot.'

'But what about the Nationalists? If they know they will expose it.'

'Maybe. Maybe not. If they foresee a lasting settlement then it won't come to light,' Philip states, leaning back once more.

'Can you see the Prods accepting that?'

'No ...but then again the leaders of the Protestant population will be given huge incentives to ensure that they do. Don't forget they may have lost considerable sums of money through Mulholland. I suspect many supposedly rich persons are sitting pretty scared and worried right now. They will jump at anything to hide their secret and maintain their lifestyle. It's all politics, Simon. And it also rests, I'm afraid, on you being found and silenced. Silenced for good. It's sheer brilliance. So simple that most people would overlook it.'

It sounds so simple. It's only my life we're talking about.

'Mulholland more or less worked on the principle of the old saying, if you are known as an early riser you can lie in bed all day. It never crossed my mind that he might be skint. The Mulhollands were renowned as rich,' I say, half laughing.

'Oh ...in the City we come across this quite often. The days of a gentleman's word or standing have long since disappeared. However, that brings me to the love element ...the passion,' Philip baits. 'Dear old Trevor Mulholland had passion ...and plenty of it. His passion was rejected. Yet he found a way not to be rejected. He kept close to this Susan Patterson. You know better than most how these things work ...the mysteries of the mind.' Philip stops and begins playing with his pipe, pushing tobacco to his liking. I couldn't be bothered smoking a pipe.

'Now,' he slaps the desk, 'pick a journalist you can trust, the first name that comes to mind and use him, don't go beyond the first choice,' he warns.

My mind immediately chose Paul. Then it registered with a large lump in my stomach. But it had to be someone outside Ireland. Matt Brown of *The Washington Flyer* is the one. Others came and went, but it has to be Matt Brown. Philip gives me time and sees I've made my choice.

'Your choice will be your partner in all of this. I'll arrange to have him meet you once you are out of the country. Start making the bones of your case, anything you need, just ask.'

I think for a moment and nothing pops to mind. Too much has happened for instant logic to pop up immediately. 'When do we move to Portugal?' I ask, lost for a moment.

'Once everything is arranged with your passports ...get the photos as soon as possible Simon. I would reckon middle of next week, not much later. Now the property in Ireland ...we need to talk business. I will buy the property from you and open an account for you in a bank in Portugal. It's a mere formality. You own a farm ...how many acres?'

I'm lost for a moment. I think of Tommy Dickson and the land I'd rented him, ten acres. 'All in all I reckon in the region of fifty acres with the house. I've rented some, how will that work out?' I inquire.
'Just change the deeds ...same agreement, no one will know,' he says, confidently. 'I believe news travels quickly in Ireland.'
'Yeah, surprise, surprise.'
'Look Simon, when this settles down I will sell you the farm back for the money I pay you,' he says, softly. I can't believe he's doing this.
'Your daughter will be here soon ...How about the ex-wife? Will I put her up in Richmond? Would that make it easier?'

I can't give an answer. I merely puff out my cheeks. I don't know what her reaction will be. I know Pauline will go along with things in Grace's best interests. I have to grant her that. But her bloody family, it'll leak out. 'We'll see what happens,' I say.
'I used the ploy of a lump sum for Grace, left by her grandmother, insurance,' he shrugs. 'Easier to explain face to face. Should be here in an hour or so. It's hell at Heathrow at this time of evening.'
'Thanks for everything, Philip. I thought long and hard about coming here, bringing this, yet I knew you were the man,' I say, moving towards him. His handshake is genuine and strong.

I leave his office and go into the kitchen. Mandy is awake, looking better with the coffee. She smiles, warmly, drunkenly, and swaying. 'Come Rogers, and try on your new clothes.'
Violet is in the garden, pulling dead blooms from her petunias. Mandy topples her stool and takes me by the hand.
'You must look nice for Grace and number one wife.'

There is no talking to her at times like this. I follow and push her out of the room while I change.
'You've nothing to fear from an old dyke, Rogers.'
'Go and lie down, Mandy.'
She bursts the door open and stands there. Her fist is pointing towards my face.
'Wise up, Mandy.'
'Wise up, Mandy,' she mimics, swaying. 'Wise up. Piss off, Rogers.' I grab her fist and her dilated pupils stagger around my face.
'You are bloody beautiful, Rogers,' she slurs, spitting all over me. I

knew what was coming next. Next her vest would be pulled up and her breasts held up for my inspection. I grab her arm and hold her.
'I know you are beautiful, Mandy. I love you, you don't have anything to prove to me.'
Her head nuzzles into my chest. 'Piss off, Rogers,' she repeats, until it fades beyond a whisper.
I set her down on the bed, like a piece of precious china. Mandy's hair dangles across her face.
    I have a quick wash and wear the shirt with yellow rings and blue stripes she had chosen. I like it.
'They will be here soon,' I say to break her stare.
'Number one wife hates me,' Mandy manages, sadly.
'No, she doesn't.'
'She does. She messed up your life before, Rogers, now she is back to do it again. And ...your latest girlfriend ...or should I say pensioner.'
'That's enough, Mandy,' I interrupt.
'Oh that's right, Rogers, defend and help the aged. So gallant. The minute she appeared you forgot about me.' Her hands rest on her heart. I can't believe this is the Mandy Drummond I know. My world doesn't make sense any more.
'I won't forget about you, Mandy. What do you want from me? I would give the world for you not to be a lesbian ...but you are. You say so. You're not available. What is it with you?'
    She begins to cry. All my thoughts hit the surface and drift into a swirling pool. A dozen years at least and we have never said these things. She probably won't remember in the morning, be back to her normal self, the rough, man-hating lesbian.
'Piss off, Rogers,' she screams again.
'Cheers.'
'Damn you Rogers,' she says throwing a kick at me. I grab her leg and she connects with a hook to my jaw. We scrap like two teenagers on the bed. I grab her arms and pin her down.
'Calm down, Mandy.'
She spits at my face and I grab Mandy's hand before she slaps my face. She grunts like a wild animal and I hold her until she is calm. I let my body relax on top of her and we hug. She's calm now, sobbing in my ear.
'Oh, Rogers, I'm pissed.'
'Get away.'
'They will be here soon, Rogers. I need a drink,' she says, with a

resemblance of her self, bouncing back. I move away and pull her up. Mandy staggers to the mirror and fixes her hair. I stand, watching her pull the ruffle out and press it all back into place.

'I will see you downstairs,' she says softly, lowering her eyes. I collapse onto the bed and wonder what is going to happen next. The whole world has turned itself upside down. It feels like my first day on this planet.

Some chatter develops downstairs. Grace's voice meets with Mandy's. I listen for a moment. It is the most beautiful sound in the world. I make my way to the landing and stare down at Grace and her mother. My eyes flick to Mandy and she catches me looking. Mandy's parents are engaged in a typically English interaction: shaking hands.

Chapter 26

Grace is Grace. Full of bubbles, hugging me and very excited about the flight to Heathrow. 'I was in the pitcock, daddy,' she beams. She gives me a blow by blow account of how the Captain flew the plane. Her eyes dance and she hasn't time to take breath. Philip ushers us into the drawing room and Grace plops herself on my knee. I twiddle my fingers through her blonde hair while her mother watches from the bookcase with suspicious thoughts. Am I being paranoid?
'Grace, did you know that we have a beautiful river in Richmond,' Philip drops in to interrupt her volley. 'The kings and queens of England have travelled along it for centuries.'
'Real kings and queens with crowns and servants? What were they doing on the river? Did they just go out like my dad and me do for a drive, only they went in their boat?' Grace asks, giving us all a glance to see if she is close to the mark.
'That's it, Grace,' Philip smiles.
'Have you seen the kings and queens daddy?'
'No ...but I saw the river.'
'Is it a nice river?'
'The best.'
'Wahoo.'
'Perhaps I could take you to see the river?' Philip says, winking.
'Only if Mandy comes too,' Grace replies.
'It's a deal, Grace. They sell beautiful ice cream at the river also.'
'Wahoo.'
 She was fond of ice cream and 10p mixes. Pauline looks well for an ex-wife: my ex-wife. She appears friendlier than I had

expected her to be and slimmer looking in loose fitting jeans. She's had her hair bobbed, too; bobbed and black.

'What's going on, Simon?' Once more I was explaining things.

'So we have to fit in with your life again,' she interrupts. Good old Pauline is leaking through. She paces around the drawing room, raising her voice.

'You don't have to fit in with my life. You need to move for your own safety and Grace's. If it wasn't for Grace you wouldn't be here,' I snap back. It works. She mellows. Pauline stands with each of her fists pushed into the sides of her waist. 'So that's why Barnsey called round to visit,' she says, reflecting.

'Yeah, I heard he called.' I blurt. 'What did he want?'

'Oh just called to see how I was and played a bit with Grace. I thought you had sent him to spy on me and Tom.'

'Wise up. Did he visit you at the caravan?' I ask.

'No but other officers called to warn me about some robberies.'

'Did they ask your name?'

'Yeah, why?'

'Figures,' I shrug walking across the room.

I pour two Scotches. 'It's Grace they would go for, maybe you ...but definitely Grace.' Pauline takes her drink and all the resentment appears to have gone from her face.

'Why can you not get an ordinary job, Simon? Jesus. ...When we were married you were never at home... and if you were you sat at the bloody computer.'

'Hey ...I don't want to get into all of that crap. Tell it to your new guy.'

'It's not crap. You took us for granted.'

'Us?' I pull myself up short. 'Look... you don't have to stay here. We can put you up in a hotel for a few days. After that you will have to move to the continent. You can't let anyone know where you are, Pauline. Your family or friends. You will have plenty to live on – I'm selling Tullydeen. Once it dies down we'll see, but Grace is in real danger. I need your word on that,' I say, 'with no compromise.'

She nods her approval.

'Is it all to do with Paul's murder?'

'Yes, and Mulholland. I suppose you saw the TV?'

She nods and walks towards the window. 'I will do anything for Grace's welfare and although we're not together any more I wouldn't like to see anything happen to you.'

'Thanks. I owe you, Pauline.'

'No, you don't. We're just parents.'
'Is Barnsey mixed up in all of this?' Pauline asks.
'Yeah,' I say. She spins around.
'He was casing you out, just in case.' She is visibly shaking, thinking that someone would want to harm her daughter or arrive in false pretences, especially, someone she had known for many years. A look of determination stiffens her body, following the shock and she looks the way she used to look when she'd made up her mind about things.
'I'll do what you think is best for Grace,' Pauline assures me.
Someone is trudging around in the hallway. The door knocks and Mandy pops her head around the jam. 'Sorry Rogers, flick on the telly, you had better see the latest, quickly,' she says.
'Are you not with Grace?'
'Was. ...Daddy and Grace are feeding the birds. It'll be on *Ceefax*, quickly,' Mandy says. She grabs the remote control and punches up teletext.
'What's up, Mandy?'
'Pearl and Susan Patterson's bodies have been found at Tullydeen, along with the body of Tommy Johnston. A search is under way for you,' Mandy states slowly, trying to soften the blow. 'You are the suspected murderer.'

    I stagger backward and slump into the chair. '*What*?' I gasp, reading the lines of luminous print. I rant silently as the facts resound off my brain. 'Armed and dangerous,' I shout, reading the last paragraph. I forget about everyone in the room. My mind has taken off, faster than Concorde. Jesus ...Pearl. Oh my God. My hands grab tightly at the roots of my hair and I want to pull it all out. They must've shot Pearl in Jersey and transported her body with Johnston's and Susan's. They couldn't take the chance of being recognised anywhere. I think of our last meeting outside the hospital and the way Pearl talked about both of us not making it. Resignation was in her voice I reckon, using hindsight. I can't cry. I'm numb, or like numb, except that I can feel things touching my limbs.
'Rogers, here ...drink this.' Mandy pours the glassful of Scotch into my mouth and it burns like hell.
'Go get Grace. Get her off the street,' I manage, midst the burning.
'Who are Pearl and Susan Patterson, Simon?' Pauline is kneeling at my knee.
'Mother and daughter,' I reply, looking at her puzzled face.

'They're bound to come looking for Grace. Thank God youse got away.'

'Jesus, Simon. What's behind this?' Pauline asks.

'Barnsey said civil war. But, I would say bankruptcy, Pauline. Mulholland has broken the bank. They have to kill me because I know. When I'm out of the way it will be business as usual. I'm going all the way. I've no choice. Now they've turned to the public, the loyal public, to turn me in, armed and dangerous,' I say in disbelief.

Pauline sits at my feet, cross-legged. For a moment I almost touch her shoulders the way we used to sit and watch television. *Sky News* carries the breaking story. I could do with the comfort. Maybe that's why she sat there. Tullydeen flashes up on the screen. Pauline rushes forward and pushes a video into the recorder and it clinks to life. The yard of my home is alive with police cars and police tape and people walking around. Barnsey is there. The fingerprint cops, too. Three men carry a coffin out of the house and place it in the back of a police van. The reporter suggests that a row had developed. Then, I had shot Johnston, Pearl and Susan Patterson. I stare in disbelief. Pauline looks at me and cuts her glance back to the TV. They're linking me to terrorist organisations.

Barnsey stands straight faced and serious, giving the general public the facts behind the triple murders at my home. It is imperative the police catch me and under no circumstances am I to be approached, he tells the camera. Stalwart citizens everywhere are to keep a lookout for me, the armed and dangerous gunman. Soon they will be phoning in sightings of me.

'I need to get in touch with Matt Brown. He'll know about it.'

'Simon, you better be careful,' Pauline states, pushing herself onto her feet.

'They've played this well. The story is a certified gluer because I'm a journalist. They've enticed every hack in the world to take a bite at this because it's one of their own. Some will sink me, others will want to support me, but all of them will want to know. They'll run and run, keeping it alive until they catch me,' I explain, downing more Scotch.

Grace bounces in and sits on my knee. Pauline announces time for bed and Grace goes with her mother upstairs. Philip Drummond is in a pensive mood. 'You'll have to move, not Portugal. However I have a place, close to here,' he says, turning to smile at me. 'They are going to town on you, Simon.'

'I'm finished.'
'Nonsense,' he quips back. 'Fix a few Scotches.'
'We can't sell the place ...I've no money,' I say.
'Forget about that Simon. We've plans to make. Have you chosen whom you will trust in your profession?'
I nod.
'Good, give me his number. We need to contact him and arrange a meeting. I'll have you out of Richmond in an hour. Someone may have noticed you, we can't take a chance,' Philip says, flicking through a diary. 'There's a good chance they will call here, once they find out Mandy is not in Ireland,' he adds.
'Will I get Grace ready?' I ask.
'I'll do it,' Mandy says.

    Violet hugs us and wishes us well. I stare at the lights of cars and shops and people making their way home, some staggering, others clinging tightly to each other. I don't know where we're going and right now I don't feel like asking. We take the M25 and the shock of Pearl's murder is starting to bite at me. I'm going to murder it with a bottle of Scotch.

'Welcome to Chertsey,' Philip says. 'This is the home of Mandy's old nanny. She's a widow now, well in her seventies and going strong. I think she'll live forever. I would trust her with my life,' Philip concludes.
We arrive in a street of semi's. It's well past midnight and the residents are slumbering. Only the planes appear to be awake, gliding overhead.
'Wait here,' he says, leaving the car. His knock is quickly answered and a lady with grey hair smiles at him. A thin lady, in a red dressing gown. They talk for a moment and he returns giving us a quick wave to leave the car. I offer to help with the bags, but he wants me into the house with Grace and Pauline. 'This is Aunt Jean,' he announces, following us up. Her face is full of life and humour. Aunt Jean shows Pauline to the stairs with Grace. Her love of children is evident. Philip leads the way to the kitchen. Aunt Jean, arrives a few moments later.
'You're very welcome here,' Aunt Jean says in her cockney accent. 'Make yourself at home.'
'Aunt Jean will get everything for you. You must stay in the house,' Philip stresses. Philip introduces Pauline and puts an emphasis on her being my wife. Not ex-wife: just wife. Pauline doesn't look up.

'Is the little one asleep?' Aunt Jean inquires.
'Yes,' Pauline smiles briefly.
'Ah ...bless her.'

Arthritis appears to have annoyed her joints, yet not her soul. Aunt Jean chuckles loudly and appears delighted to have company. A plate of biscuits arrives on the dining room table. A breakfast bar separates us from the open plan kitchen. The cupboards are brown. The fridge is covered with magnets. Grace will love those. A picture of her late husband sits proudly opposite me, in a teak dresser midst the china and numerous plates.

Philip pokes fun at Jean and she enjoys every moment. She gives as good as she gets. 'This lady means the world to me,' he says. 'I explained your situation to Aunt Jean ...you're safe here.'
'I saw you on television,' she says, giving me a stern look. 'Looks like a bad bugger,' she says, with a shrill of a laugh. She takes my hand and looks directly into my eyes: she looking at my soul. 'No one will get past Aunt Jean. No one.'
I feel a lump in my throat. People have been good to me. I still can't believe what's happened, yet I know good people are on my side. I think of the coffins appearing from the door in Tullydeen and I wonder which one was Pearl's. I think about it until my stomach gets eaten by lemons and then I have to let it go. I give Philip a few telephone numbers where Matt Brown can be contacted.
'I'll see what I can do. Self-preservation must lead the way, Simon. Do what you have to, to stay alive,' he says, leaving me and closing the door.

Aunt Jean shows us to our bedroom. It has a double bed with mirrored robes opposite it. She points to the direction of the bathroom and reaches Pauline fresh towels from the hot press. 'Goodnight, make yourselves at home,' she whispers once more and leaves us be.

'I'll take the floor,' I say, putting the bags on a chair. I catch sight of myself in the mirrored robes and I'm a sorry looking sight. My face looks drawn and murky.
'I'll check on Grace,' Pauline says. I kick off my trainers and grab a pillow from the bed and lie down on the floor, cuddling the Scotch. Pauline returns and fumbles around in her holdall. 'Grace's fast asleep,' she says.
'Simon don't be so stupid, sleep in the bed. You need a good night's rest. It's not as if we've never slept together,' she says standing in

front of me. Pauline goes to the bathroom and returns minus her jeans, which are dangling over her arm. She fumbles under her T-shirt and removes her bra. 'I've forgotten my nightie,' she scolds. Pauline climbs into bed and looks over at me.
'Are you getting in?'
'No. Do you want a swig of this?'
'No.'
'That'll not help.'
'No.'
I offer her a cigarette and she sits upright, smoking.
'Can you believe this?' Pauline smiles.
'No.'
'What are you going to do, Simon?' Pauline's eyes gaze at me the way they used to. She is beautiful and I couldn't help noticing her thighs when she returned from the bathroom.
'Fact's stranger than fiction,' I reply, swallowing another large mouthful of Scotch.

Chapter 27

My pores are crying. The alcohol is seeping through my skin.
'You're going to kill yourself,' she states, trying to take the bottle. I look at her and she decides against it. 'Ex-wives,' I mutter.
The lovely glow of booze wanders with me downstairs. I could drink Ireland dry and still be able to walk at this moment. The morning news is giving its all to slander my character to a nation which prides itself on knowing the difference between right and wrong. Before long, I feel everybody will find me guilty without a word in my defence. I imagine the headlines on the papers, *Wanted*, with my picture underneath. The front door opens and I tense up.

'Morning, it's lovely out. Got you papers. I'll start on breakfast,' Aunt Jean smiles. Have you been at my Scotch, you bugger? Bloody Irish for ya,' she laughs.
'Jesus ...if I'd known you have Scotch ...I'd have kept mine for after breakfast,' I bounce back. She hits me a slap and I salute her with another mouthful.
   Grace is still fast asleep, clutching Cornpop. The excitement of yesterday taking its toll. The smell and crackle of bacon stimulates my stomach.
'Need any help?'
'No Aunt Jean's at the controls,' she says and lets out a shriek of infectious laughter. I pick up the papers and stare at my own image, then my home, my door, with three bodies being removed from the kitchen. 'Take a cuppa up for your wife.'
   I return upstairs with the coffee and knock on the door. The wet feet from the bathroom tell me Pauline has finished showering.

She hasn't changed. Why she doesn't dry herself in the bathroom I'll never know. She always dries off in the bedroom. Seems to be a legacy of a large family, all trying to get out in the morning.

'Come in,' she says. I push the door open.

'Coffee,' I announce, reaching the cup.

'Thanks, Simon.' I throw the papers down on the bed and she looks at the front page and then to me. She takes a sip of her coffee and uses my towel to dry her hair. Bloody typical.

'Breakfast will be ready in a moment.' She's deep in thought, reading.

Grace sleeps through breakfast and Aunt Jean dampened any attempt we made to waken her. 'Aunt Jean's in charge,' she says with her infamous laugh. Philip phones to say he has arranged a meeting with Matt Brown. It would be around midnight he reckoned before Matt Brown and I met. He was flying in from New York.

Grace and Aunt Jean played Tiddlywinks and a host of other games. It was safe to go into the garden up to a point, Jean pointed out. Her neighbours could not see us if we stayed on the patio. I read the papers and drank Scotch and coffee. Jean told us of how she had worked for Philip and Violet Drummond for over forty years. The antics of Mandy growing up I felt would come in useful if I ever needed to get my own back at a later stage. Mandy would hate me knowing half the stuff Aunt Jean had told us.

Grace watched Concorde take off, roaring across the sky. Pauline was just Pauline and the day ambled in slowly. It was like a family Sunday. It was my family of a few years back. Everything's strange. It's as if nothing had happened. All the Andrews stuff, Barnsey, even Pearl. Then ...the Scotch has helped. Helped with Pauline's unfaithfulness, Big Paul and Pearl's deaths and my escape from Jersey.

Philip arranged to pick me up at 9.30pm to go to the meeting place. Pauline loses her patience, watching me labour with the pins in another new shirt.

'Give me that,' she grunts, coaxing the pins out of a thick navy polo shirt.

'Don't forget about Grace and *Jack and the Beanstalk*.'

'Forget? Think I'd be allowed to?' I laugh.

Pauline walks with me to the door of Grace's new bedroom. I read *Jack and the Beanstalk* for the umpteenth time and I try to skip a bit. Grace looks at me and points to the page.

'You missed a bit.'

'Get away,' I say, pulling a funny face. I reread the whole book and Grace slips off into her dreams.

Pauline and I go downstairs, hearing Philip arrive.

'All is ready, Simon,' he says, in his usual positive tone. He's dressed like a financier, in a black pinstriped suit.

'Be careful,' Pauline says, giving me a hug. 'Give my regards to Matt when you see him.'

I stroll towards the Jaguar and everything goes black. I struggle to keep my eyes open, focusing on the feet around me, but the darkness is reeling me in. I know the warm feeling is blood. There's no pain, just a big numbness. Pauline tugs at me, screaming. The darkness wins.

Chapter 28

I felt another human being holding my hand. I thought it was Pearl, then, I realised she was dead. It was Pauline. My body was on the journey back and my head hurt like hell. My neck was all twisted and sore. I lay still for a moment and made a check: toes were there, arms too.
'He's awake,' Pauline shouts. A man in a black suit peers down at me. He looks like a surgeon, but this doesn't seem to be a hospital. The man moves to my right side just above my appendix scar. It's bloody sore.
'Shot?' I ask. Where's Grace? Philip?'
'Grace slept through everything. Philip's outside having a smoke with her,' Pauline adds.
'Is Grace smoking?' I smile. She reflects my gesture.
'Everything appears to be fine. The scar tissue from your previous insertion helped to deflect and hold the bullet. I made the extraction. Came from a Browning,' he smiles. 'You were lucky. Throw away the fags. I will visit in a few days and in the meantime you must rest. Your wife has all the details,' he says, walking off.
'Thanks Doc,' I say, but he doesn't turn. Jesus my neck hurts.
'Be careful, Simon, you were shot on your ear too,' Pauline explains.
'That figures. Where the hell am I?'
She smiles. 'An air raid shelter.'
'A what?'
  Pauline relates the tale of our miraculous escape from the single gunman on a motorbike. He had pulled up at the gate of Aunt Jean's house and shot me twice before speeding off. Pauline

reckoned; the gunman reckoned I was dead. Philip ran at the bike and he shot at him, but missed. Luckily Grace had been asleep in the house. 'You must have been recognised in Richmond for them to know where you were. Simon this is scary,' she adds.

'Wasn't the Provos, then, or else I'd be dead. What's happening? They must've followed me here.'

'We don't think so. You've been here for two days and you're still alive,' Pauline informs me. 'You're underground, Simon …about 12 feet underground. It's class here,' she says. 'Grace just loves it …she's been sleeping in a hammock and reading you stories.'

I smile and try to comprehend everything that has happened in my unconscious absence. I summon the courage to move my hand towards my pelvis and I can feel the stitches and the swelling. Appendix two, I think. What's a bit of stiffness compared to death, and I'm sure there's something ironic about being underground, buried alive, instead of dead like most of the people that are important to me.

'Dad, you're up. Dad, this is an air raid shelter and the planes dropped bombs on England hundreds of years ago when Philip was a boy.'

'Not that many hundred, Grace,' he intervenes smiling. She affords him a smile and continues with her tale. Grace offers to read me a story and we hug. Her little fingers feel so soft as she dabs at my left ear. Her touch is therapeutic. It seems to take the heat out of the graze wound. She looks at me and then goes with Pauline to the far end of the building. From where I am the place looks like a normal bedroom except for the absence of windows.

Philip tells me that we are in an old bungalow that had been built in a twelve foot hole, dug out specifically, reinforced and then covered over again to act as a bomb shelter during the second world war. One of his old, now deceased, school friends had lived here, deep in the heart of Cheshire. 'Perhaps we'll get a few laps at Oulton Park,' he jests. Philip informs me he purchased it as a means of deflecting tax and so forth. The sale, he assures me, could not be traced to him. 'Does Mandy know we are here?' I ask. He nods and mentions the photos she had taken and their imminent readiness for our documentation.

Violet is holding the fort in Surrey. She has had a visit from the police, likewise Rory and Mandy. However Philip's brief is that he is on holiday for several weeks.

I smoke my last Marlboro on my first excursion from the shelter. I've got the bit between my teeth. Grace took me into a small plantation of trees that she called her forest. She really was having an adventure here. I breathed in the fresh air and tried to think of life on an hourly basis. Grace was delighted and had nagged at me for smoking. I figured it was maybe a sort of inborn trait with women. So far stopping was easy. Perhaps I was ready. Smoking had been causing me hassle of late. Too much coughing and time was saying *wise up Simon*. I found it hard to concentrate, but that soon faded after a few days.

Grace held my hand when I had my stitches removed. The wound was doing nicely, the surgeon with no name said. After he left, Philip appeared with the new passports and documentation. Here I was as Mark Robbins. Grace was Grace, except that her surname was Matthews like her mother. I had decided Grace and Pauline could go to Portugal. I would be going back to Ireland once I had talked to Matt Brown.

Philip had been in contact with him several times to arrange a meeting, but every time Matt had failed to show. But, dark suited individuals had not. Philip and I applauded Matt's professionalism. Matt was used to being bugged and followed. It was an occupational hazard to him. We had talked about this over a bottle of Old Comber many times. Matt had given Philip a weird message that made no sense to him, yet perfect sense to me. It was an address, a secure address that we could send items to.

I read all the papers and saw that the hunt for me was being stepped up. A possible sighting of me had been reported in Dublin and another south of the city in the foothills of the Wicklow Mountains. Matt had instigated them.

Pearl and Susan Patterson were buried at the little Presbyterian Church in Drumfiddy. I stared at the pictures of the funeral and tried to keep it at a distance. Here I was sitting, useless, with two bullets that did just a little damage. I tried to block it all out. I had to, until this was over, if I survived. Johnston was buried the following day in Antrim. He was not buried as a Loyalist hero. A mere handful of family seemed to attend the low-key funeral.

Will you put flowers on my grave? Pearl had asked. Grace comes over to sit on my knee and I just want to hold her forever and ever. She examines my ear and I smile.
'I love you, darling,' I say.

'I love you too, Dad. So does Cornpop,' she says with a shrug. I pull her close and rest my face in her hair. It smells of lavender.
'Are you looking forward to going to your new house?'
'Yeah it'll be cool,' she replies.
'Philip says it's very hot and they talk in Portuguese and there's funny money.'
'Oh, is that so.'
'And there's a beach and a pool at the house. Cornpop will learn to swim. Is mummy your wife again?' Grace asks, turning to look innocently at me.
'Em, no. No. We're just your parents …that's all.'
'Pity,' she says jumping off my knee, 'her and Tom weren't getting on.'
'Oh.'

If nothing else came from this escapade, then at least Pauline and I had stopped shouting at one another. At nights we had talked about life. Philip had disappeared back to the house several hundred yards away. Grace enjoyed us being together and made no secret of the fact. She also received theatrical daggers when she defamed Tom and his ways. It was like water off a duck's back to Grace. Pauline cooked all the meals and she is a super cook. She had always been a super cook. It was nice to be pampered and I could have been excused for thinking she was making a special effort. I smiled to myself. If Pauline knew what Grace had told me about her and good old Tom, she'd have gone ballistic.

Matt Brown kept in contact with us via the weird messages. I taught Philip the code we used, just in case something happened to me. Basically any code needs to be simple. Ours was based around old Bob Dylan songs with different parts of lyrics meaning different things. It was like a game. Hugh McWhinney, the butcher in Comber, and I had played the game for years. He might say *his best friend Frankie said he ain't dead he's just asleep*, then I would reply *let us not talk falsely now the hour is getting late*. But the secret was to decipher the meaning from that. Simple and very efficient, not many people could order sausages or the eye of silverside like that. We got some strange looks though, when his shop was full.

Twice Philip had had visits from the police to the house in Cheshire. Violet had given them the address because things were getting too suspicious with his longer absence from Surrey. It had been routine questions. Had he seen me? Had I made contact? Had I this? Had I that? Philip played the upright citizen. He lied.

It was dangerous for us to venture out. The longer we were here the more comfortable we were getting with our surroundings. That was always a good time for an attack – the element of surprise at its best. I was paranoid, but paranoid was better than dead. It happened at Aunt Jean's house. There had been no sign of being spotted and suddenly the numbness of the bullet.

Philip arrives early and appears very excited. He has a fax in his hand from Mandy. It is the lead story in *The Irish Scribe* about police corruption. It names Barnsey. 'Jesus,' I sigh, turning to Philip. 'Rory's going to town on this.'
'Perfect. It's perfect Simon. They will have to suspend him to conduct an inquiry.'
'I wouldn't be so sure,' I say.
Pauline takes the story and reads it over.
'It'll help,' she reckons. 'But Rory's putting his neck on the line literally.'
I take the fax and reread it. Rory had broken with tradition and put the Editorial, his Editorial, on the front page. He had backed up his claims with extracts from transcribed tape recordings of several meetings he had held with Barnsey. 'I'm proud of you wee man,' I mutter to myself. I choke with emotion.
'Right Philip we need mobiles. Prepay ones, no traces. Plus these two need to go.'
'Excuse me,' Pauline cuts in, hands on hips, 'these two? You too, Simon.'
'No, you would be better going yourself with Grace. I'm a give away.'
'Simon's right,' Philip quips in.
'Yeah he's always bloody right,' Pauline slams, grabbing Grace and going towards the kitchen.
Philip makes eyes and rocks on his heels, the way Big Paul used to do. 'Get the mobiles. They can go okay?' I ask.
'Don't foresee a problem,' he says, walking off. 'I'll book their flights.'
'Cheers.'

The kitchen in our underground bungalow is compact, yet functional. Pauline is making tea. She always makes tea when she's angry. One of the kitchen walls is lined with brown cupboards. The rest of the place is painted orange that was probably fashionable in the seventies. The entire place is like a time warp from a bygone era. Little photographs hang on the walls showing farmers that made hay while the sun shone. I would say post war. Big old chairs are all over the place, big brown chairs. The entire place has a red, tiled floor with mats. Pauline bounces the teapot down on the table and moves over to the yellowish dresser for some cups.

'Want any?' she mumbles.

'No, aye okay.'

'Make up your mind.'

She pours, and I watch her jeans. Pauline always looked stunning in jeans. It takes me back years to the times we made love, and the beautiful contours of her body. I can almost feel her skin.

'Do you want anything to eat?'

'Em no. No.'

She sits opposite me and cuddles her cup.

'Where's Grace?'

'Getting ready,' she says, rolling her eyes.

'Look Pauline you stand a better chance. With me about it would be curtains.'

She nods and reaches for my hand. I peck her on the lips and her tongue reaches for mine. Suddenly she pulls back and wipes her mouth. She walks to the tiny sink and looks at the wall. 'Will you come to Portugal?' she asks.

'Hopefully I won't have to.'

'Why?'

'Well if this opens up, well and good,' I begin. 'No matter what happens I'm going back to Belfast to create havoc, and to hell with the consequences. If I'm going down, they're going down, Pauline.'

'What about Grace and me? Oh so it's fit in with your life again. Grace has no dad because he's a dead hero. Is that it? Wise up Simon.'

The silence is just that. I think over my options. Probably, Pauline is doing the same. I never wanted to be a hero. I never thought any cause was important enough to die for. But now I have no choice. I can't choose to live a quiet life. It's impossible with a nation wide search going on for me. Pauline storms past me.

'Where are you going?'

'Bloody fresh air.'

I sip my tea and listen to her thumping about. She's the most clod-footed person I've ever known. There she is clip-clopping up the ladder to the surface.

'Shit Simon,' she shouts.
I sprint to the ladder, catching my scar off guard while it protests and sends little daggers to my brain. Pauline drops the hatch and almost misses her footing.
'Bloody police with dogs and stuff over at the house.'
'Is Philip there?'
'Don't know.'
'Is the hatch covered?'
'Yes.'
I run into Grace's new bedroom. She's about to speak and I place my finger over my mouth. She catches my drift. We had drilled her about being quiet in the event of this happening. Maybe they knew Mandy sent the fax or something. I think as fast as I can. We had not been seen. It's obviously Philip they suspect of involvement.
'If we stay calm we'll be okay,' I say, carrying Grace into the main living area. Pauline grabs her quickly. I'd forgotten that I wasn't supposed to lift anyone or anything.

It's well into the night and still no one has opened our hatch. Nothing sounds wrong up above. Grace has dozed off. She had spent the day colouring in and cutting things out to stick on the walls. Some were cards with glitter that would remind me of her once she had gone to Portugal. Pauline had everything packed and all we could do was wait.

Wait we did, until the trapdoor opened and a little soil and leaves dropped in. I stood with a large kitchen knife behind the ladder and was ready to lunge.
'Did you miss me?' the unmistakable voice utters.
'Philip, Jesus. The place was crawling with cops.'
'Don't I know,' he says, rolling his eyes. 'All gone now. Off to Cyprus I suspect.'
'Cyprus?'
'Indeed. I purchased two tickets for Cyprus from the local travel agent because I had been followed.'
'You old dog,' I smile. 'So they followed you back here and thought they'd caught you red handed?'
'Indeed. Any tea in the pot? Anyway I managed to phone Garcia, Mandy's sister, and she and Amy are going to Cyprus for a few weeks. Mark works in the Gulf,' Philip smiles.

We sip tea and Philip explains about the questioning. He declared his dissatisfaction with police methods and promptly phoned Professor Alex Linley and demanded respect for his privacy. Philip explained how he and Professor Alex had been at college together. Soon the call came through to move out, although Philip believed he would be kept under some sort of surveillance. However, he assures me that getting Pauline and Grace out of the country would be a tad more difficult and was of extreme urgency.

'We're all ready Philip,' Pauline says, bringing what little they had, a small blue grip each. After all they had only packed for an overnight stay in London.

'Now's as good a time as any,' Philip says. 'I shall make arrangements to have you picked up at the other end. I'll phone to make sure the keys will be there for you. Damn pity we didn't get the phones,' he rattles out.

'I have my mobile,' Pauline offers.

Little did she know that I had destroyed the SIM card; I told her the reason it wasn't working was because we were several feet underground. Pauline hates technology and the only reason she had the mobile was because Tom had bought it for her – good old Tom. The mum and Tom are not getting on – good old Tom.

'Buy some at the airport, Philip. '

'Will do.'

'Can I have one, Dad?'

'No. Not until you get a job and stop smoking,' I snarl at Grace, as her face launches millions of creasing giggles.

I kneel down and she grabs my neck and hugs me tightly. I want to savour the smell of my daughter forever and a part of me says, maybe you would be safer here. How do I know? I have to put my trust in something greater than me. It's certainly not the truth. The truth in Belfast earns a bullet. But then what's the truth? It's subjective, loaded with personal bias. What I maybe think is the truth, is another person's lie.

'Dad, you look after Philip,' Grace says, breaking from our embrace.

'I will. Will you look after your mum?'

'Of course.'

'Good.'

'Bye Simon. You take care,' Pauline says, wrapping herself around me. I pull her close and feel her soft chest squeeze into me. Thankfully I had been shot near my pelvis and sex had been out of the question. I had thought about it. Maybe it was safe to think about it because I was unable to perform in my condition. Anyway the days were long locked up underground. She feels the same as

she ever did. Then I think of good old Tom and let her go.
'Stay cool both of you. You'll be fine. Okay Grace Rogers?'
'Who? I'm Grace Matthews,' she smiles.
Philip leads the way to the surface. He waits before waving them up to the open air. It's just gone 4am and the dawn is not yet with us. I peer out from the shelter at them crossing the small bit of field close to the small plantation. I watch until they make it around the gable wall. Grace turns. They all turn and look back. The car startles the calm and I listen to the decreasing noise.

I breathe in the fresh air, although we get plenty below from the vents peeping up to the surface. My mind thinks of nothing in particular. It seems to be working, more from memory than any purpose. Perhaps it's storing the picture of Grace looking back and waving, her walking with the little blue grip across the field.

Slowly, I close the hatch and return to the five-roomed coffin. I want to speak to Rory and to everyone that's important to me. Yet here I am lost to the world, a world that has decided I'm armed and dangerous. I slap the wall, 'You harm my people and I'll be armed and dangerous,' I yell to the silence. The smell of fresh bread drifts around. Philip had brought fresh rolls and stuff to do me for several days. I grab one and bite into it while I stroll around the building.
'Shit, she's forgotten Cornpop.' Then I see the little letter with glitter on it. It's Cornpop and me and the precious smell that lingers on its fabric.

Chapter 29

The soil fell in. Black boots appear first and I push the knife against his back. The cop freezes on the ladder.
'Stop. One noise and you're dead,' I say. 'Who's with you?'
'One other,' he utters, searching for breath.
'Where is he?'
'Up there.'
'Tell him to go to the car for something. Just do it. Don't think about it.'
'Frank, get the shovel from the car,' he shouts. A muffled *okay* comes from above.
'Right. Down here. Don't turn around.'
'Look you'd be better giving ...' He doesn't finish the sentence and lands on the red tiles. A little blood trickles from his head where I'd hit him with the small bar.

I scramble up the ladder, grabbing pages and stuffing them into my coat. I try to think if there is anything lying about that could give any of us away. It's coming dawn. They must've been watching despite Philip's sense of security and phone call to Professor Alex. The dew has traced the cop's footprints back to the car. I dart for the small plantation and listen to the car door shutting. I run quickly to the gable wall of the house and close my eyes and whack him on the right temple as he passes me while praying that I only knock him out. He thuds to the ground and moans. The car keys are in his pocket and I pull the radio off his jacket and whack it into pieces.

I slam the Astra into gear and take off. Here I am like a sitting duck in a bloody panda car. I slide sideways as I brake on the gravel before hitting the tarmac. I haven't a clue where I'm going.

Philip talked of a village called Tarpoley and I drive along the narrow road in the direction that he had pointed. The roads are tree-lined and the canopy covers the sky in places with brown leaves. I come into a small village and drive along slowly. All is quiet in the early hour. I park past a hotel and fumble the screwdriver into my hand. The brown Fiesta is easy to break into. One twist with the screwdriver and the door clicks open. No alarm either. I ram the screwdriver under the steering lock and wedge the panel off. All the wires are connected to the ignition. I grab them and pull the red one out and it sparks against the metal. There's enough petrol. I take off slowly and hope that everyone has slept soundly.

The M6 is relatively quiet and the initial hints of winter are on the way. Cheshire has wonderful autumnal colour clouds and carpets. Every set of lights that appears behind me grabs my attention just in case it's a police car. The Fiesta has a female owner, I reckon. Her perfume's here, plus the scrape marks on the windscreen where her rings have dug into the glass, not to mention the hole in the carpet where her high heels rested. Hopefully she'll get it back soon with little damage. I've had a car stolen so I know what the hassle's like.

I reckon it's about 5am. With a bit of luck I'll get two more hours in the car. I'm dying of thirst and wonder about Philip. Had they lifted him or had he shrugged off their suggestions? He was one hell of a friend.

I glance over at the white stick beside me and smile. He had spent ages putting the white tape onto it. Jesus I hope he's okay. My mind is wandering a bit, like my driving, and I get a horn blast from an oncoming truck that shocks me back to reality. 'God's sake wise up Simon,' I shout to myself.

It's one mile to the next services and I decide it's best to dump the car. I'm almost reaching the end of the M6. I hope to make it to Stranraer to catch the ferry. A few cars and lorries rest in the services. I park the Fiesta behind some trucks and wipe the wheel with my coat. I glance at the mirror and place the shades on. 'Right let's go. Time to become Mark Robbins,' I say to myself. I keep the white stick under my coat until I am inside the building. I make for the toilets and fix at the papers I had stuffed quickly into my pockets. Philip and I had worked on many drafts of the text that I intended to post to Matt Brown.

It seems strange being away from my five-roomed coffin. The scar close to my pelvis is turning a lighter shade of pink. The surgeon with no name had made several visits until he pronounced me fit. When I leave the cubicle I splash water over my face and stubble. I do look different, I reckon. I had practised walking with my eyes closed. Pretending to be blind had altered my stride. I had counselled people, blinded in later life and they mentioned how they walked differently, once they lost their sight. Research evidence had backed it up too, and for some reason I'd made a mental note of that fact, perhaps a foresight. Often I had been told about my recognisable walk.

The coffee and fry are welcome. The place is basically empty except for the staff and the electronic chatter of the gaming machines. I can watch everything going on from behind my shades. Jesus... I hope the two cops don't die. I wince and think of Grace but that's equally dark. I bolt up and grab the stick and tap my way towards the door, uttering a thank you.

The Fiesta sits parked and it's minding its own business when I hitch a lift with a lorry going to Stranraer. John, the driver, speaks little and listens to Don Williams music. I doze most of the way on a contented stomach, waking to gaze at the changing colours of the forests in the distance. The autumnal landscape of Scotland is beautiful. It reminds me of the covers on shortbread tins and toffee wrappers and Sandy Shaw records that my mother played. John seems to be an easygoing type of person, large, probably about fifty with a silent courage oozing from beneath his black hair. He asks few questions. However, he wishes me luck when he drops me off at the passenger terminal. I buy a ticket for the 10.30am sailing on the Stena HSS into Belfast.

Police are all over the place and I play my role well. I have to. One wrong move now and it will be curtains. The cops are bound to be swarming all around the shelter by now, spreading the word. Surely, they know it was me hiding there, with Grace. Damn. Likewise the car will have been reported stolen. So far I'm guilty of GBH, two counts of car theft and God knows what else. Buying a bloody ticket under a false name and impersonating a blind man, I muse.

The Stena HSS is a welcome sight and a wonderful craft. It reminds me of a spacecraft, the white floating shape that I'd watched sailing up and down Belfast Lough many times. I'll never forget the first time I saw it. It literally took my breath away with its brilliant design. I had been one of the first passengers to travel on the new super ferry back then. I make for the aft of the ship and drop into one of the soft chairs and watch *Sky News*. The sailing is remarkably quiet. Most people are making for the breakfast special further up the ship. Its smell is tempting, despite my full stomach. The Irish Sea is relatively calm and the Captain forces more power from the craft once we leave the dock. He has to be careful about the wake and the waves he causes along the coastline.

I appear to have fitted in on the journey. However, will it be that simple when I dock in Belfast? The security has relaxed since the ceasefire but surely they'll check if they know I half-killed two policemen in Cheshire? Barnsey might be standing looking harassed as usual. I shuffle along to the shop and almost buy a newspaper and magazine just as I catch myself on. I fumble about and sway with the motion of the ship. Some American tourists are debating about perfume and I pick up two bags of Jelly Babies and make my way back to the soft chairs. I push in four or five at a time and devour both bags. I can never take a few sweets. Don't see the point. I'm happy when the bag's finished.

Belfast glows in the midday sun. The shores of the Lough have turned with the season and despite everything it's my homeland. A British European jet glides past the window as it prepares to land at Belfast City. It reminds me of Pearl and I flying to Jersey both times. Things seemed so different then.

Belfast is busy. The accents float over me as I make my way from the docks. *It was easy* keeps floating around in my mind. Yet it's tempered by my mother's voice saying, *pride before a fall, Simon*. The peace process was progressing in Belfast. The usual flash points had come and gone and there was a semblance of normality in Northern Ireland. Shoppers were flocking about, ones starting early for Christmas.

I book into the Manningburg for two nights. Everything within me wants to visit Tullydeen. It would be suicidal. Contacting anyone here is the lead Barnsey will be waiting for. I stroll from the Manningburg to one of the many mobile phone shops and buy a prepaid phone. Even when I was paying cash they took my bloody postcode. Well, not my postcode, rather, the postcode of a person living in Glengormley. I just played along with the guy's questions and played on the fact that I was blind. We're meant to be living in a free country. That's a laugh. People have more freedom in Russia than we do.

I saunter over to the City Hall and slap down on the bench. The guy was kind enough to activate my phone, what with my disability and all, plus he was a smart arse that liked to show off. Rory picks it up on the second ring.

Rory doesn't take a chance jaywalking. He waits until the green man appears. He enters the gardens around the City Hall and searches about for me. Good, he doesn't know me. I jump to my feet and tap the white stick out in front of me as he searches frantically, turning and glancing in all directions.
'Still slipping the sugar into your tea wee man?'
He spins around and his look says it all. He looks at me and then moves his head back about one foot to readjust his vision and get a different view.
'Simon?'
'Aye.'
He walks toward the vacant bench and waits until I arrive.
'Jesus you had me fooled. I saw ye but paid no notice to ye,' he smiles.
'Read your story about the corruption. What's happened since?' I ask.
'Nothing much. Barnsey was lifted but is suspended and basically free,' he shrugs.
'Did he come near you?'
'Not yet.'
'Did you hear anything about two cops getting ambushed in Cheshire this morning?'
'No, but I'll check.' Rory dials quickly and waits a short time for the necessary details. 'Nah, nothing,' he says.
'Strange …cops arrived where I was hiding out. I got away and stole their car. Here, take this number, just got this mobile and I'm staying at the Manningburg,' I reel off quickly.

He jots down the number and then grabs my arm and forces something into my hand. I look at it briefly and see a wad of twenty-pound notes.
'You don't have to do that,' I say.
'Just take it son. Jesus I'm glad to see you,' he smiles. 'I wish you'd get your bloody hair cut,' he laughs. Rory's face turns stern and he scans over me. 'This will all end Simon. I'm going to town on them now and I'm putting none of the crew at risk. Everyday I'll be keeping the pressure on and it's working. So don't you stop working either and don't stop if something happens to me. We have lost too many to give up now,' he says grimacing, turning away to look at the traffic.

'I've no option Rory. It's them or me. I didn't actually believe they'd kill Pearl. Just shows how naive I am. Jesus I was brought up to respect the law and the police.'

'Mass Patterson will not die in vain son. Mark my words,' he nods walking off. I want to shout after him. I can't. The reality of Pearl's murder has just hit home as sure as the pain from the bullet wound in my side does when I over stretch. Yet the muscle heals more quickly.

I saunter back to the Manningburg to shower and relax in my room with a huge sirloin steak and chips, courtesy of room service. The Belfast dusk is glowing with orange streetlights. If I had a pencil I could join them all together like a large dot-to-dot book. I'm surprised they hadn't argued about *orange* streetlights in the new Assembly at Stormont. The room is not unlike the one Pearl and I had here before. It's much the same at the Contarret in Jersey as well. The standard hotel room: en-suite; kettle, biscuits, TV, trouser press, table and the little bottles of shampoo and body lotion that Grace always liked me to bring home. Where's home? What I'd give to have her read me a story now.

I doze contentedly on a full stomach on the large bed, until the phone rings, and I come surfing back to consciousness. Absentmindedly, I pick up the receiver and mumble *hello*. As the line clicks dead my room door opens.

'Don't move, pal.'

Chapter 30

'Well now, there's a sight for sore eyes. Isn't that right Simon?' the voice utters, stepping through the two men who entered first.
'Where are you?' I ask. 'Who are you? What do you want? I'm blind,' I add, rotating my head and pushing out my arms. I can see as clear as day that it's Billy Thompson.
'Cut the crap. It was you that came to interview me in the taxi office. But maybe your memory's gone as well, heh?'
'My name's Mark Robbins. You're mistaken,' I fire back.
'Aye dead on,' Billy Thompson says, throwing an envelope down on my leg. 'Well if you're blind then you won't be able to read that. Pearl sent it,' he finishes with a wry grin. My entire body flinches and I know Billy notices. All three of them turn and leave the room.

Everything is spinning, *Pearl sent it.* I rip the envelope open. There's a compliments slip from Patterson Engineering inside. Nothing is written on it. Nothing on the envelope, either. I hold it up to the light and scan both sides nothing, except the watermark in the paper. What the hell's going on? I strut across to the desk and want to pick up the phone. But I decide against it.

The phone call, I remember. The dead line. I dial reception and inquire if they had put a call through to me. The receptionist is very polite and helpful and she confirms a call had come through asking for Mr Mark Robbins in Room 112. She was positive they had asked for both my name and room number. Her voice dropped when she told me the phone number had been withheld. I manage to utter *thanks* and slump down on the chair. Name and number ...how the hell did they know... if they know I'm here how many others do as well?

I can't work out if it's better to stay here or make a move. Am I less easy to spot out in the open or am I a sitting duck closed up in a hotel room? The door, I remember. I check the cardkey entry system and the door jam. There are no signs of a forced entry. They obviously had a cardkey too.

It's just gone eleven. My room window only opens so much and I breathe in the fresh air, if there is such a thing in the city. I pull on my coat, a long trench coat, brown, and slip on the shades. I pull the collar up so that it and my hair intermingle. I have a baseball cap that meets the top of the lenses. I check nothing of any value is left in the room: only the grip. I rub it for fingerprints. Why, beats me, it seems like a good thing to do. Nothing important that can connect me to Mark Robbins or Simon Rogers is left.

I shuffle along the hall with my eyes wide open until I come to a linen store. Quickly, I check no one is around and turn the handle, luckily it's open. The linen room has many shelves and a sink at the far end. It's big, about the size of my room. Sheets and blankets and pillows are piled high on the shelves. If I open the door I can stand behind it and peer out from the crack towards the mass of doors leading to the various rooms. From here I have a clear view if anyone else tries to enter.

Several times I jolt to life from my doze when I hear voices or movement, innocent noise, people returning from night clubs and so forth. Nothing happens, yet I stay in the linen room until the breaking dawn.

I slip back to the room and order a taxi. It's a frosty morning in Belfast, my breath rising to meet the day. The traffic is still quite light, but give it an hour or so and it will be building up. The taxi driver tries to make small talk. I decline with simple one-word answers. Soon he gives up, too much like hard work his shoulders seem to say.

Leaves and the autumnal frost greet me at the tiny church in Drumfiddy. All of my senses are fidgeting and ready to detect anything no matter how small. It's a small church painted in a light yellow with windows that start square at the bottom and then progress into points. None is stained glass. Large oak trees surround the tiny church and immaculate tarmac is bordered by neatly kept grass. Crows take off and land above me. I take the liberty of glancing around in the sunshine. Not one person is about. The lightest of skims of frost covers the grass. A mass of headstones rest before me around the wall of the church. I walk slowly along looking for Patterson. Beyond the gable wall I see the headstone of Peter Patterson. My eyes scan down the words. Pearl's name is below that of her husband and next is Susan's name.

I think back to the papers and the photos of the funerals that I had read about in the shelter and I feel like I'm going to collapse. Damn it why did I come here? I want to run, run anywhere, anywhere away from this bloody place. I aim for the church wall and lean against it. Some steps lead from a side door and I make for them. I could do with a cigarette now. It's the first time I've really thought about smoking.

It's all real, their murders. Maybe I thought I'd come here and find out that Pearl was alive. That it was all a dream. Their names are there on the headstones, engraved into the marble. There's no mistake. Everything is starting to close in. The carousel of *why didn't I do that instead* is in full circle. Why didn't I go to Portugal with Grace and Pauline …why does it always have to be me? Maybe Pauline was right, maybe I spent too long at the computer and didn't pay attention to people. *But you didn't love her*, my conscience says, *you loved Pearl*. It stops me. It stops my head. It's true. I had loved Pearl. The creaky door behind me opens. 'Penny for them,' the voice says. I spin around and a woman stands in the slice of opened door.

'Pearl?' I ask, feeling stupid.

'No, Joyce. I didn't know a blind man could read a headstone, you know' she says, smiling from the door. Her hair is brown. Shoulder length, bobbed. She steps back and that mystical smell of good wood and old churches drifts over me and I walk into the church.

'Joyce?'

'Yes.'

'But you were Pearl?'

'Yes. Oh Simon you're alive.' Joyce hugs me. It's her.

'Joyce?'

She smiles and moves from our embrace. 'Here read this,' she says, handing me an envelope. 'I believe you had mail last night.'

I take the envelope. The same kind that Billy Thompson left with me in the hotel. My body slumps down in the pew. 'What the hell's going on?'

Joyce nods to the letter and walks towards the pulpit.

My dearest Simon

By the time you read this letter I will be dead. The future is uncertain, however I had a little more foresight than most, enough of that for now.

I have followed your career closely and often marvelled at your ability and courage in the numerous stories you have written. We picked you for this job. Everyone picked you it seemed. Yes, sadly Trevor Mulholland as well.

It saddened me that Trevor turned out so much different from Tom, his father. Tom was a great man, the driving force behind Patterson Engineering and a lifelong friend to both Peter and I. His murder, along with Nancy's, was a suspicious affair. I suspected that Trevor was involved in it. He was young and very impressionable. Susan egged him on and at times made a fool out of him. I tried to talk to her about the situation and suggested that she needed to show a little more compassion. However, it fell on deaf ears. Trevor was trying to prove that he was capable. He was more than capable, but I believe he would have given all that up had he received the affection he craved from Susan, or indeed another woman.

Trevor was an odd chap. I befriended him. However, I did not know about the gun making connection at that time, nor his involvement in his parents' murder. Oh, it is painful Simon. When I did find out I pretended to myself that it was not happening. I am guilty of that. Guilty of burying my head in the sand when I should have acted.

Yes acted. Oh, I acted Simon. I was good at that. I acted during my marriage to Peter. We tolerated each other. There was one man that I really fell in love with and that was your father. He loved your mother and in those days divorce was not an option. Your father probably never knew. However, it was the main reason for leaving Tullydeen. He was handsome, genuine and just a lovely, lovely man. In fact the resemblance to you is uncanny.

I stop reading and look up at Joyce. 'Did you know all of this?'
'Yes. Keep reading, Simon,' she says softly.
'Keep reading? What are you doing to me? She loved my father, Pearl did.'
'So! They didn't have an affair, Simon.'
'So! She still loved him,' I say knowing that I sound like a spoilt kid not getting sweets. I had never really imagined my mother or father in that way. They were my parents. They didn't have sex. They were sensible. I stare around the old church, high up in the rafters and rest my arms outward with the cream paper dangling over the pew in front of me. Joyce is about ten rows forward at the front of the

church. She waits until I gather my thoughts. She seems so calm. My head is spinning, trying to put pieces together. I return to the letter. There are two pages written on four sides. I trace over the words and reread a piece until I find where I left off.

I can imagine, Simon, that you are angry with me. You were so proud of your father and he of you. The times you went fishing and the time you put Tommy Dickon's bull back in the long field. I can remember you saying: "My daddy and me weren't scared of the bull." You were so proud.

Thank you for taking on this story. I owe you so much, Simon. Well here it is. Yes for years I buried my head in the sand and lived with the remorse and the guilt of Peter's death. Until I was diagnosed with cancer. Suddenly the courage came and the decision too. The decision to rectify things as best I could. I drove home from the hospital alone thinking, 'It's over Pearl'. All that I had worried about seemed unimportant and futile. I stopped the car at the White Rocks and stared out to sea. Then I went home and phoned Joyce. She came immediately, as immediately as one can from Canada. You see no one ever knew we were twins, except us. Not even Susan. It's remarkable that I hadn't told her. Joyce and I had been separated at birth and it wasn't until the early nineties that we traced one another. God sometimes works in mysterious ways, Simon. Anyway I attended for treatment but in my heart I knew I was going to die. Don't ask me why. I just knew.

As I write this letter, Simon, I have just learned of Susan's murder. Joyce phoned to say. I am contented and know it will just be a matter of time until Susan's body is flown home with Joyce. Then we will swap places for the last time. Please forgive us for deceiving you.

I hope, Simon, in my illness I have gained the courage to put right some wrongs. Time changes us, our circumstances. There you were a little boy running up the long field to the gate when we left. I was leaving for a new life and a fresh start and you were beginning your journey. Our journeys met. We didn't.

With every best wish
Pearl

I breathe out heavily, tears smart my cheeks. My throat is closing. Joyce stands at the front of the church and looks down at me in silence.

'You're Canadian?' I ask.

'Yes.'
'Oh.'
I'm lost for words. She gives me time. Christ we're back to time. Back to a church and more dead bodies. Her heels make a piercing noise as she walks slowly towards me. Joyce sits in the pew in front and looks into my face. I chance a few glances at her. She smiles.
'Are you ready for more?' she says, as a vehicle pulls up outside the church. Three doors close and I swing around to the noise behind me. Joyce touches my arm.
'So you can read then, heh.'
'Aye.' I nod.
With Billy Thompson are the two goons that entered my room and Fast Frank Bole. Fast Frank, shakes my hand and moves into the pew behind me.
'Great work, boy. Aye, great work, boy.'
'I suppose we're having tea and sandwiches?' I ask.
'No, Simon. Need a few names to finish the job, heh. That cop that murdered Pearl.'
'Barnsey?'
'Aye him.'
'Don't know Billy. Know nothing about him …except that he lives in Glengormley in Murial Parade number ten I think. After that I know nothing about him and that stupid Escort he drives, diesel, blue.'
'You're not much use are ye, heh?' he smiles.
'No.'
    One of Billy's goons walks over to him and whispers. Joyce looks at me and Fast Frank is humming a tune, which sounds like a hymn.
'We've got to split,' Billy says, quickly.
They help Fast Frank to his feet and usher him towards the door. He stops and turns around. 'Thanks boy. Pearl Patterson was a decent soul, so was wee Peter. Aye. Just a pity the way the wee girl turned out. Aye.'
I nod and Fast Frank is gone.
    Joyce slips into the pew beside me and takes my hand she's drawing little circles on it.
'You're Canadian?'
'Yes …let's pray together, Simon.'
'What for? Peace?'
'Whatever.'

'Look how did you know I was back?' I ask. 'It's really bugged me how I was recognised. I spent ages pretending to be blind.'

'Maybe I'm a better psychologist than you.'

'You're a psychologist?'

'Yes. I just used all my excellent training and predicted your behaviour,' she smiles.

'Shit. I thought the blind man would work. That was my best shot,' I say, looking for sympathy.

'Didn't work, Simon. Had it sussed,' she snaps back.

I sit and stare at my feet. She nudges my side and whispers into my ear. 'I didn't predict your behaviour at all. It's that weird walk you have darling.'

'I changed my walk, spent ages on my walk!'

'Ahh that it,' Joyce smiles.

'What?'

'I'd know your bum anywhere,' she says, giving that little groan again.

Acknowledgements

It all began with two horses standing on six legs or something like that. The debate was never settled. Anyway, Dr Ann Long and Kathleen Murphy from the University of Ulster and K.M. Secretarial, respectively, both spent hours helping me and making me laugh.

Thanks to Treasa Coady from Town House and Country House, Dublin, who was very kind to me many years ago. I have to thank my mother, Kathleen, for the cups of tea and the walks at Delamont. It helped to get me away from a PC for a while. Thanks to Jade, for her help with the design for the cover and to Rose Stevenson, for the lovely home-baked cheesecakes, which always seemed to bring inspiration and a contented belly. A special thanks needs to go to Vinnie McCormack for our many chats about plots. Thanks to Kirk Bowe, who designed our web site, his brilliance never ceases to amaze me.

Thanks needs to go to many people, some are mentioned below. All of these people inspired me by their humanity. They are: Maggie Long; Dr Lynn Dunwoody; Roberta Bingham; Pat; Brian King; Brendan; Chris Man U; Dr Robin Davidson; Jan Daley; Therese Hughes; Yvonne; Marita; Lyn; Helen; Joy Berrenberg; Brian Duncan; Irina Roncaglia; John Thompson; Theresa Hartley; Rosemary Busby; Martin McPhillips; Diane Harvey; Dr Nicky Hayes; Marian Clulow; David McIlroy; Helen Johnston; Dr Brendan Bunting; Della Minett-Westwood; Carla McDowell; Stéphanie Rigaud; Liz Pereira; Meiling Chiu; Ken Moore; Prof. David Sines; the Bulgarian Buttercup; Renee Stoker; Pat; Tom; Gary; Dr Daniela Schulze; Prof. Hugh McKenna; Marty Cardwell; Alex Linley; Monique Anderson; Lindy Newton; Janie; Emma Clark; John Kirk; Ilona Boniwell; Vicky Gardner; Zeana Terry; Graham Pluck; Dr Jon Sutton; Jim McCourt and Donna Enright.

To Mark Stanley at Avenue Data Systems for his help with the barcode. Also, I'm indebted to the team at Editorial Solutions. Finally, to the professionalism and customer care I received from Robert Black and Maureen Allen at W&G Baird Ltd.